# WINTER'S CHILD

# WINTER'S CHILD

## Dea Trier Mørch

### Illustrated by the author

Translated from the Danish by Joan Tate

SERPENT'S
TAIL

**BRITISH LIBRARY CATALOGUING IN PUBLICATION DATA**

Morch, Dea Trier
Winter's child.
I. Title   II. Vinterborn. *English*
839.8'1374 [F]   PT8176.23.035

ISBN 1–85242–001–4
ISBN 1–85242–101–0 Pbk

First published as *Vinterbørn*, by Gyldendal, Copenhagen 1976.
© 1976 by Dea Trier Mørch. Translation © 1986 by Joan Tate.

This edition first published 1986 by
Serpent's Tail, 26 Westbourne Grove, London W2.
Published by arrangement with the University of Nebraska Press.

Printed in Great Britain by
Billing and Sons Ltd
Worcester.

# ACKNOWLEDGEMENTS

With thanks to the following women,
who have helped me with this book
through conversations, letters, and proofreading:

Anne-Mette

Jane                    Charlotte

Jenny

Hannah

Lotte

Jytte

Susie

Gudrun

Dejte

Randi

Ibi

Kirsten

## WORKS BY DEA TRIER MØRCH

# WINTER'S CHILD

The cold alien hospital night . . . that's the worst. It's so hard to get through. It's so long.

Everything that was white in the daytime is now black, and everything that was black is now white. The hospital at night is a negative that refuses to leave the eyes of the patients.

Quiet sighs, bodies restlessly turning over in their sleep.

A blue light winking. A patient has pulled the cord at the head of her bed. The night nurse comes silently up to see what is needed.

Towards morning, when at last everyone has fallen into a deep sleep, the door is flung open and a breezy voice says:

"Good morning, girls. It's six o'clock!"

The women turn sulkily over in bed, lift tousled heads from rumpled pillows, and look at each other, then sink back into the bed's cozy nest.

Two midwifery students come into the ward. They are nice girls. They don't switch on the bright overhead light, only the small bedside lamps.

The first one takes temperatures and blood pressures. The other says:

"May I listen?"

She carefully turns the quilt back and puts the cool wooden stethoscope onto the warm sleep-heavy stomach, puts her ear to the tube, lets go with her hands, and listens for the faint doop-doop sound of the baby's heart.

Then she looks at her watch, says thank you, pulls the quilt back over the patient, and hurries on to the next bed.

An orderly appears, a black silhouette in the doorway.

"Out into the sluice!"

This is one of the most difficult things for new patients to get used to, this eternal business of urine. The color, smell, quantity . . . not a single drop may be wasted.

The women go out into the low-ceilinged store where all the

clean linen is kept . . . shirts, pants, towels, sheets, drawsheets and quilt-covers. They all weigh themselves and write the result down on a sheet of paper lying on the edge of the bathtub.

A new fur coat is hanging on the wall, made with many different colored pieces of fur. It belongs to the young nurse, the one who comes in the morning to relieve the night nurse.

Then the patients can go back to bed and sleep until eight o'clock, or they can stay up and have a shower.

Breakfast is the best meal of the day. It is served at the same time every morning and yet it always seems that you have to wait an eternity for it, probably because you're so hungry. A long time has gone by since you last had anything to eat.

A small shining aluminum trolley is slowly pushed down the corridor. The patients come out of the various wards in their own dressing gowns; striped, flowered, tartan, red, yellow or blue. Black and white. They flock round the little table and the steaming tea and coffee. There is beer-bread, yoghurt, and buttermilk. There is rye bread, white bread, and crispbread. Cheese, butter, marmalade, and strawberry jam.

The patients go in and out of the wards bearing the brown wooden trays loaded generously with food.

The eggs are always boiled too hard. They are cold, the yokes light yellow, the whites pale blue. They are very different from the large-size solid country eggs Olivia is used to at home.

Olivia is on a diet. She is diabetic and must not have more than fifteen hundred calories a day. She is given her own special plate and exclaims:

"But I can't staaaaaand cheese!"

"Leave it, then," says Linda.

"We've got to economize," says the orderly. "Keep your glasses and use them over and over again."

The nurse goes from ward to ward with a dark-haired orderly, changing bedclothes and straightening beds. They plump the pillows and turn the quilts carefully, but at great speed.

Behind them comes another orderly handing out clean clothes and towels.

In Ward 0 the nurse lets up the blind with a rushing bang.

"Did you sleep well?"

"Marvelously, thanks," says Gertrude.

"Oh, hell," says little Linda. "I've got such a pain in my silly back."

"And what about you, Olsen?"

Olivia is sitting up, large and in good form, on her bed by the window.

"I go gambling every Monday, and Holger goes every Wednesday."

"What sort of gambling?" says the nurse.

"Bingo!"

"Well?"

"I put on twenty kroner every time."

"Well!"

She takes her knitting out of the drawer in her locker.

"I've been here almost six weeks now!"

"You haven't long to go then, have you, Olivia?"

"Will you go and look at my estriols?"

"You know perfectly well I can't do that."

"Doctor said my estriols have been fine lately."

"All the more reason why I shouldn't go and look at your case-sheet," says the nurse, taking the tray out into the corridor.

It gets lighter. The hospital wakes up. The hospital is an anthill. A beehive. A collectively created product. A great living organism. The sum of the people whose daily lives are in there. The sum of patients there for longer or shorter stays. The sum of buildings, equipment, and instruments. The sum of ideas that arise and develop in the place. The sum of political decisions the hospital is subject to.

The hospital wakes up and starts to live.

At half-past eight, the pale winter sun appears over the roofs and its flat rays pour into the wards, in over the beds.

They can all hear the sound of cars from the road.

A thin little woman comes in, pulling a large trolley of newspapers and magazines, women's magazines and men's magazines, crossword magazines, romances, serial magazines and horoscopes, comics, all kinds of magazines, even porn. She has fruit and cigarettes, too, and matches, soap, scent, aftershave, and a great many other things to make life pleasanter for the patients.

Olivia heaves herself out of bed with a ten kroner note in her hand.

"Hey, Olivia. I thought you weren't supposed to eat oranges?"

"Yes, but that's because my sight's got so bad."

"A *Romance* and an *Extra* for me," says Linda. "Twenty Cecils and a bag of licorice."

"*Berlingske Tidende* for me, please," says Gertrude. "And *Better Living.*"

Olivia steers her way back to bed with two oranges and the *Family Weekly* in her arms.

Linda is sitting propped up against the bed-head, her *Extra* open on the quilt in front of her.

"Unemployment, unemployment, unemployment . . . you won't be able to open a paper soon without reading that they've closed another factory."

"Oh, look . . . it says here that Prince Charles is getting engaged."

There is the calm sound of chewing and sighs, and the rustle of crisp newsprint being turned and studied in the three beds in Ward 0.

The fourth bed is empty, covered with a piece of pale blue plastic.

Rounds. The patients sit up straight, their hair parted and their toenails painted.

The consultant gynecologist comes into Ward 0, followed by the sister in charge of the department, the nurses, a couple of midwifery students, and an orderly.

Slowly and calmly, he goes from bed to bed, spending a long time on each casesheet, much longer than the younger doctors usually do, and asking questions in a quiet voice.

"Well, how are you, Mrs. Erichsen?"

"Fine, thank you," says Gertrude.

"Things look all right here. Shall we say we'll examine Mrs. Erichsen on Thursday, then?"

The sister writes it down.

"And how are things with you, Mrs. Linda Larsen?"

Linda can't get a single word out. There are tears in her eyes.

"Mrs. Larsen has pains in her back from a road accident some years ago," says Sister.

"Perhaps massage would be a good idea?" The doctor looks at her casesheet. "Let's feel, shall we?"

The midwife goes over to the bed and puts her hands flat on Linda's stomach.

"Can I go home for Christmas?" whispers Linda.

"That may be possible," says the doctor.

"Can I be together with my husband?"

"I certainly wouldn't advise it."

Linda pulls the quilt up to her face.

"Well, how are things going here?" The doctor stands by Olivia's bed and glances at the board above her head where the word *diabetes* is barely readable.

"I find it hard to see sometimes."

"We must get the ophthalmic surgeon to have a look at you."

"And Doctor, please, I'd rather not have my Caesarian on 28th, because my husband's going to bingo that day."

"We'll see."

"There are more than three hundred prizes."

Olivia looks pleadingly at Sister and raises her voice to be sure of being heard.

"My sister-in-law has just put a side of pork in the freezer."

"That sounds good."

The doctor is on his way out of the door.

"I'd really like to have my Caesarian on the 29th, because that would have been my father-in-law's seventieth birthday!"

The door closes quietly.

"Oh, how mean of him not to let me sleep with Allan," says Linda tearfully.

"In a way, the doctor couldn't care less what you do at home," says Gertrude. "It's not for his sake you're here."

"But just this once! He's not the slightest idea what it's like being married to Allan!"

"Well, you're going to have a gyne examination," says Olivia to Gertrude, screwing up her eyes. "You watch out the doctor doesn't hurt you. He's known to be a bit heavy-handed, I'll have you know."

After the round, the staff gather in the small office on the corridor.

Patients creep along with their urine glasses, looking out of the corners of their eyes at the group gathered behind the glass pane. It is like watching a silent film in which someone is sitting drinking coffee and eating cakes. Senior Sister is giving a report and watching the doctor's mouth. The nurse is sitting with her head bowed, noting down something on a colored card in a file with plastic pockets. The doctor gesticulates with both hands in a circle in the air. Sister nods, her coffee cup stopping halfway between her lips and the saucer.

The fates of the patients seem to be decided at these morning conferences, the white figures discussing *what* shall happen to *whom*? Who will soon be discharged? Who will have a Caesarian or be delivered in the old-fashioned way?

And who will have to temper her impatience and adjust to staying on in Prenatal for another eternity.

At midday, steaming plates are carried into the wards and placed on the lockers.

"Gertrude . . . d'you want a little fish?"

"I love fish."

"I can't staaand fish! We never have fish at home, neither fillets nor fish-fingers, no cold-blooded animals at all. I won't touch them . . . I just refuse to."

Olivia sits with her great broad back bent over her plate, staring at the boiled cod, the yellow potatoes, and the small plate of grated raw vegetables. Thank heavens for that . . . otherwise she wouldn't get any of it down.

Gertrude carefully pokes the bones out of her fish and puts them on the edge of her plate, one by one, then cuts the potatoes into nice small pieces of the same size.

She finds pleasure in all kinds of order. A filleted fish. A folded table napkin with sharp edges. A sharpened pencil. Order. Symmetry. That's how things should be.

When she has finished, she arranges the things on her tray, swings her legs out of bed, thrusts her feet into a pair of small pink fur-trimmed slippers, then walks lightly, her back straight, out into the corridor with her crocks.

Midday sleep is shimmering and light, like white sheets fluttering in the wind on the line. The girls lie on their backs or on their sides, sleeping soundlessly.

The long-stemmed yellow and pink tulips with their green transparent stems bow their heads and stretch out their leaves, apparently dozing in the vases.

It is better and safer to sleep in the daytime than at night. Your troublesome thoughts glide away from you during the pleasant, calm midday sleep.

The great bellies are at rest, those stomachs like small inland lakes with fish splashing about in the water. Soft nudges inside abdomens. Small hands and feet moving in shoals.

The belly is the world. The belly is the universe, with nebulae and moons and planets far inside. With membranes and swaddling clothes. The belly is a drum. The belly is a heavy cow on the ground. A huge pear-shaped muscle. A riddle.

In the middle of their sleep, the door opens. It is visiting time and the patients in Ward 0 have for once overslept.

Three people in dark clothes come gliding in to see Gertrude, who gets up saying: "Oh, I'm sorry, I haven't even done my hair!"

They put their fur coats and scarves carefully down on the end of the empty bed by the washbasin. Then they borrow a chair from Olivia and group themselves round Gertrude.

They unpack the flowers, real flowers appropriate to the time of year and the situation. They speak in subdued voices so as not to disturb the other two patients, who have no visitors.

The older woman hands Gertrude a little book and Linda hears her whisper: "You'll have to cut the pages yourself, Trude."

"Thanks, Mother."

"*Shouldn't* we try to find out if you can have a room to yourself?" the white-haired man whispers.

"Trude has no objection to being here, have you Trude?" whispers the young man with a tartan scarf thrown over his shoulder. He is sitting holding his wife's hand.

"Some people," Linda thinks, turning over on her side, away from the room and toward the window. She lights a cigarette and opens her *Romance*. The first story is called *Place of Many Stars*. She takes a deep drag at her cigarette and starts reading.

*"You must be crazy," said the pump attendant to Kerry, as he filled the tank of her red sports car. "Stark raving mad! You'll never make it." Kerry Cowper folded her arms and smiled at him with a determined expression in her blue eyes as she tossed back her long fair hair. "Why not?" she said searchingly. "I'm not the first person to drive around Australia in a car. . . ."*

"We're going now, Trude, and leaving you two in peace for a while," the mother whispers to Gertrude, pulling at her husband's arm. "Come on, let's go, George."

The parents wave goodbye.

"You've got a nice husband, Gertrude," said Olivia.

"Do you think so?"

"What does he do?"

"He's a civil engineer."

Money in that, thinks Linda.

"And the old man . . . was that your father?"

Gertrude nods.

"Does he work? Or what?"

"He's head of a department in the Ministry of Trade."

At sunset the nurse comes in to the ward followed by a long-haired morose-looking girl in a Peruvian hood and a worn sheepskin coat. The nurse helps her, shows her the cupboard, and says out loud:

"This is Marie Hansen—and this is Mrs. Olsen, Mrs. Larsen and Mrs. Erichsen."

Then she writes *needs rest* on the board and leaves.

The newcomer slowly and laboriously undresses.

She lies stretched out on the bed with her hands behind her head, staring up into the air. She clearly has no desire to talk.

From the Prenatal department's windows you can see the sun gliding downward, becoming larger and larger as it approaches the earth, the fiery ball sinking down through the watery sky, and for a moment resting egg-shaped on the roofs before finally vanishing.

Where the sun has gone down, a scarlet ribbon is left like a bandage in the sky, a piece of gauze slowly absorbing all the light into itself.

For a brief moment all the colours seem clearer . . . the buses becoming a brighter yellow, the road signs and shop signs on Tagens Road apparently luminous, before the darkness starts creeping out of the side streets, out of the porches, and rising up from basement openings.

It is difficult to get used to your evening meal being served as early as five o'clock, but that has something to do with the rhythm of the whole hospital.

The evening meal is always open sandwiches, four per patient. But you can have more if you wish.

Olivia looks with horror at her diabetic plate and says:

"God in heaven, I thought it was eel . . . I simply couldn't get *that* down!"

Gertrude drinks only buttermilk. She watches her figure. You'd hardly know she was in her ninth month.

The new girl gets herself apple purée. She walks round looking slightly aloof, coughing and blowing her nose. She has cold sores on her lip.

"Remember now," cries the nice little orderly. "Take your glasses with you from your wards. That's recycling, that is."

"Good for you," says Olivia, patting her on the shoulder. "And where have you hidden my grated salad dish?"

The new patient, Marie Hansen, is standing at the end of the long corridor trying to get her bearings. She looks out of the window down at the construction work below, at the cranes and the sheds.

The new moon is transparently violet and sharp, slanting above the roofs, looking down on the twinkling city.

She turns round and looks down the long low corridor. It is quiet and dim, with cupboards, wheeled tables and stacked chairs along the walls.

To her left is her own room, Ward 0; then follow Wards 1, 2, 3, 4, and 5. No more.

Facing Ward 0 is the w.c. and the showers, after that the spotlessly clean little kitchen. Then the office, with its great glass window facing out on to the corridor.

Marie taps on the pane and nods to the midwife standing leaning over a casesheet.

"Yes?"

"Have you any cough mixture, by any chance? I've got such an awful cough."

The midwife takes a key fastened to a chain at her belt and opens the wall medicine-cupboard. A little bulb lights up, throwing light on the small shelves of brown glasses and bottles.

Marie wipes her mouth with the back of her hand and puts down the glass.

"How many patients are there?"

"About twenty at the moment."

The midwife looks at her.

"How far on are you?"

"Seven months, but it looks more, doesn't it?"

Next to the office is the examination room with its frosted panes of glass. And that? That must be the sluice with its round porthole in the swing door.

After the sluice comes the store and another lavatory.

The last room on the right, just by the main door, is a little day room.

Marie looks inside.

Four girls are sitting in there watching television. They are knitting, smoking, and eating chocolate, all talking at once.

"But do you ever *ask*?"

"No, I'm scared of seeming silly."

"Then pull your socks up. They like answering. Shall I help you with a few questions?"

At about seven, the main door at the end of the corridor starts opening and shutting. Strangers in dark winter clothes, children and adults, split off into the different rooms and the nurse is kept busy finding vases for all the flowers they bring with them.

A woman with clear-cut features and a tailored suit and thick glasses opens the door to Ward 0. She stands quietly by the wash-basin and lets her gaze wander from face to face.

"Hullo, Mother!"

"Hullo, Linda."

"So you found time to come?"

The tailored suit sits down on the chair by the bed. It is silent, the silence lasting just too long. Linda smooths the quilt with her thin hand, trying to find something to say. She very much wants to be friendly, but it's hard to start.

"Here are some apples for you," says her mother, staring through her thick glasses at the wall beside Linda.

"How's Dad?"

"All right."

"And Anker?"

"Haven't seen him for a long time now."

As always when Linda is with her mother, she feels a painful tension, a never satisfied need.

Gertrude's husband comes in through the door like a breeze, his tartan scarf flapping behind him.

He bends down and whispers something to Gertrude.

"Ha-ha. No! Not really. . . ."

"Yes, promise, and you should've seen. . . ."

He has one hand on Gertrude's shoulder, a catalog from a carpet firm in the other.

"What do you think of this one?"

"Well . . . but what about the dining room?"

A girl in a long-haired afghan fur is leaning right over at the head of Marie's bed. They have their heads together and are whispering and giggling. You would think they were sisters, they are so alike.

Only Olivia, as usual, has no visitors. She takes no notice and holds her knitting right up to her eyes. Even if she pulls the table lamp right up to her work, as if third-degreeing herself, she still drops stitches and mumbles: "Damn!"

There is a radio built into each of the lockers, arranged so they can only be listened to through small earplugs on a cable. Marie tries hers out. She finds Program One and lies back on her pillow with the plug in her ear, her eyes closed.

". . . for Vietnam's rice continues. The National Liberation Front has now captured the fourth largest town in South Vietnam in under a week. The large number of villages taken by NLF recently is part of the destruction of support points Saigon has been using to launch their attacks and attempts to retake the liberated area. When the fighting takes place in the Mekong delta and around Saigon, it appears that in these areas especially the boundaries are fluid between what South Vietnam's provisional revolutionary government and the Saigon government control. At the same time the rice harvest. . . ."

"Time for your jab now." The midwife is standing by Olivia's bed with a hypodermic raised.

Olivia smiles with her bad teeth, puts down her knitting and gets out of bed. She crosses her arms and lifts up her hospital shirt and the midwife sticks the needle into her white flesh. Gertrude shudders and turns her head away.

"Now you can go back again, Olsen."

"Oh, don't you want to feel the baby, Rasmussen? Oh, please do!"

"All right . . . lie down, then."

The midwife bends over Olivia and places the palms of her hands on her stomach, pressing down carefully, letting her hands glide gently and yet firmly round the great muscle.

"There are the lower extremities," she says. "Hm, perhaps it weighs a bit more than six pounds? It's quite cozy, anyhow."

The patients love it when the midwives feel their stomachs.

"Holger's coming on Sunday," says Olivia, adjusting her shirt. "I'm so pleased, so pleased, I can't find words to describe it. It's terrible being without him for a whole fortnight."

"What does he do, your husband?"

"He's a workman. He's been on social security for almost a year and a half now. He used to work for Skelskør Orchards . . . but then they suddenly didn't need him any more. He's at home now, looking after our son."

Olivia points proudly at a photograph in an "antique" plastic frame of a small fair curly-haired boy with a teddy bear in his arms.

"We've got my disability pension, of course, but that doesn't go far. It certainly doesn't if we want to do something for the baby."

"With both disability pay *and* unemployment, you really *ought* to be able to make ends meet," says Gertrude, putting down her hairbrush.

"But you see, Holger's got a bad back. He got it from heaving sacks a few years ago. And he has to go for treatment in Skelskør . . . and the house, the house we live in, that's not cheap, either."

"But all the *same*," Gertrude goes on stubbornly.

Suddenly the others see a glint of anger in Olivia's good-natured face.

"It's no fun getting public money, I'll have you know . . . we used to be free!"

"Is there anything wrong with public money?" Marie asks.

It is the first time they have heard her open her mouth.

"We're too well-off, *that*'s what's wrong," says Gertrude, plucking the long fair hairs out of her brush. "There are lots and lots of people who don't want to do anything!"

Gertrude taps her paper with the tips of her fingers, as if she had got it from there.

"I was sacked from my job when they heard I was pregnant," says Linda in a thin voice. "I was working for a huge firm as an office assistant, and I was pretty good at it, too."

"How old are you?" says Gertrude.

"Twenty-one."

"Goodness, and having a child so soon?"

"I've never thought about anything else since I had an abortion last autumn."

Linda hides behind her *Romance*.

*One Saturday morning when she was waiting for Don to come to her apartment to say that he had bought the air tickets, Will had come instead with a letter. In a few scrawled sentences, Don had almost carelessly explained that he didn't think he was mature enough to marry. . . .*

There is a storm that night, ragged clouds racing past the new moon, the wind crashing against the windows, slapping wires against the hospital panes . . . sending icy drafts under the doors and along the floors. It whistles and sweeps through Prenatal's corridor, through the corridor of ill fortune. The wind crashes against the windows like birds flying astray.

Linda whimpers in her sleep.

An ambulance sends its wail up through the night and stops somewhere far down.

Marie cannot sleep. She coughs and finds it difficult to breathe. These damned colds. They lay her out completely three or four times a year.

She turns the episode that has brought her into hospital today over and over again in her mind.

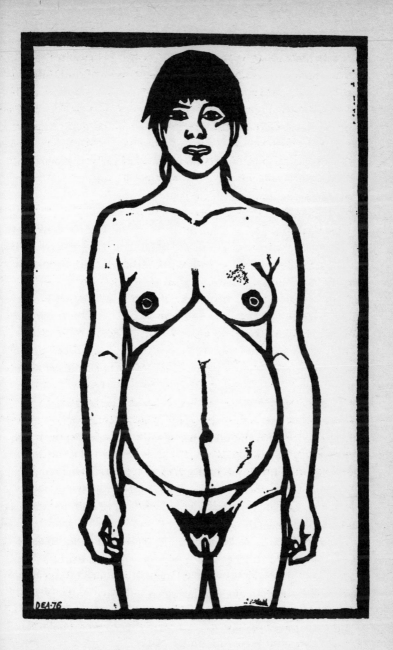

"Perhaps you're a month earlier than calculated," the fair-haired doctor had said.

"No, that's not possible, I'm sure I won't be having it until at least the tenth of February."

"May I examine you?"

He feels, carefully, then looks at the scans that have already been taken.

"You've too much amniotic fluid."

"I don't feel well, either."

"It can be a strain on both you and the baby."

"How?"

"It can inhibit development of the placenta. I don't think we can let you walk around like that. I think you'd better come in today. Can you? I mean . . . your work . . . would you like to go home and say goodbye to your husband first?"

"I'm not married, and my parents live in Jylland . . . but I must tell them at work."

"Where do you work?"

"At a kindergarten in the city."

*Inhibit development of the placenta.* She feels faint, as if she were sliding down a slope. She who was so proud of her stomach. So there *was* something wrong. It wasn't just exaggerated fancies.

Here in the dark, she tries to push her unpleasant thoughts aside, lying on her side, bunching the quilt in under her back for better support . . . wishing sleep would creep up from behind and enclose her, take her in its arms and carry her out on to the great gray ocean.

But just as she is about to slide into the land of nothing, she is again whisked up to the surface.

*Inhibit development of the placenta.* The placenta is essential for the baby's life. She switches on the bedside lamp and listens to the wind. If only she had a watch. It must be about four o'clock, too late to take something to make her sleep and too early to get up, the most cruel night hour between before and now.

Suddenly Linda sits up like a phantom rising from the grave. She spreads her arms out, the sleeves far too long, and says: "Oh, no, no, no."

Ward 0 is square and light, the walls gray, the ceiling white. Through the venetian blinds, you can see down on to lower and older buildings, the old military hospital with red brick walls and a red tiled roof.

Marie looks round the room. Large Olivia and small Linda are in the beds by the window, and alongside Linda is Gertrude with her yellow fairy-tale hair.

Alongside Gertrude's bed is their wardrobe, and alongside Marie's bed is a washbasin.

On the wall above Olivia's bed is a Kodak color photograph of two pale gray kittens, giving an impression that life is twee like a kitten.

Otherwise there are no pictures in the ward, apart from those standing on the patients' lockers.

"You're to go to the ophthalmic surgeon, Mrs. Olsen."

The nurse opens the wardrobe door and gets out Olivia's brown coat and brown lace-up shoes.

"Here you are. It's on the note where you're to go. Up the main stairs and then take the lift down to the ophthalmic department."

Olivia's tall stooping figure is in the middle of the room, her long white legs solidly planted in brown shoes, like two trees in wooden boxes.

She raises a long finger and points at Linda.

"If the paper trolley comes, you'll get that for me, won't you? I'd die without it."

Linda waves her *Romance* at her.

Baska wipes and wipes the floors with a wrung-out floor cloth. It is incredible how a floor has to be washed to be clean enough for a hospital.

Baska is wearing a green nylon overall with short sleeves, and slippers. Her mouth is dark red with strongly touched-up lines. Sometimes she stands still, her arms resting on the floor-scrubber, looking thoughtfully out of the window, her gaze fixed on eternity.

"Baska . . . Baska!" the patients really like her and are always trying to attract her attention.

Sometimes she makes private purchases for them.

"Baska, how long is it since you left Poland?"

"What?"

"How long have you been in Denmark?"

"Six years."

"You're a great patriot, the way you stick to your own language!"

"What?"

"Yes!"

Linda is lying on her back, holding her magazines straight out in front of her. She has almost finished *Place of Many Stars* and notices a sweet tingling up and down her spine.

*Kerry whispered: "I feel so peculiar . . . so weak and peculiar. The whole thing seems crazy and impossible." Rick held her away from him, so he could gaze tenderly into her eyes. Then he stroked a few untidy fair curls away from her face and let his fingers lovingly run round the shape of her ears. He quickly ran his fingertip down her nose, then jokingly pressed the tip of it. "Crazy!" he murmured. "But not at all impossible." Then he pulled her to him again in a tight embrace as he gave her a long and passionate kiss, so she could not doubt that he loved her, or that she loved him. She sighed happily as he smiled down at her, and suddenly it seemed as if the future that had looked so sad and un-inviting now contained a million brilliant promises. Like the sky above them, Kerry thought, as Rick pulled her up in front of him on to his horse. The future would be a place of many stars. THE END.*

Linda puts the paper down and looks up at the ceiling, thinking about Allan. If only Allan sat on a horse and rode through Australia like Kerry and Rick and. . . .

Then she was interrupted by Baska moving her locker and the lamp cord to clean the floor.


"Olivia! It's not certain it's that bad . . . you mustn't take it so much to heart."

But Olivia can't get a word out.

Little Linda is sitting on Olivia's bed with her thin arm around Olivia's broad bowed back.

"He said it so clearly . . . that my sight's got worse."

"Think about the baby you'll soon be seeing."

"But what if I lose my sight!"

They sit in silence, staring ahead, Olivia sniffing and wiping her nose on her sleeve.

"I want to be able to see Holger and Kalle and the baby."

Linda hands her a paper napkin. She's almost crying herself. Suddenly she has a good idea.

"I know what! I'll read your horoscope to you."

Olivia crawls into her bed.

"Yes, if you like. I'm Leo."

"Listen now," says Linda cheerfully, opening *Romance*. *You are bursting with ideas that you are dying to carry out in reality. This is all to the good as long as you know how to weigh things up carefully before spending too much money and time on something that will not produce what you expect of it. You will have luck in gambling this week.*

"Hell, and I can't get to bingo, either!"

"Read Pisces . . . read Pisces, too," cries Gertrude from her corner by the cupboard.

"Here you are then. Listen to Gertrude's horoscope: *It looks as if there may be certain changes in your home.*

"I'll say!"

"*But be careful that you don't take on more than you can cope with. Your finances seem to be stable now. Try to keep them like that.*

"Try to keep them like that! Try to keep them like that!" says Gertrude with gusto.

Marie has not heard much of what has been said. She has been lying on her back reading her green pamphlet. At the bottom of the page there is a drawing of a hand lifting up a factory with a smoking chimney. She has to read the last paragraph three times before she understands it properly. Even then she doesn't entirely grasp its meaning.

*What is meant by the means of production being used as capital? Are means of production and capital not the same? No, capital can take on various forms, and it can also consist of the means of production. But the means of production are not in all circumstances capital. By means of production are meant the quantity of all the tools, buildings, raw materials, etc., of production, that man uses in production.*

"Are you seriously reading *ABC of Political Economy*?" says Gertrude.

"Yes. Do you read *Berlingske Tidende* seriously?" says Marie.

"You're a nursery-school teacher, aren't you? To be quite honest, I wouldn't be too sure about letting my child go to *your* kindergarten."

Marie smiles.

"You aren't a Communist, are you?" says Gertrude in horror.

"Holger's a Communist," exclaims Olivia. "And I vote for them now and again."

"What do you think *Allan* votes . . . now he's unemployed!" cries Linda from her window.

"Heaven preserve us!" exclaims Gertrude, holding her cheeks. "What sort of ward have I got myself into?"

The nurse comes in with a large sealed envelope.

"Why are you all looking so agitated?"

"We're not."

"Here," she says to Linda. "You're to go to Ultrasound. Here's your casesheet. You mustn't open the envelope yourself."

Nothing wrong with a bit of class struggle in the Prenatal department, thinks Marie. So Gertrude couldn't possibly send her child to *my* kindergarten. She can't help smiling. They've been working for more than a year and a half now on collective management structure. It has not been easy. Five sets of parents have already taken their children away, and both the part-time teachers and the practical assistant have resigned. But two new ones are to start on the first of January, good people, with a few years' experience. As long as they cooperate. . . .

But being taken into hospital has not made things any easier for the others. Women having children is one of the greatest burdens on a small place. Now they would have to find a replacement six weeks earlier than anticipated.

Recently there have been a lot of meetings. Meetings with parents and staff. Meetings with teachers from other institutions. Meetings in the union. Not to mention meetings of the family groups into which they had now divided the kindergarten for better opportunities to talk about individual children. She had been to an average of four evening meetings a week in the last four months, and on top of that her study circle and lectures on political economy . . . so it had all become simply too much.

She had caught a chill and was tired, then had gradually felt worse and worse.

Marie is not married. Unmarried mother—a self-evident thing. More than half the parents in the kindergarten are not married, both single fathers and single mothers. Our time seems to run away from marriage.

She is expecting a child with a friend called Zacharias. Zacharias is a Greenlander. He's at the teacher's college and plays the drums in a Greenland beat orchestra. Their great prototype is the Sume group and their new singer Rasmus Lyberth.

Marie and Zacharias have not tried living together, but they've talked about finding a commune with other people who have children. A collective . . . they might well do that.

The child is not planned, but neither is it unwelcome. When Marie found she was pregnant, she had been very pleased.

Twenty-eight, that's the perfect age for having a child.

If only this business of the fluid hadn't happened.


Linda is in Ultrasound in Ward 5. She is lying on a narrow bunk and has had her abdomen rubbed with groundnut oil. She is waiting for it to hurt, but it doesn't hurt. It just tickles.

Nevertheless, Linda tenses every muscle in her body and clenches her fists, for she has never learnt to relax.

A young man with a black moustache begins to move a metal arm back and forth over the skin of her stomach. The metal arm is suspended in the same way as a dentist's drill.

The young man glances from her stomach, where her navel sticks out like a little plug, to a radar screen about the same size as a television set on a low table in front of him.

With the aid of an echo-sounder, a picture of white spots and lines comes on the screen. Now and again, he lets go the metal arm and takes a picture of the screen with a Polaroid camera. A moment later, he pulls a wet photograph out of the camera with a bang and hands it back over his shoulder to a fair-haired woman who has been watching all this time.

They speak quietly to each other. Linda can hear that they are talking about their Christmas and New Year holidays.

The telephone rings. The fair-haired woman answers, listens, raises her head, and says quietly:

"It's from the Prenatal clinic downstairs. They're asking if we can confirm a fetus mortuus?"

"Did you say *fetus mortuus*?"

"Yes, the patient has a heavy feeling in her abdomen. Pregnancy reactions are positive . . . presumably because the placenta is still intact. Hullo—yes."

She jiggles with her foot.

"Can we confirm a crack in the cervical spinal column? Yes, I think so. Ask the patient to come up at once."

She puts the receiver down with a sigh. Heavens! Then she catches sight of Linda lying as quiet as a mouse on her couch.

Linda has heard everything, but not understood what the conversation was about. She is lying there staring at the radar screen. She plucks up courage and asks about what has been occupying her thoughts all the time.

"Can you see my bad back?"

"No."

"Can you see if it's going to be a boy or a girl?"

"No. But we can more or less calculate how far you've got. And we can see the placenta and the baby's position."

"Would you like to have a picture of your child?" says the fair woman. "Look, here you can see the head and body quite clearly, and that's one arm. . . ."

As Linda goes out of the door, slightly cold and with stiff legs, her casesheet under her arm, she passes a young couple. Both are wearing arctic jackets with large fur collars. The man has his arm around the woman's shoulder. Her face is dissolved in tears.

"Isn't he nice, the young man in Ultrasound?" says Olivia.

Linda has noticed long ago that Olivia looks at men.

"Yes, he's quite nice-looking."

"Well," says Olivia, screwing up her eyes. "Did you manage not to look at your casesheet?"

"Olivia!" says Gertrude. "You can't do that sort of thing. It'd be a breach of trust!"

"If I could understand a word of what's in it, then I *would*," says Olivia.

Marie has gone into the day room for a change. She is sitting in an armchair, a newspaper on her knee.

There is a patient in a blue dressing gown sitting on the sofa, her cheeks hollow and her stomach not especially large. If you hadn't known it, you would never guess she was expecting twins.

Her husband is sitting beside her, a sturdy square man, known in Prenatal as Terrible Olfert, although he doesn't know that. That is what Linda says, anyhow.

The couple's youngest son, five-year-old Little Olfert, is sitting on a chair, playing with an elastic band.

The tears are pouring quietly down the woman's cheeks, but it seems to make no impression on the man.

"Don't mind me, Yvonne," he says. "You have a good cry. I'm the one who should be crying. Who the hell do you think's going to answer the phone while you're away? You tell me!"

"Couldn't your mother give a hand?"

"Huh! She knows nothing about the business."

"I know it's difficult for you."

"I'll say it is, hell, yes. A little business like ours can't afford one of us away."

Terrible Olfert bangs the table so that the ashtray jumps.

"Wow!" cries their son.

Yvonne stares emptily in front of her.

"They say if I discharge myself, it'll be on my own responsibility."

"Then *be* responsible, woman."

Linda and Olivia are standing in the bathroom brushing each other's hair.

"But I heard it," says Olivia, in a drawling voice.

"Ultrasound! Are you sure?" says Linda with a hairpin in her mouth. "Can it do damage?"

"Definitely. They say that in Sweden they've stopped using it completely."

"Oh, no, no," whimpers Linda.

The shower curtain is crooked. The bathroom is shabby and the things in it don't work as they should.

The day room is empty, but the television is still on, a silent blue test picture quivering on the screen.

The low table is a mess of ashtrays and cigarette ends, chocolate papers and crumpled-up cellophane.

Yvonne straightens the cushions, switches off the television, then sits with her shoulders hunched up to her ears, staring ahead of her, dreading the night that is now creeping up round her.

Then she gets up and gathers her dark blue dressing gown closer round her. Slowly she goes out into the long night-empty corridor.

The office is empty, but the light is on. A pair of glasses and some knitting are lying on an open magazine.

She goes down to the big window and stands with one hand at her side and the other on her back, staring down at the building-site far below. Cranes and scaffolding lie there in the dark, one small strip-light revealing the roof of a shed and the edges of some timber.

Orion can be seen in the sky between patches of cloud.

## WEDNESDAY 18 DECEMBER

The round had reached Ward 2. There is only one patient in there, Signe Dahl, a potter from Lejre.

"Can we have a description?" says the doctor, nodding to

the young midwife standing by his side with her hands behind her back.

She goes over to the patient and puts her long clean hands flat on the side of the patient's stomach. The hands glide up under the breasts and then back to where they started from. Then they glide down toward the patient's groin, carefully feeling the part of the fetus farthest down in the womb. Slowly, the hands move upward to note the various parts of the fetus. Finally, she turns her back to the patient's face and with all her fingers feels the lowest part of the womb.

"I don't think there's all that much fluid," she says, looking up at the doctor. "Weight . . . well, perhaps 1,800 grams."

"That sounds about it."

The patient sits up.

"I'm worried in case my estriols were low for several months . . . that is, *before* it was discovered."

"Theoretically that could happen, but I think we can exclude the possibility."

He smiles.

"What are you reading?"

He takes the top book off the pile.

"*Handbook in Ceramics and Earthenware*—well, I'm glad you're not wasting your time!"


"Hullo, Baska!"

"Hullo, Signe."

The Polish cleaner is the only member of the staff who always uses the patients' first names. It's not done, although the practice is gaining more and more ground. Patients are supposed to be addressed by their surnames and as "Mrs," regardless of age or status.

"I buy vegetables for you," says Baska, putting a cardboard box on the locker. Under a piece of pink tissue paper are two avocados and a lemon.

"What about the salt?"

"Here!"

"You are lovely, Baska. Thanks a lot."

The nurse sticks her head through the door.

"Signe Dahl . . . you haven't by any chance used Mrs. Larsen's urine container, have you? Something doesn't quite match up."

"I hope to goodness not," says Signe in horror, gathering her kimono around her.

"There's a letter for you, by the way—here."

The envelope is large and white with a lot of stamps all over it.

"It's from my children."

"How many have you got?"

"Three girls, six, four, and two."

"Heavens," says the nurse. "Haven't you had enough of it?"

"No, but we didn't really mean to have any more."

"Where do you live?"

"In Lejre, in an old school where we have a pottery. We're both potters. We lived in Copenhagen before."

She spreads the contents of the letter out on the quilt. There's a blurred photograph with a crooked skyline and a peculiar little bit of knitting from the eldest girl, a paperclip from the middle one, and an incomprehensible cramped drawing from the youngest. Finally there is a short handwritten letter from her husband. She reads it twice, folds it up again, and puts it in her locker.

Then she tapes the children's little things on to the wall, which will soon look like a museum.

She is plagued by that old guilty conscience of hers. Here she is, lying in bed, and at home they have to manage everything themselves. Jacob has to look after the children and at the same time do the work, the throwing, the drying, and keeping the kiln going. But they have to have something to live on. Thank heavens he works at home and doesn't go out to work.

She had become pregnant by accident, so to speak.

The first seven months of pregnancy had seemed thankfully to be quite ordinary, Signe feeling both well and happy. She had carried on with her glazing work and had also started with Jacob on a new series of pots.

She had gone for a checkup at the National Hospital, where she had had her three children, and then it had been arranged that she could have her fourth there as well, in spite of them having since moved out of Copenhagen.

But one day at the beginning of December, they had suddenly telephoned from the hospital. From the analysis of her last urine sample, they had found that her estriol figure had fallen dangerously low. She must come in at once.

Jacob had driven her into town.

"What are estriols?" he asked in the car.

"Some kind of hormones excreted in the urine . . . they tell you something about how the placenta is functioning. And they should be *high*. But mine are low, they say!"

At the National Hospital they were met by the doctor on duty.

He said there was something indicating that not all was well with the fetus, and also that it weighed no more than 1,200 grams.

A Caesarian had been arranged for, and her type of blood brought up.

Signe had said that they should not go to a lot of trouble.

"What do you mean?"

"I mean you mustn't induce me . . . if the baby is in a bad way and is also very small. Nature will have to take her course."

"Now listen. If the baby is suffering and the womb itself does not push it out, then perhaps it's better the baby is delivered by section and is put in an incubator. . . ."

Signe thought for a moment.

"If you do a Caesarian now . . . then the child is not to go into an incubator!"

The doctor looked at her in surprise.

"But you might be risking that the child survives anyhow . . . and in considerably worse circumstances than it would *in* an incubator!"

"Am I not allowed to decide about my child?"

"No."

The doctor shook his head.

"You could have decided to have an abortion . . . but once a child is born, the responsibility is then ours."

"And where's the borderline between abortion and a child?" Jacob had said.

"At 1,000 grams . . . we usually calculate. But some babies with an even lower birth-weight have survived."

When Signe had at last adjusted to a Caesarian being the only way out, the operation was called off as quickly as it had been decided on.

Another diagnosis was made. The situation, they said, seemed to be better than had at first been presumed.

Instead she was to go into Prenatal and see how things went.

Before Jacob went home, he squeezed her hand and said: "We'll have to take things as they come. Just think about yourself now. Don't worry about us."

From then on, he has had to cope alone with everything at home.

Fortunately, his mother lives nearby, but she is nearly seventy, so there are limits to what they could burden her with.

Now Signe has been here for almost two weeks, and against everything she had believed, she is enjoying it. It is marvelous that for the first time for many years, six in all, she is able to take a complete rest. To sleep, to doze, to read and have a bath. To have food brought and everything arranged for you. To be able to talk to people she would otherwise never have got to know.

But she is moody. Sometimes she is tormented with worry and anxiety. Four children in a row . . . that's too many, too short a time between births. She has not had time to recover and she is also really rather too old. She is thirty-six and finds it difficult to vegetate together with her children. Jacob finds it easier.

It had gone well three times. Can one ask for more?

She thinks about her three girls, healthy, sturdy, happy children.

She knows the number of deliveries increases the risk of complications in pregnancy and birth. Pregnancy number two—that's the best one. That's what they usually say here.

Perhaps her glazing work has done the damage in some way or other? She and Jacob have always worked with traditional glazes, quartz, china clay, and red lead with iron or copper oxide added.

Some years ago, Jacob had had lead poisoning, and they had both taken that calmly. But in July, she had twice felt the tips of her fingers turning cold and insensitive, a sure sign of early poisoning.

That was July, and she wasn't even three months gone then! And all the fetus' vital parts formed during the first three months of pregnancy. . . .

She has now persuaded Jacob to work with nothing but frit glazes, a previously blended mixture of quartz and lead, so that the lead is never in its free form. The new glazes are not as good as the old ones, but they are acceptable.

Jacob! She misses him dreadfully, more than any of the others. More than the children, and more than her work.


*The ambitious young officer was noticed by his superiors and advanced unusually rapidly. He was sent to France and Russia, and on his return home, he married one of Queen Sophia's ladies-in-waiting. He moved naturally and with grace in those exalted circles, satisfied with his surroundings and with himself. In the course of time, he benefited from the turn of fortunes in the Dean's home that had become suspended in his mind.*

Gertrude tries bravely to overhear the crude, to say the least, conversations between her fellow patients.

"Well, in the four years since our first, I've hardly dared to sleep with Holger. I've lain there as stiff as a board and been so scared it'd all go wrong again."

Gertrude fixes her gaze firmly on her book.

"But haven't you got a pessary?" says Marie with interest from her corner by the washbasin. "Or condoms? That's easy enough!"

"We tried that five years ago . . . and we got Kalle! At *once!*"

"What about a coil?"

"No, thanks very much. You get cancer from them . . . I've read that in the papers."

The papers, the papers, thinks Marie. Isn't it incredible how they misinform people?

Linda puts on an experienced expression.

"What about the pill then? That's O.K., isn't it?"

"The pill!" says Olivia, flaring up. "Do you think I want an embolism? Me! I've enough to put up with already!"

She puts a hand on her knitting with a sigh and goes on: "But it's just as tough on Holger . . . he could *never come*! I once told our doctor, and do you know what he said?"

"No?"

"Not a word. He didn't say a thing. He just gave me a prescription for my nerves. And that's no great help, is it? Anyhow, not for Holger."

Marie studies Olivia, her hand under her chin.

"When I got pregnant again, I nearly *died* of fright," Olivia goes on. "I didn't find out until I was about three months gone, and then it was too late. And the first one was so difficult, so difficult to get. . . . Heavens, I wouldn't be without Kalle for all the gold in the world."

Olivia smiles with her blue front teeth at the picture of the little boy in the plastic frame.

"They've advised us that I should be sterilized, now that I'm having an op anyhow. They say it will make things better for us."

Olivia clicks her tongue.

"I should hope so, for Holger's sake."

Shivers run up and down Gertrude's spine.

"But it's not advisable to have more than two children if you're diabetic," says Olivia. "They say. The third one might be weakly. So now Holger and I've signed on the dotted line that I'll be sterilized."

"Does it hurt?" says Linda anxiously.

"They *say* it doesn't."

Olivia is proud she's the one who can tell the others so many medical stories.

"You must get pregnant very easily," says Gertrude, raising her head from her book. "It took me eight years."

"But I'm grateful for the children I've got," Olivia says thoughtfully. "Because when you're diabetic, you're not allowed to adopt them."

The conversation comes to an end.

Gertrude opens her book again and goes on reading.

*Achille Papin, the great singer from Paris, had sung for a week at the Royal Opera in Stockholm and there, as everywhere else, had astonished his audience. One evening, one of the court ladies, who had dreamt about an adventure with a great artist, had told him about the wild grandiose countryside of Norway. His romantic mind was inflamed by her description and on his return journey to France, he went round the Norwegian coast. But he felt. . . .*

"Is it good, that book?" says Linda, as she peels an apple.

Gertrude does not reply.

"Gertrude, is that book good?"

"Marvelous."

"Is it a novel?"

"It's *The Banquet of Babette*."

"You know, I once read a fantastic book called *Live Well and Die Young*. You should read it."

The midwife called Rasmussen comes in and asks if there is anything they want for the night.

She goes from bed to bed with her yellow wooden stethoscope, listening to their bellies.

"Ten—eleven—eleven—that's how your baby's heart's beating," she says to Gertrude. "Like a little pocket watch. You're in good shape."

"Do you think good enough to have a Caesarian on the 29th?" says Olivia in her singing voice. "As that'd please Holger so much?"

"I can't tell you that," says Rasmussen, turning to Marie.

Marie looks up from her green pamphlet, grateful for the interruption. She marks her place with her nail at the sentence: *in addition, there are certain middle groups, technicians, intellectuals, etc., who certainly work for wages, but who are rewarded according to rules that are different from the workers', and so. . . .*

She lies back and immediately feels unwell. The midwife notices.

"Don't you like lying on your back?"

Marie shakes her head.

"What's that sore on your lip?"

"Only a cold sore."

Marie touches her mouth.

Carefully, Rasmussen feels her swollen belly.

"You've certainly got a lot of fluid," she says quietly.

"Can't you drain it off?" whispers Marie.

"No, it just regenerates again. And there's always the risk that the patient goes into labor afterwards."

"Why do I have to lie down and rest?"

"So the baby gets more nourishment. So there's better flow through the placenta. Can't you see that?"

"Can the baby be damaged by all that fluid?"

"No, no. The fluid can't damage the fetus, whether there's too little or too much."

Rasmussen raises her head.

"I can't find the heartbeat . . . I'll just go and get the amplifier."

The heartbeat! A jab goes through Marie.

The midwife comes back with a small apparatus, which she places on her patient's stomach.

At once, she can hear the sound, as if someone had turned up an old radio. They could both hear a rushing sound, like a distant train.

"That's the movement of the bowels," says Rasmussen matter-of-factly.

"Listen . . . listen to that soft blowing noise in time with your pulse . . . that's the uterine sound. Here . . . now you can hear the heart, can't you? Listen to that little locomotive, how it's working!"

Marie is filled with joy. She starts coughing and tears come into her eyes. The little dunk-dunk-dunk is her child turning round in the ocean. It's alive. Its heart is beating.

Rørby and Rasmussen of Prenatal are like the famous number seven pair in the six-day bicycle race.

Rørby and Rasmussen are afternoon nurses. They meet every day at three o'clock and stay until the night sister relieves them at eleven.

They work two weeks at a time, and then have two weeks off.

Rørby is an assistant and Rasmussen is a midwife. What the patients daren't ask the day staff about, and what they haven't understood at examinations, they bring up in the evening.

Rørby and Rasmussen make time to talk. They often joke and make everyone laugh. Both of them have children and can put themselves inside the painful nagging thoughts filling their patients' uneasy heads. They understand pregnant women. They speak their language, and they are prone to sentimentality.

After working hard to put the department and patients right for the night, Rørby and Rasmussen go home at eleven. Prenatal becomes slightly emptier and poorer after they have gone, the anonymous hospital atmosphere beginning to seep into the wards again and hang over the beds.

Before Signe lies down to sleep, she thinks about how she has come to regard this hospital.

She really likes it all. The food, which is so different from what she's used to. The room temperature, which is far higher than the one she lives in every day. The staff and her fellow patients, each of whose life stories is an adventure.

All her adult life, she has worked and planned, moving purposefully from one point to the next. She has always been busy.

*That* is what Signe finds so especially good about being in hospital . . . just having time to herself, having no responsibilities and a chance to think.

She lies awake for a long time, enjoying the stillness as she stares out into the darkness.

## THURSDAY 19 DECEMBER

Karen-Margrethe is lying on the couch in the examination room behind the frosted glass, her flowered dressing gown over the back of a chair. She can see a speculum and a pair of forceps, a glass of tampons, and a spray-bottle on the little table beside her.

She is lying on her back with her legs raised in straps, her feet in hospital white socks. There is a rubbery sound from the gynecologist's gloves and the nurse puts her light cold hand on her stomach.

The doctor looks up in the air and inserts his gloved forefinger

and middle finger into the patient's vagina. He feels her womb and the opening of it, with his other hand noting anything external on her belly. Carefully he presses downward and inward, feeling for her child.

Karen-Margrethe tries to relax. She turns her eyes upward and tries to slacken her limbs, breathing quite calmly, noticing his hand inside her, far away, and to her surprise feeling a slight glow of pleasure somewhere between her womb and her heart. ·

He talks quietly to the nurse and she jots things down on a card.

"Thank you . . . you can get down now."

He takes off his gloves and looks through the full file.

"You're forty-one, I see. And your husband?"

"He's fifty-two."

"And this is your first child. Have you been pregnant before? No, I can see here that you haven't."

"We never thought we'd be able to," she whispers. "We're so happy about it, both of us."

"Do you ever get headaches, or feel dizzy?"

"I've felt dizzy now and again."

"Do you have blurred vision?"

"No, but sometimes I seem to . . . how can I describe it . . . to have a kind of *insistent* headache."

"We'll look after you, don't worry."

He smiles at his patient with his brown eyes and she smiles gratefully back.


Every single day since Karen-Margrethe had definitely known she was pregnant, she has thought about her stomach. Every single day . . . many, many times. About what's inside there, what it looks like, how it is.

She is happy. She gathers extra strength and manages a great deal more in the business than she used to. Her stomach is round and tight. Her doctor is satisfied. Her blood pressure is slightly high, but her blood count is normal. Her urine is normal. There's no edema. Only a headache now and again. Everything has been registered as *perfectly normal*.

How marvelous it is, to be normal!

Until her ankles started swelling, and then, a few days later, further up her legs. Her blood pressure had risen and some albumen appeared in her urine. Suddenly a lot more interest is being taken in her. Had she had migraine? Yes, occasionally.

She is brought into Prenatal, and they write *pre-eclampsia* on the board. That means poisoning in pregnancy.

But Karen-Margrethe feels perfectly secure. Nothing can disturb her joy and anticipation. They will help her. And everything will be all right.

"If you don't mind . . . I'd love to be present at the birth," her husband has said.

"Do you really mean that?"

"Yes. You'll have to make up your own mind, of course . . . but I'd like to be there."

"I'd simply love it if you were there," she says. "It'd be marvellous. It'd be a great help. Then we can be together on everything from the very start."

Karen-Margrethe puts her flowered dressing gown over the back of the chair at the end of her bed and looks at her neighbor, seventeen-year-old Connie from Hundestad.

Connie is asleep, her quilt slipping down on to the floor. Karen-Margrethe carefully replaces it.

"Here," says the nurse, sticking her head round the door. "You are to have phenemal, fifty milligrams."

A heavy book trolley is wheeled into the department, a tall bearded young man dragging it along by a handle; behind it an older woman with glasses, in a white overall and slippers.

The trolley stops by the large window and Ward 0.

"Would you like something to read?"

"Thanks, I've got something," says Linda, quickly putting her hand on her magazine in case they should take it away and replace it with some deadly boring book.

"What about you?"

"It hurts my eyes to read," says Olivia. She's holding her knitting right up to her screwed-up eyes.

"Have you anything on childbirth?" says Marie.

"Yes, I've got one here called *Obstetric Psycho-Prophylaxis* . . . it was written by a midwife here in the hospital."

The librarian hands over a thin little book bound in blue plastic.

"Can an ordinary mortal understand it?"

"Have you got anything by Isak Dinesen?" says Gertrude.

They can hear through the open door the young man suggesting books to the staff.

"What about Agatha Christie . . . worth reading? Or Maria Lang? I'm sure you'd like Sjöwall and Wahlöö." *

The older librarian gets ready to leave.

"Tell me, what do people read when they're in hospital?" says Marie. "I'd very much like to know."

"Well, now. What do they read, what do they read? Preferably not too heavy books. They have to be read in a day or two. Patients like exciting novels best, really. True stories from the Second World War, about spies, submarines, sabotage, and smuggling. Or crime, or funny books. Memoirs do well, too. Lots like women authors. And knitting patterns, of course, and books about home decoration."

"What about more egghead stuff?"

"People just don't read serious stuff. They haven't got the energy. The only people who read them are the patients in the psychiatric wards."

"What are you going to call your baby?" little Connie says.

"Something really beautiful," says Karen-Margrethe dreamily. "Yes, something really nice. We'd thought Brian . . . or Benny."

"How can you be so sure it's going to be a boy?"

"It is! That's definite! They've done a chromosome analysis of

---

* Maria Lang is the pseudonym of the Swedish mystery writer Dagmar Lange (1914–), who has published about forty volumes since her debut in the 1940s. Maj Sjöwall (1935–) and her husband, Per Wahlöö (1926–75), also Swedish mystery writers, wrote an acclaimed series of novels about the Stockholm police detective Martin Beck. One of them, *The Laughing Policeman,* won the Edgar Allan Poe Award for best mystery novel of 1971. In the Martin Beck series the personality changes in the detective mirror Sweden's political, economic, and social changes over a period of time.

the waters and they asked us if we wanted to know the sex of the baby."

"But why?"

"They did it because the chromosome combination can tell them if the child is a mongol. And the risk of having a mongol is greater when you're older."

"Why?" says Connie, putting her hand to her cheek. She is not certain what mongol or chromosome means. Karen-Margrethe might just as well have said that they had investigated the mongol combination to see if the child was chromosomed. But it doesn't matter, because Karen-Margrethe is nice to talk to. For the first time in her whole life, Connie is being treated as an adult.

"It's something to do with women's ovaries getting old, while men's sperm is fresh every time," says Karen-Margrethe. "And it's also something to do with the placenta developing less well the older you get. "But I don't really know. I'm so grateful they look after us so well in here. They'll manage, I expect. It's like being in Majorca. Don't you think so?"

Connie nods energetically, although she's never been to Majorca. She just wants to say yes to everything Karen-Margrethe says.

When Connie had come in, she had been told that she must not move. They checked on her contractions, put her on a drip, and gave her an injection that would strengthen her baby's lungs. For a few days she lay with her feet raised and was given only liquid food, so that her bowel movements should not irritate the fetus.

She wasn't even allowed to go to the w.c., but had to call for a nurse every time. That was especially difficult to get used to, the business of bedpans, and being washed so carefully with lukewarm water and soap by other people who kept asking her if the water was all right.

Then the drip was taken away and she was given pills four times a day to stop the contractions.

Gradually her womb has settled down sufficiently for her to get up and go to the bathroom on her own.

Not that Connie can understand what all this interest taken in her is about. Would it really make any difference if the baby were born a month or two too early? They'd just put it in an incubator!

The sun is pouring into the ward. Connie looks out at the clear December sky. She's been told she can probably go home for Christmas.

She opens her magazine and happens to see a couple of sentences. *It is very important you protect your skin from the sun when winter-sporting. If you are going on a skiing holiday or if you like skiing outings, you must use a cream with a high protection factor, because the snow reinforces the effect of the sun and. . . .*

Connie yawns, her eyelids already heavy . . . protection factors, chromosomes, mongols and Majorca. She lies down and pulls the quilt up round her ears. Marie nods to Karen-Margrethe as she passes the open door.

In her white dressing gown and plastic sandals, she walks to the main stairs, the massive shaft through this stone pyramid.

The lifts rush up and down. Stretchers are wheeled from one department to another. Doctors, nurses, and midwives hurry up and down the stairs, always busy.

The sounds on the steps are cold and hard. The patients feel shattered whenever they venture out there, mostly to telephone from the kiosk down in the entrance hall by the great main door.

The main door constantly opens and shuts and visitors look alien and padded as they come in from the cold in their winter clothes. They stand with a hand on the banisters, gazing round with apologetic, almost self-effacing expressions on their faces.

Marie queues for the telephone. She wants to phone her sister, Eva, and Zacharias, to get them to help with all the things she has committed herself to in the coming weeks. She will not be leaving until she has given birth. She has to face that.

An icy wind comes whistling in, wrapping itself round the patients' bare legs.

"I've got permission to go home," says Gertrude radiantly, when Marie comes back to the ward.

"Lucky sausage," says Linda.

Gertrude gets a leather bag out of the wardrobe and empties her locker. Carefully, she packs every article, one by one.

"Do you want my tulips? It seems a pity to throw them out. And look . . . I'll put my papers on the windowsill here."

"I'll hand in your library books," says Marie.

There is a knock and Gertrude's husband sticks his head in, an embarrassed look on his face.

"Are you ready?"

She nods. He throws her overcoat over his shoulder, picks up her bag in one hand and opens the door for her with the other.

"Best of luck to you all and thanks for everything . . . perhaps we'll meet in Postnatal?"

"Must be marvelous to have such a chivalrous husband," thinks Linda. "Carrying your things like that, and opening the door and being nice and considerate. Allan would *never* learn . . . not even if he stood on his head."

While plates of boiled beef, peas, and parsley are being handed round, the dark-haired nurse makes the beds at tremendous speed. The dirty linen is flung into a bag, then the bed covered with a piece of transparent blue plastic . . . almost sealed.

"Lord, we're rushed," exclaims the nurse, clutching at her forehead. "It's always like this just before Christmas. People have babies by the dozen out of sheer nervousness and stress."

Karen-Margrethe has been told to eat two eggs a day, apart from the ordinary food. But she finds it hard to get them down, especially when she is not supposed to take salt. There is no salt in Prenatal, and Karen-Margrethe would never dream of breaking the rules.

Connie eats eagerly, and she's also got some salt in her drawer. She keeps the piece of beef till last. It's a long time since she's eaten anything so delicious. Not since her younger brother's confirmation in the spring.

She doesn't think much about what it'll be like to have a child. A child . . . that's just something you have. At first it's small and then it grows bigger. It doesn't make much difference what you do, it'll grow all the same.

The oldies were stunned when she'd first told them she was going to have a baby. Her father had stamped up and down shouting that she was a chip off the old block. But in the end her mother had said: "One more or less won't matter. We'll probably manage. But mind you don't go doing it again, do you hear!"

"What about watching television this afternoon, girls?"

Rasmussen is standing in the middle of Ward 0, her wooden stethoscope under her arm.

"We usually go down to the day room," says Linda.

"But today I'd like to help you fix up a set of your own."

They accept the offer with pleasure, and Rasmussen starts shifting the furniture about, beds, lockers, and chairs, extension cords and plugs.

The beds are then placed—that's what's so difficult—so that each patient can lie comfortably with a good view of the screen.

"Don't bother about me, Rasmussen dear," says Olivia. "I can't see it, anyway."

The television set is switched on. It flickers and trembles and the picture appears on the screen.

"Can I join in?" Signe comes into the ward with a pot of tea in her hand. "Anyone want any?"

Rasmussen pulls the big armchair out for her.

Marie takes a bottle of schnapps out of her locker.

Linda offers round licorice and cigarettes. She and Signe both smoke like chimneys, and both of them have a guilty conscience about it.

Almost the best thing about watching television is talking. When the television is on, you seem to be able to think better, to have more ideas, to feel more alive.

"What did they do in the old days, Rasmussen?" says Signe. "When women had babies and you couldn't make incisions and stitch like you do nowadays?"

"Well," says Rasmussen, leaning against the cupboard. "What did they do? You just lay in bed until it had healed again, all crooked, too. Your grandmothers didn't look all that good down there, I can tell you."

"Oh, no!" says Linda, putting her hands to her cheeks.

"But in the old days your lying-in was for much longer than nowadays," says Rasmussen. "In the seventeenth century, they reckoned a woman needed forty days, the equivalent of the forty weeks of pregnancy."

She turns down a financial debate a little and continues.

"During those forty days, both woman and child were considered unclean. The child was a heathen until it was baptized, and the woman until she had been churched."

The Middle Ages seem to appear on the whitewashed walls behind the beds.

Marie is following Rasmussen with her eyes all the time.

"Do you know, this, by the way—

> *Forty weeks the Jesus child*
> *was carried inside Mary Mild*"

"Do you know any more like that, Rasmussen?"

"Yes, one. I know a little prayer that's good to say when you're about to give birth:

> *Mother Mary lend me those keys of thine*
> *to open the door to these loins of mine*"

"I'll remember that, when I get to that stage," says Marie. "I'm sure that'll help!"

"It always helps."

"But what did they do when things went wrong?" says Signe.

Rasmussen patted her wooden stethoscope with the palm of her hand.

"You had to loosen all the knots, first on the person giving birth, the hair-bands and tapes and ribbons on her clothes. Then they loosened or opened everything else in the room, sashes, belts, buckles. Yes, the drawers had to be pulled open, and the cupboard doors, too."

Linda creeps halfway down under her quilt. Olivia lifts her knitting right up to her eyes.

"I'm glad I'm having a Caesarian."

"And if that didn't help, then you tried the windows!"

"There must have been an awful draft."

"Yes, but if the child wouldn't come out . . . now, now, don't get nervous. We're good at coping with that sort of thing here, I promise you. If, for instance, the child was lying in the wrong position, then the man of the house was sent out to chop some equipment or other to pieces . . . a plough or a sledge. That helped sometimes."

Marie lights a candle on her locker, and Rasmussen's shadow appears on the wall.

"Shall I stop?" she says.

"No, don't," says Signe. "It's like watching a horror film on the television."

"But when the baby was born," Rasmussen went on, "they hurried to close and tie and buckle up everything in the room again. That couldn't be done too quickly. Otherwise you risked the baby being a changeling."

"A changeling?" says Linda.

"Yes, should there be anything wrong with the newborn baby, they were convinced it had been exchanged."

"How worried they must have been about birth in those days," says Marie, her hand up in her hair.

"Yes, and there was also a remedy. But that was dangerous! If a girl wanted to be certain of an easy painless birth, then, in great secrecy, at midnight, she had to crawl through a magic tree, where the branches had grown together and formed a hole. The birth would then be easy. But the price was high, because her child became either a werewolf or a witch. And the witches, we meet them then whenever we have nightmares: a witch's ride."

The ancient anxiety over birth is there amongst them in the ward. They shake themselves, but companionship warms and protects them, just as it had protected them in the Middle Ages.

"Heavens, is it really half-past nine already?" says Rasmussen. "I must be off."

Signe gets up and turns up the volume. While she is up, she gives a drink to anyone who wants one. They all sit back in their beds and chairs to watch a 1966 Swedish film, *My Sister, My Love*.

A stretcher is brought into Ward 0 and wheeled over to Gertrude's empty bed.

A heavy dark figure eases very cautiously off the stretcher on to the mattress. The porter puts a coat and a bag on the end of the bed and places a pair of slippers on the floor.

The woman is black-haired with a plaited knot at the back of her neck. She has golden-colored skin, heavy eyebrows, and red cheeks. She is squat and very overweight.

She looks a typical guest-worker's wife, robust, humble, anxious not to attract attention.

It is quiet in the ward for a long time, a silence only broken when the nurse comes in with a raised hypodermic in her hand.

"How's my blood sugar?" says Olivia.

"Your insulin dose has been changed . . . but leave that to us, don't worry."

The nurse goes across and introduces herself to the newcomer.

Olivia lets her shirt fall down over her long bare thighs and plucks up her courage.

"Are you Italian?" she asks the newcomer.

"?"

"Rome? Well . . . are you from Yugoslavia, then?"

"!"

Olivia makes an effort to remember the geography of Europe. "What about Greece?"

"What about Africa?" says Linda, rising with a groan from the pillow. "Perhaps she's one of those Arabs?"

"No, no, Turk! I Turk!" exclaims the little stranger with a wide smile. At last she has understood the question.

"Do you speak English?" says Linda, her head on one side.

"Sprechen Sie Deutsch?" says Marie from over in her corner, closing her green pamphlet.

The Turkish woman shakes her Turkish head.

"Parlez-vous français?"

"Little Danish, little bit Danish," she says, her face flushing, and she shows her little bit of Danish by holding up her thumb and forefinger with half an inch between them in front of one eye.

The door opens and a tray of white plastic mugs is brought in.

"Tea for Linda."

"Coffee for me, please," says Olivia.

"You wanted cocoa, didn't you?" she says, nodding toward Marie's bed. "And what does this little mother want, then? Hullo, and welcome," she says, going over to the Turkish woman and shaking her hand.

"Pst! Do you live in Copenhagen, you, the new lady?" says Olivia, her cup of coffee in her hand.

"No, Næstved . . . husband work very fine factory."

"How much does he earn an hour?"

"Olivia!" The nurse looks cross.

"What's wrong with asking? What does her husband get per hour . . . your husband . . . how many kroner?"

Olivia stretches out her hand and rubs her middle finger against her forefinger and thumb. The Turkish woman understands that.

"Sixteen kroner," she says innocently.

"Huh!" exclaims the nurse, now no longer able to contain herself, either. "Damned fine factory, when the minimum wage for unskilled workers is about nineteen!"

They knit and knit and knit. Their knitting needles send their special knitting-needle frequency out into the quiet afternoon of the ward. Marie is the only one not knitting. She is lying on her side with her back to the others, struggling to concentrate on the chapter on surplus value and profit:

*The relationship between surplus value and variable capital or what is the same, between surplus value and the sum of wages, is called the rate of surplus value. The same way, the relationship between excess working hours and necessary working hours can also be expressed by the fraction $\frac{M}{V}$.*

Linda goes over to Olivia.

"Look, I've got to the sleeve. Should I start decreasing now, or what?"

Olivia shows her. Olivia's good at knitting and other handwork and it's no small quantity she's done since she's been in hospital.

She has told the others that her dearest wish is to open a little crafts shop in Skelskør.

"It's my dream. But where shall I find the money?" she sighs. "Tell me that."

Olivia is knitting something bright green, Linda something in pale nondescript colors and the Turkish woman something in radiant cyclamen red.

Marie has her nose in her pamphlet. *In our example, the rate of surplus value is 100 percent* $(\frac{25,000}{25,000})$. *The surplus value rate expresses the degree of exploitation.*

"Look," says Olivia. "Won't it be good? It's going to be a skirt for the floppy doll my niece is having for Christmas."

"Floppy doll?"

"Yes. One of those that flaps its arms and legs about like a real child. It costs seventy kroner . . . but Holger and me and mother-in-law and my sister-in-law have gone shares on it."

Signe comes into the ward in her black kimono, her short hair sticking out in all directions as if she'd lain on it in the night.

"Look!" she says to Linda, slapping a thick library book with satisfaction. "*Natural Childbirth* . . . you should read it."

"Can't be bothered."

"But you *should* know *something*."

"I'm having a Caesarian, thank goodness," said Olivia loudly and self-confidently. "I had one last time, too. So I don't have to know anything whatsoever!"

She holds the doll's skirt right up to her eyes and smiles to herself.

Linda looks appealingly at Signe.

"I've had an abortion . . . I don't know *what* I should know. Do I have to read that boring old book?"

"Yes, you do. You should know about the various stages of birth, the dilation period, the expulsion period, and the afterbirth period. Otherwise you won't have the slightest idea of what's happening."

"She's right, you know," says Marie from her corner.

"Oh, I'm so scared, I'd rather know nothing."

"You certainly ought to," says Signe, so firmly you'd think she's a schoolteacher. "Birth isn't something to run away from. In some countries women lie screaming like animals . . . just because they think that's all part of it. And because they're so frightened. But here we don't scream any more . . . that stopped years ago, because pregnant women go to prenatal classes."

Marie turns the corner of a page that starts: *The relationship between surplus value or profit and total capital, i.e., the sum of constant and variable capital is called the profit rate* . . . then turns to Signe.

"Come and sit over here for a while, will you?"

Signe gathers up her kimono and lights a cigarette.

"You see, I've got something called hydramnios," Marie whispers. "That means *too much amniotic fluid*. What do you know about amniotic fluid? Is it something that is produced once and for all?"

"No," Signe replies. "As far as I know it's produced all the time. The fetus absorbs it, and some of the water goes back to the mother."

Marie looks intently at her, her finger touching the cold sore.

"What's the matter with you? How long have you got to be here?"

"They estimate the fetus is 1,800 grams. They probably won't let me go home until it weighs 2,500."


"Lovely lovely flowers. Me find vase."

The little Turkish woman has had an unexpected visitor.

"Look Habiba . . . lovely lovely vase."

A small woman in a bright red suit hung with glittering imitation jewelry walks on, bouncing rubber soles round the room, making herself useful. Her head is large and not diminished by a yellow candyfloss hairstyle.

She pours water into the vase, spreads the flowers round the edge with her stubby little fingers, and straightens the lamp on the Turkish woman's locker.

"Habiba's tummy . . . very fine?"

"So her name's Habiba?" thinks Marie. "Heaven knows what nationality the other little lady is . . . with that language she speaks? She sounds Danish."

"Doctor-man . . . what says doctor-man?"

"Very fine!"

The little Turkish woman nods with her bun, pleased to be able to deliver such important information.

You would think her guest was Ringo Starr, with all the glittering rings she has on her fingers.

"Not be afraid . . . not be afraid."

"No, no," says Habiba politely. Neither has she even considered being afraid.

"And damn me, if Manchester United didn't go and win two-nil."

Allan is sitting on Linda's bed, trying to tell her something that will cheer her up. Before he came, she was quite happy, but he had hardly come in through the door before her face took on a troubled expression.

"I thought Manchester had lost," he says, flinging out his hand.

"What about the electricity bill?"

"Don't worry, the father of the family will see to that."

"Have you been drinking?"

Linda moves a little away from Allan and looks at him with reproachful eyes.

A young man with long black hair and high cheekbones is sitting by Marie's bed. He is wearing an anorak and a blue seaman's sweater. He is holding Marie's hand in his, looking round smiling.

"I hope you understand . . . it's a terrific chance."

Marie nods.

"And because we've got the job because of a cancellation, we've had no notice. We're off by air the day after tomorrow. The whole orchestra . . . *with* instruments but *without* equipment. They're paying for the lot. In exchange, we get nothing except our keep. But don't you think it sounds good?"

"Yes, it does," said Marie, somewhat subduedly.

"We start in Godthåb and then go on up the West Coast. We're playing every night at a hotel. And perhaps we'll go south to Julianehåb. It'll be marvelous to see the family."

"When do you think you'll be back?"

"We're coming back at the end of January. That'll be in plenty of time . . . you're due on the tenth of February, aren't you?"

"But what about college?"

"*That*'s not so good. They don't seem to be terribly understanding about the need to develop special Greenland-beat starting from the vaigat music.* But to hell with them. I'm going anyhow, and I don't care what they say."

"What if they chuck you out?"

Zacharias shrugs his shoulders and tosses back his long black hair. He smiles at Marie. He is a couple of years younger than she is, and for him life is still wide open.

"I've been to get a new drum-set from Super Sound. I'll pay for it over three years. It's great! Even the Sume drummer can't better it."

"Now you sleep, little one," says the Turkish woman's guest hoarsely, leaving the room waving and turning round several times.

"Me come again soon."

Habiba takes up her cyclamen-colored knitting and sits with it in her hands, staring thoughtfully ahead of her.

Terrible Olfert has brought their two boys, Middle Olfert and Little Olfert, to see their mother.

The whole family has in some way clustered itself together on the day-room sofa with the anemic Yvonne in the middle.

The television is on full blast, but no one is listening.

"Makes me sick to see you all strutting about here doing nothing," shouts Terrible Olfert. "And all at the expense of the taxpayer."

He stubs his cigar into two in the ashtray.

"Things'll go to hell if you stay on here. What are we going to have to live off? Tell me that . . . have you thought about that?"

* Vaigat is a kind of rock music in Greenland.

Yvonne blinks.

"A small business like ours. It'd soon be swallowed up by the big boys. And now . . . what with bad times and unemployment! Can't you get that into your thick head? You must get yourself discharged!"

He gives his wife a nudge in the side and shakes his head violently.

"Wow!" yells Middle Olfert.

"Dad, can we go home now?" says Little Olfert.

"The boys'll be neglected, you'll see."

Both children are rather fat. They take after their father, and they also seem to take his side all the time.

Middle Olfert pulls his brother's hair.

"Stop it!" howls the younger one.

"Behave yourself . . . you young pup!" says his father, slapping the older boy's head, then putting on a miserable expression.

"I never get anything decent to eat. And the canary's water needs changing. And I can't be bothered to look after the guinea pig, I'm telling you."

"Poor little mite," says Yvonne, her face looking quite withdrawn.

"Now just you look at this."

Terrible Olfert slaps a Progress Party card down on the little table.

"I got this this morning. Just you wait . . . in a couple of years, I'll be a member of parliament."


"Heavens alive, is that little Larsen weeping buckets over there?"

The sounds of suppressed sobs are coming from Linda's bed.

Nice little Rørby stops with a tray of empty mineral water bottles.

"Now listen."

She puts the tray down, sits on Linda's bed, and starts winkling the patient out of the tangle of sheets. Then she bends over the tear-stained face and whispers:

"What's the matter? What's troubling you?"

"It's . . . it's Allan," hiccoughs Linda. "I'm so scared of what he'll do while I'm in here. . . ."

"Silly old thing," says Rørby. "Don't you know that all wives are afraid of what their husbands get up to when they're in hospital? And it's just the same with the husbands . . . they lie there all the time speculating about what the missis is up to at home."

"But . . . he's . . . he's been drinking every time he comes here."

"So what? He misses you. It's not easy for him, either . . . don't forget that now."

"But he's not paying the bills," stammers Linda. "I'm so frightened everything'll go to pieces at home. . . ."

"She's probably not far wrong," thinks Marie. "Something or other's no doubt going on in that little two-roomer."

"Oh, dear, the way you all brood when you're here in Prenatal," exclaims Rørby, rising to her full stout little height. "Dry your eyes, now, and I'll get you a cup of tea."

"Was he Japanese?" Olivia asks.

"Who?"

"That nice boy who came to see you?"

"Oh, him. No, he's a Greenlander. He's the father of our baby."

Olivia clicks her tongue.

Marie is lying in the dark with a hand on her stomach.

You, my little one, lying in there, in my womb, how are things with you? Am I about to hatch out an incomplete little life?

What does it matter, really, if the child isn't quite as it should be?

Yes, it does matter, because human beings love to create something perfect. A carpenter wants his table to be stable and stand firmly on all four legs. The painter wants the wall to be painted evenly and well; he won't stand for slapdash work. And it's like that for a woman, too. She wants a lovely child that looks right and knows everything a child should know. You can't blame her for that.

A chilly breeze comes through the ventilator.

Karen-Margrethe is standing under a hot shower, letting the water trickle down over her stomach. That nice round stomach. It is almost as if the baby enjoys being in the shower. She can feel it pitching and tossing, then suddenly kicking out, almost like getting a stitch.

Nothing, not even the thought of the slowly increasing pregnancy poisoning, can discourage Karen-Margrethe, so certain is she they will do everything humanly possible to help her here in the hospital.

What more could anyone ask?

She hums a tune she has heard on the radio.

Karen-Margrethe regards her pregnancy as a windfall. She and her husband had long since given up hope of having children, and they have never done anything to find out the cause of their childlessness. Every fifth married couple suffers from involuntary childlessness; that was something they just had to come to terms with.

Instead, they had adapted to a life with each other, the two of them on their own, and their work in their stationery business they have developed together.

When they had discovered she was pregnant, they had at first been uncertain and confused. She was old enough to be a grandmother! Yes, a very young one, the doctor had said politely. There was no real question of a termination, as she was already in the twelfth week of pregnancy, as far as they could make out.

The doctor had said that they would have to have the chromosomes of the fetus examined to make sure that the child did not show signs of Down's syndrome, because statistically the risk increases if the mother is over thirty-eight, he told them, especially if she is just approaching the menopause.

Karen-Margrethe was sent to St. Joseph's Hospital, where they extracted a sample of her amniotic fluid with a long needle through the abdominal wall.

The result would be sent to them within the next four weeks.

The following weeks were not easy. She and her husband had explored almost every single possibility and had finally decided that even *if* the fetus should turn out to be mongoloid, they did not want to have the pregnancy terminated. Considering their age, they would prefer to have a handicapped child to none at all.

Then it turned out that the chromosome count was normal. Did they wish to know which sex the child was? Yes, indeed they did. It would be a boy.

Now Karen-Margrethe had abandoned herself to the joy to come, and her mother had also been so happy! "I'll look after the baby when you're at work," she had said. "Don't worry about that." Her mother is seventy-two and a pensioner. She has been a cleaner all her life, and can no doubt cope with taking care of a little grandchild.

Her husband is busy equipping a nursery at home. He has done the papering himself and is making a baby-table and shelves for the baby's clothes.

He visits Karen-Margrethe in Ward 5 every evening, and it's hard to say which of them is the happiest.

Karen-Margrethe turns off the tap, takes the warm towel off the radiator and wraps it round her body. She straightens the shower-curtain . . . it is falling off its rail. A small foot, or is it a hand, butts her just below her navel. She presses it lightly with her hand, as if they were greeting each other, the two of them.

"Hey look!" says Olivia. "Now here's something nice . . . *this year's babies and their first Christmas*."

She holds the open magazine up close to her eyes.

The girls gather round her bed.

"Look . . . look at Sonja Oppenhagen, isn't she pretty? And that baby with the cheeks," says Linda, clapping her hands. "And Ulf Pilgård is celebrating Christmas with his wife Gitte and their two small boys, Mikkel and Christian . . . who is only four months old. Isn't that great?"

"And there's Peter Belli and June," says Olivia, pointing. "Ha-ha . . . with pixie hats on. Isn't he sweet, that one with bristly hair?"

"And Pia and Peter from the radio," says Marie. "Have you seen them?"

"Lord, just listen to this!" Linda snatches the magazine from Olivia's hand and reads aloud: *Princess Benedikte's ex-lady-in-waiting, Lykke Hornemann, now married to Count Werner von Schwerin, has three children to celebrate Christmas with at their handsome home in Skåne. Martin is five and a half, Carl Johan three and a half, and little Sofia a year old on the first of January.*

"Oh, let me look," says Marie. "Vivi Flindt's youngest is going to be called Vanessa."

"Vanessa?" Olivia tries out the name. "Vanessa . . . hmm. . . ."

Linda bends her head over the magazine.

"William Rosenberg . . . that's who married Pusle's mother, you know, Jeanne Darville. . . ."

"She's fantastic!"

"He's married again . . . she's studying Danish at Odense University and they've got a daughter called Katrine."

"Yes, and just look at the jersey she's wearing," says Olivia, screwing up her eyes. "Just like the one I'm knitting, isn't it? Isn't it exactly the same model?"

"Oh, fancy getting into a magazine with your child," Linda exclaims, her eyes radiant.

She is already imagining next year's Christmas number. On the center double-spread, there is a color photograph of her and Allan in pixie hats, and a fat little child. The caption says:

*We usually spend Christmas in Tenerife, says Linda Larsen, ex-office assistant, but we are staying at home this year for the sake of the baby. But that is also very pleasant. Relations are coming and we will be seven for Christmas dinner and Allan is going to decorate a really old-fashioned Christmas tree. . . .*

Sister is standing in the middle of the ward with her hands on her hips.

"I hear there's a rumor going round that ultrasound can be damaging."

Olivia peeps at her over the edge of the magazine.

"Isn't that right?" says Sister. "Have you heard anything about it?"

"Yes, we have. . . ."

Linda nods.

"Then I must put an end to such rumors, in all seriousness. It is *nothing remotely* to do with the truth!"

"You never know."

"Perhaps not, but now you all *do* know!"

The place is quite high up and was once a school. Now there is a pottery in the old gym.

Signe is homesick for Lejre. She is lying on her back with her hands behind her head, staring up at the ceiling. She had thought it fine to have a room of her own, but now she doesn't mind any more. She would rather be down in Ward 0, if there is a vacant bed.

She goes round her own house in her mind.

It is the same story every year. The bare cracked soil and black trees surrounding it. The fruit trees blossom first, then the lilac and the chestnuts. Then come the hawthorns and elders, and finally the garden closes in, thick and impenetrable, for the rest of the summer.

In the dark workshop, in the evenings, they can see the yellowy pink transparent light of the sky through the windows. Even if the sun has long since gone down, the light stays, the dark silhouettes of the trees and leaves against the window panes.

Signe and Jacob often want to take a walk at night, but they never do, in case one of the children wakes and calls them, waking up the others.

In many ways, the children limit their world.

"Let's hope no one comes tomorrow," says Jacob before going to sleep. "Let's hope we can be ourselves and not have to talk to anyone. Just be alone with the children and sit for ages over the dinner table."

"Some people have to spend their whole pregnancy here," says the night nurse to Marie. "Without even getting out of bed. Imagine that! They stay here from the moment their pregnancy is confirmed until they are delivered. Naturally they sometimes get 'hospitalitis,' but they're tough, those girls, I must say."

The night nurse pokes at her gray head with her knitting needle.

"I could tell you about a woman who had nine miscarriages. Yes, nine! The tenth time she came in here and was in bed for eight and a half months."

"But didn't she have a flabby, weak baby?"

"No, not at all. It doesn't affect the children. She had the prettiest little girl imaginable. See for yourself. That's her, there."

She pokes with her knitting needle at a color photograph on the notice board. The photo is of a large round infant with a rattle in its hand, and with *Happy Christmas* underneath it in professional photographer's lettering.

"That was her firstborn. She was forty then. That's how strong the desire to have children can be."

The night nurse smiles.

"And you know what . . . a month ago, she had a boy. What do you say to *that*."

"She must have a good husband."

"Yes, she has! He's an engine-driver, and is totally involved in it all, otherwise it wouldn't have worked."

Marie looks round, feeling guilty that she is taking up the night nurse's time, but at the same time, it's nice to talk, so she plucks up her courage and goes on:

"But it's awful, isn't it, when you think about what women used to have to go through? When you think of the suffering involved in pregnancy and birth . . . the price they had to pay, and *still* have to pay, I suppose?"

"You *could* say that, when you see some of the women who come here. But don't forget this is a special department, my dear. Generally speaking, pregnancy has nothing to do with illness at all."

"But I can't help thinking about all those women who die in childbirth, or whose whole lives are ruined by it. Or those who've seen their babies die. Does anyone ever consider what great burdens they've borne?"

The night nurse looks sharply at her, like a bird, her head to one side.

"And what about pregnancy outside the womb?" Marie goes on. "And the fetus lying crookedly, and being strangled by the cord, and . . ."

Marie stares in front of her, her eyes wide.

"And birth cramps and rhesus negative . . . and German measles . . . and cleft palate and clubfoot and oxygen shortage and. . . ! Why is pregnancy such a frail affair? Why are the risks involved always played down . . . at all levels . . . so much? What's the reason for that? *That's* what I can't understand."

The night nurse turns up her transistor radio.

"Now just you come down to earth, will you? You're thinking too much about such things. Even here in this department, where the most difficult cases are, about *ninety-seven percent* of births are normal!"

Thank goodness the night is soon over.


## SUNDAY 22 DECEMBER

It's the fourth Sunday in Advent. There are small bottle-green Christmas trees all over the hospital, hung with fairies and plaited red and white hearts and cones, gold stars and colored glass balls.

Olivia has got up early. Before breakfast, she's had a bath, washed her hair and put in curlers. Then she rubbed body-lotion all over her, put on clean clothes from top to toe, and cut her nails.

She has tidied up her locker and smoothed her bed. She has taken her brown coat out of the cupboard, brushed it down, and hung it back again.

For today Holger is coming to see her, all the long way from Skelskør . . . as they had agreed when they last saw each other two weeks ago.

At exactly twelve minutes to twelve, Holger is there in the doorway, a pleasant little man with black hair, a long white face and long teeth. He is wearing a brown suit and a tie, a blue raincoat over his arm. He smiles bashfully.

Olivia blushes and puts down her bright green knitting, pleased and confused, as if he had taken her completely by surprise. She touches her curled hair with the tips of her fingers and slowly swings her large legs out of bed.

They greet each other rather distantly, and she goes over to the cupboard to fetch her brown coat and lace-up shoes.

There they stand, dressed and radiant in the middle of the ward, a queen with her consort on her arm. Olivia leads her Holger through the door and out into the corridor. Slowly and with dignity, they glide down it, Olivia nodding to right and left through the open doors.

For the moment has at last arrived . . . they are to have breakfast at the new patient-café that has been opened in Blegdam Road, in the tall skyscraper that can just be seen from the windows.

"Heaven knows what husbands really think of their wives slowly swelling up and becoming more and more voluminous, more and more carnal and shameless," thinks Marie. "Their eternal talk of symptoms and this and that . . . it must be an extremely peculiar experience."

What does Holger think of his Olivia, as she has been for months, weak and smiling, brooding on her great egg? Does he regard her pregnancy as an illness? As something he is partly to blame for . . . because he's made her fat? Is he proud or ashamed? It's hard to know.

But he clearly protects her while she sits brooding in the nest, as best he can. Perhaps most do? It is something called 'parental instinct.'

Unless, like Terrible Olfert, they prefer to shove the eggs out of the nest in order to have more room for themselves.

Allan and Linda are sitting side by side on the bed. They have put the quilt round their shoulders so no one shall see they are holding on to each other.

"What about that LP he borrowed?" whispers Linda.

"Oh, he's borrowed so much since you've been away."

"Will we get it back?"

"When he's sober, perhaps? Ha-ha."

"How much did you drink yesterday?"

"Was it half a case?" Allan always asks questions instead of answering, which is irritating.

"What time did the others go?"

"Was it about three?"

"Did you remember to pay the rent?"

"No; that's a thought, of course."

Linda falls silent and stares through the dark slats in the blind at the chalk-white December afternoon, white as the room, white as the bed.

Every single day, she hopes Allan will come. And every single day she feels sorry for him that she's here and it's a hell of a long bus trip for him to visit her. And every day she feels the same stab of jealousy, of anxiety, disappointment, and irritation when she sees him coming into the ward. He's not like the men she reads about in magazines. Far from it! He is cruder, less considerate, he drinks, and never says he loves her.

Deep down, she knows perfectly well the child she is expecting means nothing at all to this twenty-two-year-old expectant father. He hadn't wanted it. But he thinks, *what the hell*, when Linda did.

Linda reckons everything will change when their first child is born. Then she'll be a real woman with a little child on her arm, and Allan will grow up and be more considerate and hard-working. Linda is looking forward to both of them creating round this child the loving atmosphere and security she has never in her lifetime even come close to having. All her pains, her bad back and uncertainty, everything will simply dissolve when she first holds that little creation of hers in her arms.

Allan looks down at her thin legs and puts his hand on her knee and gives it a friendly squeeze.

"I've mended the door of the kitchen cupboard," he says.

Linda nods. Allan wonders what he can tell her now that might interest her.

"You know," he says. "You know that uncle of mine, the one who lives in Hjøring. He's heard there's no more work for him after the fifteenth of February. They've sacked a hundred workers and office staff. And they're moving the factory to Roskilde."

Linda isn't listening. She suddenly interrupts him and whispers: "Look, see, over there. . . ." She nods in the direction of the Turkish woman.

A large company is assembled round the Turkish woman's bed. A man is upright, thickset and square in blue clothes, at the head of Habiba's bed, his eyes dark and lively. He is looking at his five-year-old daughter, who has got up on to the bed into her mother's cozy arms and is now lightly patting the large stomach.

At the foot of the bed sits the family's fair-haired friend in her bright red suit with all its ornaments, making encouraging little cries.

But because she is there, they don't think they ought to speak their own language. No, they have to stick to their common guest-worker's dialect that their Danish friend had mastered to perfection.

The man hands his wife a brown paper bag. She takes out a crochet hook and a small ball of crocheting thread and gives him a smile of gratitude.

Their daughter, Fatime, becomes impatient. She jumps down from the bed, crawls underneath it, and says peep-bo and cuk-cuk in Turkish. Then she goes to the foot of the bed and starts doing gymnastics on the foot-pedal. Her father hushes her and tells her she mustn't mess up her clothes. The child smiles with her brown sparkling eyes. Then their fair-haired friend gets down on the floor, catches the child, drags her over and dumps her down on her mother, who is almost knocked breathless by the unexpected gesture. Habiba's eyes fill with tears. The hubbub round her bed is almost more than she can cope with.

"Me help," says the Danish woman. She can perhaps help the man and wife speak to each other; that's probably what she was thinking.

"You eat chocolate mum-mum." She takes a large box of chocolates out of her bag and hands them round. Little Fatime stuffs her mouth full with more than she can swallow.

When there is nothing else to talk about, both Habiba's husband and their fair-haired friend start looking round the ward to find something to do or someone to talk to, because it's rather too early to go home.

"Would you like a chocolate?" says their friend, stopping by Marie's bed. Marie can't contain her curiosity.

"How do you know them?"

"Oh, they lived in my apartment for two years in Vender Street . . . before they moved to Næstved. They're the nicest and best behaved people you could think of, Habiba and Ibrahim are. We Danes . . . we have a lot to learn from them."

The man comes over and stands by Marie.

"I've been five years in Denmark. Wife two years. I send money home . . . cash . . . bank . . . Istanbul. Every month. Very fine. Three more years in Denmark. Then home to Turkey."

He slices through the air with his flat hand.

"Now they're hoping for a son," says their friend, smiling broadly. "They've got a daughter. Isn't that right?"

She turns to Habiba and smiles:

"Boy very fine, eh?"

The little Turkish woman is sitting straight up in bed, her bun loosened and the black plait down her back. She puts the palms of her hands together, turns her eyes up to heaven, and says:

"Allah, Allah!"

"Oh, yes, I forgot. That's something Allah decides, that's right. Ha-ha. But perhaps he'll be friendly just for once."

"Two children," says the husband, a modern man. "Two children very fine. One boy. One girl. Very fine."

Down in the day room, Middle Olfert, Yvonne's son, is lying with his feet up on the table, deep in a comic book. Now and again he pulls a long thin strip of bubble gum out of his mouth, cries "Wow!", winds it round his forefinger, and stuffs it back into his mouth.

There is a smell of peppermint and dirty socks round him. His mouth moves as he reads.

*"It is my knightly duty to fell the monster," says Sir Gawain. They ride on and suddenly they come upon a gigantic crocodile. Sir Gawain at once lowers his lance and bravely charges at the monster. . . . Prince Valiant gallops quickly forward to rescue him. Sir Gawain is thrown to the ground. At the last moment, Prince Valiant flings his net, diverting the monster's attention away from Sir Gawain.*

Terrible Olfert and Yvonne are sitting side by side without saying anything, he blowing out great clouds of smoke, she playing with the belt of her dressing gown.

Suddenly he exclaims:

"The guinea pig has eaten its babies."

During the night, the Turkish woman has severe pains, twisting and turning in her bed, groaning. Marie can't decide whether she is asleep or half-awake and trying to control her anguish and pain. Like a great injured animal, she lies struggling with herself.

Marie rings for the night nurse. The blue lamp winks. The night nurse phones down for the midwife. Marie goes out into the corridor to wait, to have something to do and not just lie there taking no initiative.

Far down by the door out onto the main stairs, two white angels come into sight. Two tall, slim midwives . . . two white and starched young women in white wooden-soled shoes and knee-length stockings.

Soundlessly, they go into Ward 0 and over to the foreigner's bed. They whisper to each other, fold back the quilt, and feel with their cool hands over the large swollen belly.

They feel the patient's pulse and listen through the stethoscope, whispering.

"Are you having contractions?"

"?"

"Are you having contractions?"

"She probably doesn't know what contractions are."

"Hurts!"

"Look, she has a lot of swelling. . . . Does it hurt when I press here?"

"Hurt . . . hurt," whispers the Turkish woman unhappily.

"And here? Does it hurt there?"

"Can you see? She's got eczema. She must see the dermatologist tomorrow."

"Don't you think we should calm her down?"

They give her something to make her sleep, covering the heavy body carefully with the quilt and putting out the light as they leave the little room.

Their care and cool hands seem to have been enough to calm Habiba. She puts her hands under her cheek and closes her eyes. The white angel has taken away her anxiety and loneliness. Now she can sleep. Her little black plait lies on the pillow like a kitten.

A moment later, her calm Turkish breathing can be heard . . . as regular and heavy as the waves in the Bosphorous.

Marie can't help thinking about why the midwives are so beautiful.

She realizes what it is after a while . . . it's because they are so young. They are student midwives. Is youth really beautiful in itself? Or is it their special work that gives them that look of clean airiness?

## MONDAY 23 DECEMBER

The professor is doing his rounds from ward to ward, discharging patients.

"Go easy on Christmas food," he says. "Remember now, not too many rich things."

The patients with small children at home must make sure they don't get too exhausted. They should preferably lie on a sofa and get others to do the work for them, and they must report back to Prenatal on the first or second day after Christmas.

He walks, tall and imposing, past the small decorated trees, and goes into Ward 0, heading first for the foreigner's bed.

"Do you speak English?"

Habiba shakes her head.

"No? What about French? Parly you français? No? Habler you espagnol, perhaps? Nor sprechen Deutsch? Well, now."

Habiba looks at him with a trembling smile on her lips.

"Little bit Danish," she whispers, almost inaudibly, holding her forefinger and thumb up to her eye to show how little.

"The patient has been here for two years," says the sister. "She finds it difficult to make herself understood. But I think she'll get all the help she needs from the others in the ward."

"But things are looking fine," says the professor. "Has this patient anywhere to go for Christmas?"

"She lives in Næstved."

"Then we'd better keep her in."

The professor smiles and goes on to Linda's bed, his hands behind his back.

"You want to go home very badly, don't you?"

"Oh, yes I *do*."

"All right, but be careful, now, won't you?"

"And you . . ." he stops by Olivia's bed and glances briefly at her board. "How are you feeling, Mrs. Olsen?"

"Oh, Professor, *wouldn't* it be possible for me to have my Caesarian on the twenty-ninth, because that would have been my father-in-law's seventieth birthday?"

Olivia looks as if she is speaking to royalty.

"Hm . . . the twenty-ninth. That's a Sunday. I doubt it very much. I think you should stay here, too, now it's so near. And you, what have *you* got to say?"

"Christmas means nothing to me," Marie hurries to say. "It's neither here nor there to me."


"It's too bad," says one orderly to the other. They're standing in the corridor, watching Terrible Olfert, who has come to fetch his pregnant wife.

She has at last given in and has had herself discharged *on her own responsibility* before Christmas Eve.

They walk along the corridor, followed by Sister. Yvonne looks lopsided and all wrong in her coat. Terrible Olfert is polite and is carrying her case, looking triumphantly at the staff and patients. At last the wife has shown some courage and heart. He has good reason to feel proud.

He thumps her delightedly on the back and cries, "Cheerio, then," as they go out on to the main stairs.

Now Yvonne can go home and look after her go-ahead husband and their two go-ahead children, the telephone, the guinea pig, and the canary. Instead of lying here, playing at being Cleopatra with all those women's libbers.

The corridor is uneasy. A midwife and an orderly are in Ward 5. The door is wide open. A fetal monitor stands by the window bed, its cable wriggling like a hosepipe out to the plug in the passage alongside the little Christmas tree.

Karen-Margrethe lies in bed looking lost.

She has the machine's belt fastened round her waist.

Her contractions are irregular. They are being drawn in dancing vibrating curves on to a broad strip of paper, which slips to the floor with a little ticking sound.

Karen-Margrethe stretches out her hands in front of her.

"It's flickering in front of my eyes . . . I can't see very well."

The midwife takes her pulse and blood pressure, listens to her abdomen, and nods to the orderly already standing with one foot in the corridor.

Little Connie goes over to Karen-Margrethe and gives her a great big hug.

"Look after yourself," says Karen-Margrethe.

A white stretcher is pushed through the glass door at the end of the corridor.

Then Karen-Margrethe is taken away.

## TUESDAY 24 DECEMBER

"Have you heard? Karen-Margrethe has got her baby boy!"

Trusting Karen-Margrethe has got her little Brian.

Olivia knows most about it, because she's spoken to Baska, who knows someone who cleans in Delivery.

They did a Caesar on Karen-Margrethe. They realized the fetus was suffering and her estriols had fallen. She is already back in the postnatal ward. The boy weighs 2,700 grams. Just think, born on the twenty-third of December. What a birthday. Poor child!

Well, he will be all right with those parents.

While the crowd is gathered out in the corridor, the little Turkish woman, who doesn't understand what it's all about, goes from bed to bed, smoothing quilts and shaking pillows and throwing crumpled bits of paper into the wastepaper basket in Ward 0.

It is her way of showing gratitude.

"The boy's in Neonatal."

"What's Neonatal?"

"The unit for newborn babies."

"His heartbeat's weak . . . Baska says."

"Does that mean anything?"

"Not necessarily."

"And his father and grandmother have already been to see him . . . they were shown him through a glass window."

"I'll go down and see Karen-Margrethe in the postnatal ward," says Connie, who already has her coat on. "Because I'm going home today. And I won't be back until I'm due."

All through the day, patients go home one by one. Signe is fetched by her husband and their three little girls and, for a brief while, the corridor is filled with their laughter and shrill little voices.

Linda takes a taxi home to Allan.

One after another, they vanish through the main door, their cheeks red and flushed, their hair newly washed.

By the evening, only Olivia, Habiba, and Marie are left.

The orderly tries to make Christmas as nice as possible, mostly for Olivia, because the Turkish woman is not used to a Danish Christmas, and Marie has said that she doesn't mind either way.

Greek folk music is coming out of the office. The orderly has been given a tape for Christmas by her daughter.

The notes bounce cheerfully round the white hospital walls, as if you could see the small white churches of Greece, the sheep and flocks of goats, and the wide green plains.

Marie wonders briefly what Habiba thinks about when she hears that music? But there is no sign on that dark face.

Habiba is sitting on the chair at the end of her bed, just as if she were outside her door at home in Turkey, watching the passersby. The television doesn't interest her. Occasionally she lifts her head and smiles in a friendly way to the others.

She is crocheting with a tiny piece of strong white thread. Length after length, slowly but surely, the finest lace trimming. It is for the five-year-old Fatime's wedding-dress.

Marie feels like getting drunk. The orderly has said they can have as much red wine as they like, and as neither Olivia nor Habiba drink, there are already three bottles lined up on Marie's locker.

But she has heartburn and that takes away some of her desire.

She gives Zacharias a thought. He's probably at some hotel in Godthåb with the others in the orchestra. But maybe some of them have relations in the town?

The orderly comes in with cakes and oranges and chocolate in colored silver paper.

Olivia takes two large bars of filled chocolate.

"Just this once, then I seem to see better."

"Where are Holger and the little boy?"

"They're with my brother-in-law and sister-in-law . . . they live quite near."

Some time during the afternoon, a pale girl is brought into Ward 0. She has had a miscarriage and should be in Intensive Care. But Intensive Care is closed and Prenatal has taken over its duties.

When the orderly is not in the ward pouring red wine into glasses, she is out in the office playing the same tape over and over again. She leans back in the office chair, listening to the Greek dance music, dreaming back to the little café kept by Stellio and Michaelis.

The sponge fishermen are singing and dancing on the sand in the moonlight. The nearest two hold a little handkerchief between them and dance straight-backed and with quick steps between the tables, so people have to pull in their chairs. The retsina glints in the carafes, crickets chirp, low shield-shaped olive trees are silhouetted against the full moon.

Stellio has put his arm round her waist. She leans back against his warm chest and sips wine and slowly smokes a Greek cigarette as the water laps against the small stones.

Two large ships are anchored in the silvery bay.

## WEDNESDAY 25 DECEMBER

The rain slashes against the window, belting out of the sky. Christmas rain and slush. Typical blustery wet Danish winter weather. Cars swish along, constantly driving up and away again.

At the bus stop in Tagen Street opposite the hospital, people stand holding their headgear with one hand, their other arms at their waists, leaning against the wind to stop themselves from being blown over.

The bus stops with its hissing windscreen-wipers, spews passengers out on to the pavement, and sucks others up.

The wind is roaring as if through long pipes, the sound coming nearer and nearer, then colliding with the hospital windows, which flap and shake like sails, like a great tent the wind is about to blow away.

Marie is standing at the window.

Deep down below on the tiny fragment of pavement, she can see a small figure walking along in the wind. It is Karen-Margrethe's mother on her way to see her grandchild.

## THURSDAY 26 DECEMBER

Signe is chalk-white in the face.

"The boy's dead."

"Who?"

"Karen-Margrethe's little boy has died."

"No."

Signe nods. Marie stares at her.

"It can't be true!"

"They operated on him this morning . . . there was nothing they could do . . . something to do with his heart."

"Where's Karen-Margrethe?"

"She's been given a room of her own . . . her husband and mother are in with her."


## FRIDAY 27 DECEMBER

There's a full moon that night.

The storm has abated and the moon is shining above the National Hospital. The face of the moon is calm, melancholy, with thick cheeks and half-closed eyes that have much too much to think about.

Life can be short. Some don't even manage the short journey between fetus and life.

Karen-Margrethe's little Brian died on the fourth day, a small light extinguished in the incubator. Now he's gone.

Nevertheless, his parents and his grandmother, who just had time to see him a couple of times through a pane of glass, will never be able to forget him. They will never be able to forget the little face that seemed so familiar to them. That was like themselves. They would never be able to sweep aside the picture of the tiny sleeping creature weighing 2,700 grams, lying in the incubator with his legs curled up under him.

But they will not be able to tell anyone that. Grief cannot be shared.

They had only just begun to dream of a life with him. We'll do this, and that, and that, and when he's older, we'll do that.

All her life, ever since her thirteenth year, Karen-Margrethe has menstruated with absolute regularity. She has had the same cycle, year in and year out. This calm moon-cycle has been broken for the first and last time before her menopause, by this child, which she has nurtured, if not completely, inside her body for the past thirty-seven weeks.

The full moon stands above the hospital with its head on one side, looking like a baker.

There are only twenty-five years left of the century. Karen-Margrethe has not been able to give those twenty-five years to her son.

Life is not trivial. Everything that happens is relevant and brings with it a message. Every little life is part of a great plan. It is almost impossible for individual human beings to take it in.

## SATURDAY 28 DECEMBER

"There's no doubt the hourglass runs out much more swiftly for women than for men."

"I'm not quite with you."

"I mean," says Signe. "Women can have children until they're about forty, can't they? But that's not to be recommended, is it? Because we all know women become more and more incapable of giving birth and the children get more and more weakly. I've always thought I'd have my children before I was thirty-five, and now look! I'm already thirty-six. Time goes so quickly."

"Yes," says Marie. "I turned cold when I realized that here they regard you as a late primigravida if you're over twenty-seven! I'm twenty-eight!"

"Yes," Signe goes on. "What I wanted to say was that women— *before they're thirty*—must have decided whether they want children or not. They can't allow chance to rule. That'd be too risky."

"Why?"

"Because if they really want children, but don't work purposefully toward it, it can happen very easily that they can't get pregnant for a couple of years, for instance, however hard they try. That's what they call 'infertility problems.' And then suddenly, the bell goes, and there's panic-stations, and it's almost too late. Then the situation can be really painful."

Signe passes Marie a table napkin.

"I think that in that way women are differently *placed* from men. Women live under time pressure. Although it's not true men go on being just as good at bringing up children and just as fit to be fathers, until they're quite old. . . ."

Marie nods. Signe is sitting up in bed in her black kimono, propped up against pillows.

"Women's most fertile years, the age when birth is easiest and the children healthiest is somewhere between eighteen and twenty-five. But if she wants any kind of further education, say until she's twenty-five, then the ideal age has already passed. Then she's only got a short time after she's finished her education to decide whether she really *wants* children or not. And if she does, she finds it hard to *use* the education she has just had. I think the pressures are too great."

Marie pours out some wine.

"That makes our situation rather different from men's . . . and I don't think it's been touched on nearly enough in the women's movement."

"Yes," says Marie eagerly. "I've thought a lot about childbirth being a school subject."

"Of course."

Marie chews on a match.

"I know a lot of girls who've decided not to have children . . . and I respect them enormously for it."

"Yes, indeed. What I'm against is that many men and women don't get together to *think* out the problem.

"Do you think men have the same need for children as women do?"

"They haven't the same physical need, of course. Naturally, they've no need of becoming fertilized, having a child inside them, nourishing it and feeding it. But as soon as the child is born and they've seen it and felt responsibility for it, then I think they have the same desire to live with it, protect it, and bring it up as a woman has. You can say what you like, but I think it's instinctive."

*It is the three-hundred-and-sixty-third day of the year today. The sun rises at 8:42 and sets at 15:42. Lighting up time is 16:12.*

Marie is lying on her side with the newspaper stretched in front of her in one hand. *Washington (AFP). On Friday President Gerald Ford started to. . . .*

If only my estriols would go on being relatively high?

*The Saigon area is suffering from an acute shortage of rice, including rice for the million members of the armed forces, and are doing everything either to loot or destroy the rice in the liberated zones, hoping in this way not only to acquire rice for themselves, but also to stop the mass flight of people from Saigon into the liberated zones.*

Here in prenatal, they should have one of those little flags the newspaper kiosks put out when the evening paper has arrived. On it should be: estriols have come. They're fine all along the line. No need to worry. Love from the Serum Institute.

*Gradually, as the time for the proposed election of the constitutional assembly in Portugal approaches, there is a growing political awareness.*

Think of being in Portugal now! That must be exciting!

*Preparations are being made for parliamentary elections on 9th January. About a third of the voters are expected to vote differently from in 1973. If a third of the votes at the coming election move in an appropriate direction . . .*

In an appropriate direction?

*. . . then the vigor of parliament can be restored. It is the responsibility of voters to see that this happens.*

Well, thanks very much . . . it's the responsibility of voters to see that this happens!

*There are eleven organizations altogether behind the attempt to coordinate the work for the coming International Women's Year: the Red-Stockings of Copenhagen, Women's Front, Thilders, Danish Women's National Council, Democratic Women's Association of Denmark, the Lesbian Movement, the Women's Association of Denmark, the National Union of Danish Students, SF Women, VS Women, and the Danish Communist Party's Women's Branch.*

And I dreamt of a quiet well-prepared Leboyer birth! What a hope! Laughter and voices are coming from the end of the corridor. A short stocky man with dark curly hair goes into Ward 2, followed by three little girls in voluminous jerseys and anoraks.

"Hullo, Mum!" say the girls, crawling up on to Signe's bed. "When can we see our baby sister?"

"Soon, soon," says Signe. "I'll probably be coming back home for a few days first. Won't that be nice? Then we'll get everything ready for the baby."

"She can have my toys if she likes," says the middle girl.

"Dad's made a house for us," says the big one. "Out in the workshop behind the wheel."

"Is it tough going?" says Signe, feeling soft all over. "Aren't you exhausted?"

"No, not too bad," says Jacob. "They're sweet really. As long as they don't squabble, there's no problem. They do everything they can to help me . . . it's quite touching."

The girls chatter away, arranging themselves in the bedclothes, unpacking small gifts they have wrapped up themselves for their mother before leaving on the long journey from home. They all sit up on her bed as if in a compartment on a train on an ordinary journey to somewhere in a green summer landscape.

"Every night, all four of us get into the big bed and read picture books and watch television. The only problem is that they go to sleep too late," he says, nodding in the direction of the youngest one. "I can hardly get her up in the mornings."

"Granny has made a Happy Families for us," says the middle one. "We're all going to play it tomorrow, she says."

"Would the children like something to drink?" says Rørby. "What about a poisonous green soda water?"

"Yeeees, pleeeeease!" all three of them squeal. "A poisonous green soda water!"

They are given plastic glasses and spill it all over the quilt and the floor, so Jacob finally has to put a stop to it. For a moment everything is chaotic, and an anorak slips to the floor into the soda water and gets soaking wet.

"They don't get washed all that well, as you see," says Jacob. "And neither is the cleaning done properly at home, but you'll forgive us, I suppose."

Signe sits with her youngest in her arms. The child puts her warm cheek against her mother and her hand on her breast. It is only a year since she was being breast-fed.

"Lie still, Olsen, otherwise I can't do it!"

Olivia wriggles on the sheet, while Rørby shaves her between her legs.

"Lord, how it tickles!"

"Go on, Rørby, don't hold back!" cries Marie from the wash basin.

"No, leave a bit for Holger," says Linda.

"Holger can wait," groans Olivia. "The worst of it is that it takes so long to grow again and then it prickles like hell in between."

"Now you're to have an enema," says Rørby, gathering up her shaving tackle. "And you mustn't eat or drink anything from midnight on. Remember that now, Olsen dear. Nothing . . . no eats or drinks!"

"Oh, I can have one bit of sugar-free chewing gum, can't I?" Olivia says appealingly to Rørby.

"No, you can't. Chewing gum is enough to set the saliva secretion going."

"So you mustn't think of anything that makes your mouth water, either," says Marie, pulling her quilt up behind her back.

"Today's the day Holger's dad would have been seventy," says Olivia.

## MONDAY 30 DECEMBER

The day Olivia is to have her Caesarian, she has a bath early in the morning, washes her hair, and changes her clothes. It is not the twenty-ninth, as she had hoped, but she has got used to that and is happy and excited all the same. The long journey is coming to an end. Now she is on her way in and the consultant has promised to wield the knife himself.

She has planned everything down to the minutest detail. Her toilet bag is packed and her overcoat has been rolled around her slippers. The green knitting is in a plastic bag and the magazines thrown away, after the knitting patterns have been torn out. The photograph of Kalle has been wrapped in paper and put into the pocket in the big bag.

An hour before breakfast is served, Olivia is given an injection in her arm and a glucose drip is set up to give her twenty drops a minute.

At eight o'clock, she is given her ordinary insulin dose.

Habiba is sitting on the end of her bed. Her back straight and her hands in her lap, she sits watching the activities in the ward.

With signs and gestures, Marie has explained that Olivia is going to be sliced open today with a large knife, and she does not understate it when she shows how large the knife is. Habiba's brown eyes are round like marbles.

"I'm scared to death they'll forget to sterilize me," says Olivia, who is stretched out flat.

"I know what!" says Signe, who is leaning against the doorpost with a cigarette in one hand and a box of matches in the other. "We can draw a dotted line across your stomach and write *cut here and remember to sterilize me*. I'll go and get my red felt-tip."

"Yes, you do that," says Olivia, smiling.

Her cheeks are slightly redder than usual.

Baska comes shuffling along in her green nylon overall. She puts down her bucket and broom, leans in toward large pale Olivia and says: "Nice time, have really nice time."

Olivia is lying all packaged and ready, as if to be sent off from the station, when the porter appears with a stretcher at ten to nine. She is transferred with dignity onto the stretcher and her parcels, her bag, her brown lace-shoes, and the brown overcoat are all placed at the end of it.

She is tall, her feet protruding beyond the end of the stretcher.

The moment she leaves the ward she has lived in for the last two months, a small tear makes its way out of the corner of her eye. She smiles and raises her hand to wave as the stretcher is wheeled away down the corridor.

The others stand, watching her go. They can't help thinking that in a short while Olivia will be given an anesthetic. The doctor will be wearing his blue operation gown with a mask over his mouth and a cap on his head. At exactly 9:30 the incision will be made, first right down the abdominal wall and then across through the womb, and the little creature will be lifted out into the daylight like a cork being taken out of a bottle.

A little Olsen, who will live in a farmworker's house somewhere near Skelskør, with a good unemployed man as a father, with a nice large mother who has an invalidity pension and is slowly losing her sight, and with a curly-haired older brother called Kalle.

The good news comes in the afternoon.

Olivia has had a big girl with black straight hair and weighing 3,400 grams, and everything's gone well. The baby has been put in the ward for the newborn babies. But there's nothing remarkable about that . . . all diabetics' children are. It will have to stay there for twenty-four hours or so for observation.

Everyone is happy and relieved and thinks the doctor and Olivia together have made a fine job of it all.

Habiba smiles with her round cheeks, claps her hands and says: "Very fine!"

## TUESDAY 31 DECEMBER

The remaining patients, now only Habiba and Marie, spend New Year's Eve in Intensive Care. They are to be there for two nights, as it is Intensive Care's turn to be on duty. Prenatal is closed so that the whole staff can have a break.

Brilliant red, white, and blue balls of fire rising into the air and exploding like suns in the night can be seen from the hospital windows. Rockets go whistling up between the buildings and there is a constant wail of ambulances. People are enjoying themselves and casualty departments are all open, their staffs doubled to tend to the nation's injuries.

They can hear bang after bang, like cannon-shots, and series of Chinese crackers go off in Tagen Road and the quiet side streets.

The television is on in the sitting room.

Arm in arm, Marie and Habiba sit listening to the Queen's New Year speech.

Habiba doesn't understand a word of it, nor of the program in which six actors give thanks for the past year. She contents herself with giving Marie's arm a friendly squeeze.

There's a Christmas tree with electric lights on beside the television set. The day room in Intensive Care is nothing special. There are some nice pictures that no one looks at. Modern art. Marie has never understood it. The furniture is brown, varnished, and cold.

A cheerful porter comes into the room and plumps down on the sofa beside Marie, streamers in his hair and confetti all over his shoulders. He hauls a small bottle of Pernod and a cracker bomb out of the inside pocket of his white jacket.

"Haven't we met before somewhere?" says Marie.

"Oh, there's lots of ways of meeting people," he says, blowing on a horn. "No, you've probably never seen me before."

"Didn't we go to the same school?"

"No, we didn't. I'm from Bornholm and you're not."

He looks at Marie with his head drawn back, as if she wished to assault him.

A gigantic bang comes up from North Avenue and Marie hugs her thick waist to stop the sound waves penetrating her.

Then a great crackling comes from the porter's pocket. He takes out a small radio and listens to a *hullo-hullo-64-to-Delivery-Ward 2*.

"Ah me, then," he says, rising unsteadily, and clicking his heels, he puts his hand to his forehead. With a *Happy New Year*, he goes out, a streamer flapping behind his ear, leaving behind him some of the confetti and his half-bottle of Pernod.

"As soon as you do get a chance to look at a man," Marie thinks, shaking her head, "he starts looking at you as if you wanted to seduce him."

Habiba sighs deeply, her mouth open.

Marie lights the cracker bomb. It says *poof* and sends eight little paper flags and a plastic tortoise flying out on to the low table.

On the television, Victor Borge is conducting the Royal Theatre Orchestra at the concert hall in the Tivoli Gardens, accompanying a singer called Marilyn Mulvey.

A young man in a striped tie and velvet jacket slips into a chair in front of the television. A moment later, he leaps up and looks out into the night, watching all those suns rising up over the roofs. Then he slips out into the corridor, glances both ways, then comes back and throws himself down into the chair again.

"I've been in the delivery room with my wife all day," he says. "But now they've sent me out. She's had second stage contractions for an hour, but the baby won't come out."

He straightens his tie nervously.

"And now they're doing a Caesarian. I think it's too bad. First all those pains. She's been through nearly the whole birth. If only they'd known beforehand . . . that the head was in the wrong position, she wouldn't have had to go through all this!"

"Have a glass of Pernod," says Marie, pouring some out of the porter's bottle and adding some water.

"It's too bad for her."

The announcer's voice says: *It is a quarter to one and we are now broadcasting a program of dance, words and music . . . to end our New Year's Eve programs of entertainment with a chivalrous homage to young womanhood, at the beginning of the International Woman's Year. . . .*

The young man scratches his head and knocks over his Pernod. Habiba pats Marie on the cheek and makes a sign to show that she is off to bed.

Suddenly a little nurse comes tripping by with a baby's cot.

"Hey, father . . . come and look at me!"

The young man in the velvet jacket leaps into the air and rushes out into the corridor.

Inside the cot lies a small red-faced baby boy, his two small fists clenched and his forehead bearing clear signs of pressure.

"Oh, what a smashing little thing! Oh, isn't he lovely," says the father, doing a couple of dance steps and flinging out his arms.

The nurse sets off with the cot, then turns her head and says over her shoulder:

"Your wife will come round in an hour."

"What a smashing little boy," the father keeps saying. "Oh, how lovely. . . ."

A mixed choir sings a hymn and then there is the loud heavy sound of the City Hall clock striking twelve.

## WEDNESDAY 1 JANUARY

It's snowing, great feathery flakes floating in an unbroken stream down from the white vaulted sky spanning the city like a glass dome.

The building site is deserted, the great crane standing like a primeval lizard rising out of the cement mixers and sheds.

It is pleasant lying in a hospital bed gazing at dancing snow-flakes. It is balm to the soul, as if your thoughts are dancing with them.

Marie and Habiba are alone in a large empty room; outside in the long corridor, midwives float past now and again.

Habiba has something they call an ice-hand low down on her abdomen, a transparent plastic glove filled with iced water. It makes her skin stop itching and is pleasantly cooling. The mid-wives in Intensive Care have been so very inventive.

Habiba turns to Marie and smiles with relief.

"Very fine!"

Marie is sitting on the edge of the bed with her lower arm resting on the locker. She is making a little book for the Turkish woman. She is trying to portray in pencil the most important con-

cepts: contractions—amniotic fluid—stitches—breast-feeding—
milk. It is not all that easy. But she's *going* to do it.

"You're going to have a little Danish lesson in a minute, Habiba."
"What?"

A midwife comes into the room.

"Do you think you could explain to your friend that we're
keeping her in Intensive Care? She won't be going back to Prenatal. It's been decided to induce her tomorrow. With a drip."

Marie starts drawing a bed. The Turkish woman is lying in it
with a baby inside her, a drip hanging on the grid above her head.

Marie is convinced that if she had been in a hospital in Turkey,
then some Habiba or other in the next bed would have held out a
hand to her.

It's like that. Solidarity between people will always exist. That's
a fact.


## THURSDAY 2 JANUARY

Marie feels she is losing her grip. Most of the time she lies dozing.
At night she can't sleep, and in the daytime she can't keep awake.

Her whole body prickles and hums, the fluid pressing from
within and expanding her ribs, and if she occasionally gets out of
bed, she has to lean right back to be able to keep her balance.

Habiba is lying in the other bed, a drip of yellow fluid hanging
above the head of her bed. Habiba is happy . . . something is happening now. She lies looking at the little "word-book" Marie has
made for her.

Marie is fetched back to Prenatal by an orderly. It is good to come
back again and see the familiar faces appearing, one by one. Signe,
Linda, and all the others, totally exhausted by their holiday.

"How was it?" Sister asks.
"Great!"
"Did they look after you properly over there in Intensive Care?"
"Oh, yes . . . I was just as pampered as I am here. But when I

86

said I had heartburn, do you know what they gave me? This! A transparent plastic glove and a suppository as big as St. Paul's. I'm going to keep it as a souvenir from the National Hospital."

"What have you done with Habiba?" says Linda.

"She's staying in Intensive Care," says Marie. "They're starting her off today. With a drip."

### FRIDAY 3 JANUARY

"Good morning, girls. It's six o'clock."

"Oh, can't we sleep a bit longer?"

The ceiling light shines coldly down on Linda, Marie, and a new girl brought in during the night. Why has the orderly turned on the light in such a brisk way? She could have made do with the light over the wash basin. As if it weren't bad enough being woken just when you've at last got to sleep.

Linda sits up with her hair all over the place, bends over, then with her hand over her mouth, she rushes on her thin legs to the w.c. and is sick without even having time to lock the door.

A student midwife hands out thermometers and the patients sleepily stick them in their mouths. Then the student midwife lightly touches the patients' wrists just above their thumbs to feel their pulses.

Finally, she fastens a clammy rubber cuff onto the patient's upper arm, pumps it up, and reads off her blood pressure.

Temperature, pulse, and blood pressure are noted down on a piece of paper and then entered into their casesheets.

"I'm bleeding," says the new girl.

"Give the pad to me," says the orderly. "I'll show it to Sister."

"My name's Marie. What's yours?"

"Tenna," she says, looking at Marie with a pair of calm gray-blue eyes.

In the morning-blue corridor, Linda appears from the w.c., wiping her mouth with her arm and heading for the sluice. She opens the door with the circular porthole in it, stops by the shelves of urine glasses, and finds her own. Larsen, it says, Ward 0. She feels sick again, but her stomach is empty. So she goes back to the w.c. once again, the glass in her hand.

In the store, Marie is on the scales, her feet bare and cold. The young nurse is looking at the scales. She is the one whose smart fur coat made of multicolored pieces hangs on the wall.

"Are you sure?"

"Yes, certain. I've put on half a kilo since the day before yesterday. I weighed seventy-two kilos then, and now I'm seventy-two and a half. You can see for yourself!"

"What about your clothes . . . aren't you wearing more clothes today?"

"No, I had nothing on but shirt and underclothes."

"And how much did you weigh before you were pregnant?"

"Fifty-five kilos." Marie has tears in her eyes.

"We must tell Sister . . . it seems too much to me."

"Are you upset about something?" says Signe.

"It's this damned fluid . . . more and more of it. Why else should I have put on weight?"

"But haven't you any fluid in your body?"

"Not really . . . you can see. My face looks perfectly ordinary. And look at this. . . ."

Marie pulls up her sleeve and shows Signe her long thin arm.

"There's certainly no water in that arm."

The consultant looks at the sleeping patient with his brown eyes.

"Shall I wake her?" says the nurse, putting her hand on Marie's shoulder.

Marie sits up in bewilderment.

"The patient has put on a lot of weight," says Sister.

"Are your fingers or feet swollen?"

"No, not at all," says Marie, pulling the quilt aside so he can see her thin legs. The sister grasps her ankle and presses her thumb into the skin.

"No, no accumulation of fluid."

"How are you otherwise, Mrs. Hansen?"

"I've begun to get rather tired. I sleep badly, even with sleeping

tablets. Late at night is the worst. The fluid presses against my bottom ribs and I feel as if they were breaking. I lie twisting and turning, but can't get comfortable. It doesn't matter as far as I am concerned . . . as long as I know things are all right for the baby."

The doctor nods and leafs through her casesheet.

"We can send you to Ultrasound and see what results they come up with this time. But if it gets too bad, we'll have to consider inducing labor."

The winter light falls in the ward, a thin January light that throws no shadows and doesn't show the shape of things.

"How's everything here?"

The doctor is standing by Tenna, the new patient with the gray-blue eyes.

"I've got bad pains in my side . . . I've had them since yesterday morning."

"May I see where?"

"Here, but it's hurt all through my pregnancy," says Tenna in a low voice. "As if I was being stabbed with a knife every time the baby moves."

"Yes, things like that shouldn't be felt. Let me see," he says, leafing through her file. "Second birth. Yes, and you were brought in last night with pains and bleeding? And the pains have stopped, have they? We must do an ultrasound examination as soon as possible."

Sister writes it down.

"And you, Mrs. Larsen, are you about to lose patience?"

"I lost it ages ago," whispers Linda, pulling her quilt up over her ears.

"But you're looking very well, and your baby's growing as it should. As everything is going so well, I think I can discharge you today."

Linda's face brightens into a huge smile and the quilt slowly sinks down on to her small stomach and the spindly body.

"Is that really true?"

"Yes."

The long weary broody time is over. Now she can go home to Allan. Now life can begin again.

When the round is over, the nurse sticks her head inside the door and says to Marie:

"Perhaps you'd go and see the Turkish woman in Intensive Care? She'd like to see someone she knows, I'm sure. You can take a shortcut through the Delivery corridor."

Marie brightens, swings her legs over the edge of the bed, tosses back her long brown hair, and puts on her white dressing gown.

"Did you hear that, Marie?" says Linda. "I'm going home today! Oh, how pleased Allan will be!"

In white knee-length stockings, white dressing gown and white plastic sandals, Marie walks with her bouncing stomach out onto the main stairs, goes down one floor and stands outside the actual Delivery Department . . . the place you do not go into unless you are in labor. *No admittance*, it says on the door, and *Please ring the bell*.

A student midwife opens the frosted-glass door. Fortunately, Marie already knows her.

Marie tries to look purposeful and self-confident as she silently eases her way into the dim corridor. To her surprise, it is very quiet. She had thought she would hear loud cries and wails from the various labor wards, but on the contrary, it's quite silent. A midwife hurries soundlessly past her, a tray in her hand. A disheveled stretcher stands outside one of the rooms, as if it had just been deserted by someone. Marie walks past a little kitchen and notices the smell of toast.

She is again on a main stairway. On the other side of the lift it says *Intensive Care* above the door.

She goes past open and closed doors, at one seeing an empty white bath, at another a young girl lying reading, a bottle of soda water on the locker beside her.

In the large room with four beds in it, where she had slept over the New Year, a stout little figure is sitting silhouetted against the window. She turns her head . . . it is Habiba, in her cyclamen-red nylon overall. She gets up and embraces her friend.

A hefty midwife in white clogs comes over to them.

"Could you possibly tell her that she is to take pills now? We're starting with the first series in half an hour."

With the help of a few drawings in the little homemade word-book, Marie succeeds in making it clear to Habiba what is going to happen to her. The drip has not worked. Now she is to have pills instead.

Habiba is getting tired. Her eyes are bright and bloodshot, the little black plait lying slackly over one shoulder. She scratches her elbow and neck.

The big midwife comes back again.

"Well, has she understood?"

"Yes."

Marie looks at her and suddenly says casually:

"Tell me, can too much amniotic fluid damage the fetus?"

"Oh, no," says the midwife, smiling. "Not at all. It's more the other way round. Too much fluid can be a sign that the fetus *is* damaged."

Marie clutches her throat . . . now she knows!

The midwife has no idea that in one single sentence she has revealed the truth, the truth Marie has been seeking for weeks.


A tall, strongly built patient in an orange toweling dressing gown comes into the ward. Marie and Habiba look at her. She raises her hand in greeting as she supports her stomach with her other hand. She goes over to the window and looks out at the tiled roofs and red brick buildings.

"Isn't it awful trying to get the time to go by?"

She clearly wants to talk, so Marie obliges, her hand on Habiba's shoulder.

"When are you due?"

"Anytime now."

"You don't look that big."

"No, I don't really. But it's probably because I'm quite tall."

"Why are you here?"

"They've got me in for observation for pre-eclampsia . . . I've had trouble with my eyes."

"What sort of trouble?"

"A sort of double-vision, I think it's called."

She smiles and pulls a bag of salt pastilles out of her pocket. She is happy and does not look in the slightest worried.

"I think it's great giving birth."

Marie makes a hunching movement. If only I could be like her, she thinks, like in a fairy tale.

"My name's Veronica," the girl says. "What's yours?"

"Marie . . . and this . . . this is my friend, Habiba."

They all shake hands.

"Did you go to prenatal classes?" says Marie.

"Oh, yes," says Veronica. "Of course. Both here at the hospital with the midwives, and at the women's center. It was great. I'm well prepared. And I've seen a couple of films, too."

"Why are you having it here in the special department?"

"Because I'm a late first delivery . . . I'm thirty-one. And I wanted to have it here. I really did my best to get in. The girls I know who've had their babies here have always enjoyed it."

"Is your husband going to be with you?"

"Yes, he's also taken part in the examinations and prenatals, whenever he's been able to get time off from work."

In Ward 0, Linda is emptying her locker and cupboard. She has thrown the wilting flowers into the wastepaper basket and put the vases back in the sluice.

Then she packs the last things into her case and puts the great stack of magazines on to the window sill.

Linda is wearing a tight yellow blouse, a red miniskirt, nylon stockings and high-heeled red shoes. It is always astonishing to see each other in private clothes, almost more intimate than seeing each other naked.

"We're due at the same time," she says to Marie. "So we'll probably meet again in the delivery ward. Won't that be great?"

"Regards to Allan! And have a good time."

The moment Linda has disappeared, orderlies start making up

her bed. All the old bedclothes and the mattress itself are removed and replaced with clean ones with brisk professional movements; then the bed is sealed with a pale blue transparent plastic coverlet.

Hot food comes in on aluminum trolleys along the corridor: liver and fried onions and mashed potato. Locker-tops are swung out over beds, the overhead grids put up, rattling and metallic.

"Can I have mine in here with you?" says Signe.

"Come on in," says Marie.

They eat in silence, then Signe says to the new girl:

"Have you got any children?"

"Yes, a girl of three."

"How did her birth go?"

"All right really," says Tenna. "Though it was much more painful than I'd expected. That was in a private clinic. It took a long time, but it was all right. Anders was with me all the time, which was nice. But you know what I thought was awful?"

"What?"

"Being cut. I had no idea about things like that beforehand. No one had told me it was common to be cut or stitched in one way or another."

"But why was it so awful?" says Marie.

"I had two cuts, one on each side. It wasn't that I felt it, but that I heard it. It sounded like when you cut into . . . a fish, for instance. Yes, a fish. It was almost as if they'd clipped into my face . . . in the mouth. That my mouth had been cut open . . . that's what it felt like. And I also got a walloping black eye. But Anders took it all quite calmly. He stood watching the midwife stitching me up and said: 'It's a craft in itself. I'm a craftsman, too. Can you do your work properly?' She wasn't at all offended, just said 'Yes, yes, I'll do a good job.'"

"Does anyone want any milk?" Marie is holding a carton of buttermilk in one hand and one of fresh milk in the other.

"But they say it heals better if they cut you than if you tear."

"Did they use a local anesthetic before they stitched?" says **Signe**.

"Yes, I didn't really notice anything. I think if I had been prepared for it, then I wouldn't have minded so much."

"Did you have to have the stitches out?" says Marie.

"Yes, and that was damned unpleasant," says Tenna, wiping her mouth with a table napkin. "When we got home, we found there were a couple of stitches further in. So Anders phoned the hospital and told them his wife had stitches in still, and what should we do about it? They'll go away by themselves, they said. So Anders took them out."

Marie shuddered.

"You know, lots of Anders's workmates who have been present at their children's births don't want to sleep with their wives any more."

"You can't mean that!" exclaims Signe.

"Yes, they say they've had enough!"

Tenna scrapes her plate clean.

"How shitty of them, but that really can't be common," says Marie. "That means they regard their wives as . . . well, as a kind of sex object."

"But Anders and I've never had a problem. We can't look at each other without. . . ."

"How old are you?"

"Twenty-two, and he's just twenty-two, as well."

Tenna looks at Marie with her calm gray-blue eyes, then a spasm flashes across her face.

"Oh, hell. . . ."

She drops her knife.

"There's something or other darned wrong," she says with tears in her eyes. "I'm oozing and I've still five weeks to go."

She pulls the cord above her head.

The nurse opens the door.

"Could I have a bedpan, please?" says Tenna.

Signe starts gathering up the crocks.

She picks up the tray and opens the door with one elbow.

Marie gets a woman's magazine off the window sill.

She opens it up and is soon gripped:

*She felt two brutal arms around her. In one crazy moment, he again became a man. He was no longer ashamed and forced her to submit. He crushed her mouth down with a demanding kiss. Melting with gratitude, she let him undress her and with his large hands, he burrowed his way through to her naked flesh. Even before he had taken off her clothes, he was on top of her, forcing on her. . . .*

"Finished," says Tenna to the nurse.

She puts a cloth over the bedpan and leaves the room.

*. . . forcing on her his weight, his desire and movements. A sudden cramp made him rigid, motionless. When she half-opened her eyes, she saw Pierre's face crumple into an expression of ecstatic pain. Waves of desire continued inside her, then faded away, transformed into a need for tenderness and protection. . . .*

Marie felt a kick inside her . . . *he crushed her mouth with a demanding kiss. . . ?*—now the child was off swimming again.

When Signe is back in her own ward, she goes on thinking about what they had talked about in Ward 0, the things all patients in Prenatal think about incessantly.

About their sex life in relation to birth. About *vita sexualis*, as it is called in medical language.

Immediately after her first child was born, she found herself shaven, maltreated, torn, flayed, and sewn up! She had felt slayed. She had not thought reality would be as harsh as that.

For weeks she had been frightened even to bend down and look at her swollen and patched sexual parts. Not until a month later, when her body had calmed down, did she dare look at herself down there in a mirror she had put on the floor.

She had wondered whether they would ever sleep together again. The constant flow of fluids from pregnancy, the newborn infant at her breast, the endless exhaustion. Everything seemed to put obstacles in the way.

Neither men nor women really know anything about a woman's vagina. A dark and mysterious place, as puzzling as the starry sky. The work of the gynecologist and the astrologist are both equally far from the ordinary mortal's understanding.

But childbirth throws its merciless light on a woman's sexual organs. The vagina is revealed and demystified, and if either partner's sexual life has been exclusively based on this mystification, it is bound to fall to pieces. Naturally.

That was probably why Anders' friends that Tenna had mentioned no longer wished to sleep with their wives, after they had seen for the first time the raw mincemeat between their legs. The pinup girls of the newspapers and then a real live birth . . . they don't really go together.

Signe has talked to Jacob about whether he was scared about their sex life when he had seen his first child born.

"No, not at all," he had answered in surprise. "I don't really connect the two things, birth and sex. Do you? Sex life has nothing much to do with the sexual organs. You mustn't think that. It's to do with relations between two people."

Remarkably enough, they had started to sleep together again, even more relaxed, pleasantly, and simply than before, if not quite so frequently, because of the children.

And yet a great deal has changed. Sexuality is no longer so much self-knowledge. Not so self-centered. And not so essential.

When Marie slips into Intensive Care that night, her heart thumps so that she feels someone must be able to hear it. She is sure the Turkish woman has started and is already in the delivery ward.

One lamp is alight in the big ward where Veronica is, her orange dressing gown hanging over a chair. She is asleep and doesn't know a man is sitting at the head of her bed, his coat over his knees, stroking her hair. Then he turns and sees Marie and nods almost imperceptibly.

In the opposite corner of the room, in the darkest spot, a small lonely figure is sitting on a chair, her knees trembling, her all too large belly hanging between them. The cyclamen-colored overall is open, and her white hospital shirt rises and falls over the heavy dark breasts. Her lips are yellow and stiff from the pills that at intervals during the day have been put under her upper lip. Those stupid pills. They have not worked.

When she sees Marie, she starts crying, her whole sturdy little body shaken by despairing sobs.

Marie takes her hand. Habiba gets up heavily.

Together they go on a short night tour of Intensive Care, through the wards, out into the corridor, down to the door and back again.

They can't say much to each other, and anyhow there isn't much to say. They can only show affection and friendship to each other, a quite elementary emotion that spans over language and nationality and their whole background. They walk slowly, arm in arm, with their great swaying stomachs.

They walk past the little office where a couple of midwives are leaning over cups of coffee, casesheets and index cards. They walk past cupboards and trolleys, past a low sofa, past a ward with no lights on.

A midwife comes along with a high child's cot on wheels, followed by an agitated young man in a white shirt and flapping tartan scarf.

"Where can I find a telephone?" he says, turning round in confusion.

"Right down in the entrance hall by the main door. It's a pay phone."

He rushes out of the door.

Marie has recognized him at once. It's Erich Erichsen, Gertrude's husband.

"Look, isn't he sweet?" says the midwife. "He's just been delivered by Caesarian, and now his father has gone down to tell *the whole world*!"

Half hidden by the covers lies a fine newborn infant, complete and beautiful, with a large well-formed head, soft silky hair and a pink curved mouth. He grunts and tries to suck his fist. With a complaining wail, he starts to cry. The midwife picks him up carefully and puts him against her starched breast. The child falls silent immediately. She walks round humming a little tune. Habiba and Marie stare at her.

"What's happened to the mother?" says Marie. "I know her. We were in the same ward in Prenatal."

"She's been taken to the recovery room."

"And the father?"

"He'll probably go home to bed."

"Where's the baby going to be, then?"

She's hoping the midwife will ask her if *she* would have him for the night.

"He'll be taken down to the postnatal department with the other babies."

"What if he stays awake all night and cries?"

Marie gazes at the little Erichsen, who an hour ago was lying protected and safe inside his mother. Is he to lie all alone in his starched bed all night? Surrounded by nothing but air and material and light, things he simply doesn't know about? Now and again, someone will pick him up and change him. Change this tiny boy, whose connection with the outside world has up to now gone only through his and his mother's common umbilical cord.

The baby starts whimpering again. The midwife lifts him up and puts his soft head against her neck. He calms down and is quiet. Even this alien creature, just by holding him close to her, can make him feel secure.

The midwife eases him carefully under the covers. He does not wake, but goes on sleeping his extended fetal sleep.

"Well, we must get on," says the midwife, setting the cot in motion. "We can't stand here all night."

Marie notices the perspiration breaking out all over her. Let me come, too! Let me look after him tonight! Let me sit with him until Gertrude wakes—the cries go through her head.

There they are, one tall and one short patient, in hospital clothes and their own peculiar dressing gowns, their hair untidy, in slippers and stockings that fall round their ankles.

The cot moves away from them, and the two patients grow smaller and smaller and smaller.

### SATURDAY 4 JANUARY

Baska is talking Polish over the telephone when Marie comes into the office to fetch her letter. She has noticed that Baska often telephones . . . whenever there's an opportunity and they are not too busy on the wards, and especially when Sister isn't there. Baska chatters away in her gibberish, drawing with her finger on the pane of glass.

Marie creeps up into bed and opens her letter. Zacharias is in Søndre Strømfjord, playing with his orchestra in a hotel every evening. They're trying to write their own songs, but they're not being very successful. He sends lots of love from them all.

She doesn't find it hard to read his handwriting. It is large, done in script, and open and clear.


"Why do you keep thinking something's wrong with your baby?" says Signe, putting aside *Handbook in Ceramics*.

"It'd be terrible if there were!"

"Yes, but even here, where they have all the complicated cases, they say nearly all births are normal."

"They *say* that, yes. But I don't believe them."

Marie tosses back her hair and goes on:

"Perhaps nearly all births are normal here, but then perhaps the child isn't quite normal? And they don't tell you that, either. The world wants to be deceived. I think if one asked, they would say there are no statistics."

She gazes out at the great dancing snowflakes.

"They say nothing . . . so as not to frighten us."

"Yes, of course. It's not their job to go round scaring the life out of us. On the contrary."

They look at each other in silence, Marie silhouetted against the white morning sky. If only she had a watch. It embarrasses her that she never knows the time.

She puts her hand on Signe's large pile of books. It's incredible how little she has read in the time she has been here.

The world outside the hospital, the world written about in newspapers, magazines, journals, and books, seeps and filters through to patients in Prenatal, into their minds layer by layer. No one reads papers here. They buy them, yes, and skim the headlines, but they don't read them.

Stacks of books are taken into Prenatal and stacks of books lie there unread. The patients can't concentrate. They prefer to chat or watch television.

Reality does not penetrate . . . *not here . . . where a wholly different reality makes itself felt.*

"Do you think?" says Marie, looking straight at Signe. "Do you think one would have the slightest chance of doing away with one's baby, if one wanted to?"

"You mean if the baby's very damaged?"

"Yes."

"I've often thought about that. But to be honest, I think it'd be very difficult, because they take the baby over to the postnatal wards at once. And it's under constant observation."

Signe tugs at her hair.

"One can only hope it dies naturally. One could say that to the doctors, too, if only one dared."

"One could suffocate it with the quilt," says Marie, looking almost appealingly at her fellow-patient.

Signe involuntarily glances at the open door.

"Or let it die of cold when one's first got it home," Marie goes on.

"Yes, if one had the courage to do that."

"Or drown it in the bath. Lots of babies die every year that way. In the old days, they lay on them. Or simply put them outside. I can't see what's so wrong with that. There's an ancient tradition of women doing away with their babies. And I think they have a right to."

Signe looks at Marie. "I'm older than she is," she thinks. "I must try to get her to think along different lines. This is crazy." She says nothing for a while and then goes on:

"Don't forget, Marie, that for every hour that passes, you become more tied to your baby, even if the baby is in poor shape. Nature has arranged things like that, so that we're able to protect our offspring."

"So it must happen quickly?"

"Yes, I'm sure of that."

"If it happens here, do you think they'd report you to the police?" Marie tosses her head nervously.

"I doubt it, somehow. I don't think they would. But that all depends on the circumstances, doesn't it?"

Signe pours some wine into two glasses, spilling some on to a copy of *Information* underneath them.

"But if you have the courage to take the life of your own child, then surely you must be courageous enough to face the consequences."

"If you can think that far . . . yes."

"There must be an incredible purposefulness about doing away with another person. Not everyone could cope with that."

Outside the window, the snowflakes dance together, as if kept up by a warm current of air, like down from a quilt swirling round in a whirlpool.

"I'll tell you something," says Marie earnestly. "If you have a very handicapped child, then you can't just say you don't want it, can you? They would presumably do what they could to make you acknowledge the child. Don't you think so? Of course! They couldn't do anything else."

She squeezes her fingers so they crack.

"But then if you thought such a child would destroy your whole life, then I think the mother is *the only person* who should be allowed to do away with it."

The hand with the glass of red wine stops in midair.

"Yes. Mmm." Signe tries to collect her wits. "Yes. But perhaps just that child might become the greatest joy to you. It might become the one you will be more fond of than anyone else in the world, even if it is seriously mentally handicapped, for instance."

"But is that kind of love reasonable to base your life on?"

"What on earth do you know about what's reasonable to base your life on?" says Signe. The red wine has made a black line on her upper lip.

Marie straightens up.

"I want to live as a free person. I have a right to that. Even if I perhaps know perfectly well that the *individual freedom* we're brought up to believe in is one of the great bourgeois illusions. Well . . . but I want to work, I want to look around, I want friends and to live life fully . . . to realize myself . . . isn't that what it's called? And tell me, don't you think most men, fathers too, want to keep that right?"

"Yes, I'm sure they do. But they don't actually live very freely, whatever you think. Don't you think most people find the greatest freedom within certain limitations? Children are a limitation, and it would be a lie to maintain anything else. But it's only to the good there's a framework to one's life. When the world is small, it becomes more concentrated."

"*Maybe* you're right," says Marie, excitedly. "But I want my child to leave me one day. As I was separated from my parents. A badly handicapped child is with you all through your life. No one can be free of that."

Signe lights a cigarette and pushes the packet over to Marie, who shakes her head. She doesn't smoke.

"I'm convinced," she goes on, "that in many cases, you do the child the greatest service by helping it into another existence . . . it's sentimental to believe otherwise."

"You're not a child specialist, are you? You don't know what science can do for your child. You're not in a position to evaluate the opportunities for your newborn child."

"You mean to say they can force a child on you that you don't wish to have?"

"Yes, in some ways. I think they can, as far as I can make out. But at the same time, you simply don't know what you *do* want before you've seen your child and you've been able to think it over."

"You mustn't take all my courage away," whispers Marie.

Signe blows out a large ring of smoke.

"In one way, I think a bargain is a bargain. You can't both wish for a child and keep the right to choose when it comes. You have to take things as they are, and try to make the best of the situation. Those are conditions we're subject to, even if I think you're right when you say the *woman* in the end bears an unreasonable share of the burden and responsibility."

*Am I lying here saying this?* Signe thinks, wiping her mouth with a corner of her quilt. Heaven knows, all those thoughts have gone through my head, too. I'm deceiving her like everyone else. She's right!

Marie looks out at the whirling snow, her hands on her huge stomach.

"We'll be having something to eat soon," says Signe, stubbing out her cigarette in the ashtray.


*This is one of the most recent pictures of Princess Elizabeth and Richard Burton, taken at a moment when they were relaxed and happy on holiday in Casablanca. But even then, the smile has become more rigid, the atmosphere chillier.*

Marie devours the picture magazine.

*Burton himself says: "Elizabeth and I have decided that we will not see each other too often. Elizabeth Taylor and I were together at all hours of the day, and look what happened?"*

One nurse says to another:

"Is it really true?"

"Ask the orderly down in the delivery ward . . . it was a breach."

"They heard a cry?"

"That's what I'm telling you. The waters had broken. The body had emerged and there was air in the womb. The fetus was crying quite clearly in the mother's womb."

"No, that's *too* much," says Sister, who is just passing them.


"Habiba."

"Maria."

Marie pulls a chair up to the delivery couch. She strokes the Turkish woman's hand and looks into her anxious brown eyes, where the veins have drawn their fine red network over the yellowish whites. Her hair is loose and flowing darkly out over the pillow, beads of sweat standing out on her forehead.

In a corner of the delivery room, on a chair, is her folded cyclamen-colored overall, her slippers and her bag.

The Turkish woman puts a finger to her mouth, which is dry and cracked.

"Is there anything I can moisten her lips with?" Marie asks the student midwife on duty, a fair-haired girl with bobbed hair and gray eyes.

The student midwife hands Marie a jar of vaseline.

Every time a contraction comes, Habiba closes her eyes and sighs heavily.

"How's it going?" Marie asks, her heart thumping. "Is everything as it should be?"

"Yes, yes. She's just so overweight, it makes the birth rather long drawn-out."

Marie strokes Habiba's hand.

"She's got a lot of fluid in her body, hasn't she?"

"Yes, she suffers a lot from edema, and she also has that silly itch. But I think that'll go when the delivery is over."

Marie looks at Habiba. Great drops of sweat are hanging from the thick eyebrows. On the table at the head of the bed is the little homemade word-book.

"How big do you think the child is?"

"Hard to say, because she's so big, but I shouldn't be surprised if it's around nine pounds."

"How's it going otherwise, do you think?"

"Oh, fine. You look as if you're having twins."

"Yes," says Marie, flushing. "Have you phoned her husband?"

"He's on his way in. It's lucky for him it's Saturday."

Marie puts her hand flat on Habiba's large firm stomach. She notices how the contraction comes from above, just below her breasts, continues down over her stomach, then pushes down toward the loins. It is a faint ripple, a trembling, a light electric tension; as if Habiba had a vision . . . as if she were in communication with something supernatural. A message goes from the heavy Turkish body to Marie, who is her medium.

The contraction goes back up over her belly to its starting point at the top of the womb.

A midwife has come in and is talking quietly to the student midwife, leaning over the desk, her hands on the back of a chair. Simultaneously, they turn round to the bed.

"Now we're going to break the waters," says the student midwife. She is holding an instrument rather like a knitting needle.

"Roll over on your back. That's it, and then let your legs fall apart, and relax completely."

Marie helps Habiba turn over. When she sees the flaming red of eczema low down on her stomach, an irritation that has made the skin quite raw, the room starts spinning.

Habiba is shivering all over.

"Just lie still. It doesn't hurt."

She doesn't understand what they are saying. Marie squeezes her hand.

The midwife and the student midwife place an elbow each on Habiba's knees and lean over between her legs.

At the next contraction, the fetal membrane bulges out and they stick the needle into the tough white balloon.

The membrane bursts with a little pop and the water pours out in a great warm wave.

The tension inside her is relieved, the rigid feeling gone. Habiba can suddenly breathe more freely. She sends a trembling smile out into the room at the student midwife, who is wiping her forehead with a cold cloth, and she says:

"Very fine. Thank you."

"Now things'll get going."

The snowflakes are still dancing outside. The contractions start coming more and more quickly in over Habiba. She is a Turkish shore and the waves of the Black Sea are rolling over her sand. She is a gravel pit and the gravel is rushing down into the pit. She is a heavy cow and the veterinary surgeon is feeling in her with his long gloved hand.

There is a light knock on the door. Ibrahim comes in and hurries over to Habiba.

Marie slips out into the passage.

A fair young man with bright eyes is sitting on Tenna's bed, bending over her with one hand on each side of the pillow. He has put a little bunch of red and white flowers into a glass on her locker.

His forehead is against hers and his nose against hers. Then he wags his head from side to side as he looks in her eyes.

She starts and laughs when she finds his hand under the quilt.

"Anders!"

An afghan fur, a huge pair of mittens, and a fur hat are lying on Marie's bed. Eva has pulled a chair over to the bed, and Marie looks at her sister. Eva is so young. It hurts Marie that Eva should see such an irregular pregnancy. Hydramnios. Is that something to tell a young girl who has never even been pregnant?

"How are they managing at the kindergarten?"

"They've got a replacement. A man of thirty-two, someone who's left the rat race. He's an architect, really. But now he wants to look after children, anyhow, for a while."

"Is he married?"

"Divorced, with one child."

"Are you getting any reading done?" says Eva, picking up *ABC of Political Economy*. Underneath it is Pablo Neruda's *Memoirs*.

"Well, I've managed to get through those two books, but I can't get started on anything else. I've borrowed several books from the library and other patients, but they have no effect on me. I can't keep my thoughts together. The only things I want to read are the weeklies. The magazines and Sunday supplements slip down easiest, and send you to sleep quickest. You get so tired of being in hospital! Sometimes I think, God, how ever shall I manage when I get home?"


"No, that can't be right?"

"Yes, it is. Ask Rasmussen yourself."

"4,500 grams?"

"Yes, Habiba's baby girl weighs nine pounds. She's got long black hair and black eyebrows, they say. She's in Neonatal. Habiba is diabetic, did you know?"

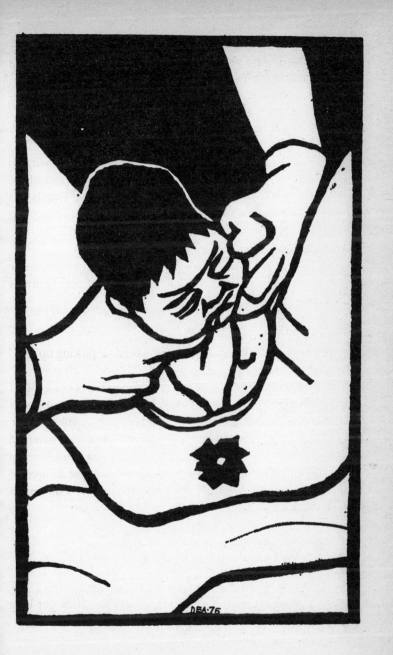

III

"No."

"But everyone says the baby's fine."

"So Allah decided it was to be a girl after all."

What was Zacharias doing in Greenland? Was he being tempted? Perhaps two Greenlanders get on better with each other than a Greenlander and a Dane? Perhaps there is a special Greenland style?

As long as he doesn't come home with venereal disease!

Marie wants a man. At night she imagines there is one lying beside her under the quilt. His cool body is lying right up against her. Her great stomach does not stop her from thinking about him inside her and all round her.

Her grief at the thought of the threatened little life she bears inside her is one thing. The desire for sex is something else. It gets stronger for every single shimmering black-and-white hospital night that passes. It drives her forward, forward to her release, to the day when the child is thrust out of her body.

Those wretched sleeping tablets. They haven't worked. Marie turns her head from side to side. She has pushed a corner of the quilt in under the small of her back to give her better support. Her ribs are being pressed out and she is finding it difficult to breathe.

She can't get through this night. The blinds cover the window. If only she could have seen the stars and the Turkish half-moon over Tagen Road.

Tenna whimpers in her sleep.

In the small hours, Marie starts up with her hand over her mouth. She has been dreaming that she was walking down the delivery corridor, which looked more like an old-fashioned gallery outside an old house, in the hope of being invited into the room Habiba is in.

The student midwife with the page-bob and gray eyes comes out, and with a wave, beckons her inside.

In the bed under a heap of quilts is Habiba, her eyes worried. She is in labor, but is not moving.

Marie crawls up into bed with her, and tips them both out onto the floor. There they lie, in a tangle of quilts.

Habiba looks at her, dumb with grief.


## SUNDAY 5 JANUARY

While it is still dark, on the night between Saturday and Sunday, Veronica is woken up in Intensive Care by the sound, or rather the sensation of a small bang. The tense feeling inside her fades and the bed turns warm. She sits up, wide awake, switches on the bedside lamp and throws the quilt aside . . . the sheet is wet. Her waters have broken.

Her waters have broken and the time has come. After all those months! How marvelous! She pulls the cord at the bedhead and the duty nurse comes soundlessly into her room.

"I think my waters have broken."

"May I see?"

"Look it's pinkish."

"That's the show—good enough."

In her orange toweling dressing gown, Veronica walks up and down the floor of the delivery room, from the door to the high labor couch, from the window, past the bed to the door, slowly back and forth to get the contractions going.

The indistinct outlines of two buildings can be seen from the window, a couple of windows alight, which looks pleasant out in the darkness.

The duty nurse opens the door.

"How're things going? Have your contractions started?"

"Yes, I think so."

"Try timing them—note how long the time is between them."

There is a clock on the wall opposite the bed. It is five past eight. The hospital is coming to life now, whitecoats in pairs moving diagonally across the yard.

She hears a low cooing. Are they pigeons? Is there a cornice outside the window? Or is it women in pain? There must be several others in labor round about, mustn't there? She longs not to hear sounds from the other wards.

When the contractions come, she puts her forearms on the bed and leans over it, in the way she has been taught to relax.

A small cot on wheels is standing in the corner. She's been over to have a look into it several times. It has a red check quilt and a yellow furry cover, a white tape with a handwritten number on it hanging from the edge.

That's it, isn't it, just like that—a natural consequence—there will be a child?

"Are you getting tired?"

"Yes, my legs are."

The nurse closes the door behind her.

"We've decided to give you a drip to hasten on the contractions. When your waters have broken, there shouldn't be a too long gap before the birth starts. We must check your data, too."

She opens the casesheet.

"Veronica Andersen, secretary, born 2nd January, 1944, in Hillerød. Is your husband to be present at the birth? Yes. Shall we telephone him?"

It is nine o'clock and growing lighter.

Now at last she can get up and lie on the bed. A stand is fastened to the bedhead and a bottle of clear liquid hung upside down. A hypodermic needle is stuck into the back of her right hand and the fluid to activate contractions runs through the tube into her body.

Veronica longs for something to happen. She has been drawn to this day for months and months, as to a magnet.

A thin, colorless young girl is sitting in silence on a chair beside her bed. In one hand she has a black ballpoint and with the other she registers the contractions in the patient's abdomen. A stopwatch is lying in front of her. Every time the stomach wall hardens, she writes a figure on the paper.

She is uncommunicative, either shy or cross. Veronica notices she's not concentrating on the job.

The minutes crawl by. Time passes slowly. The hands creep laboriously round the clock on the wall. When she has a contraction, it hurts at the base of her spine, as when she has her period. It would be nice if someone came and read her a story now.

The girl looks at her nails.

In between contractions, Veronica is just as usual, the pains stop and she can doze a little.

The girl gets up and leaves the room.

Anxiety creeps over Veronica. She is alone. She is growing cold. Suppose something happens.

She has heard about women being left quite alone in labor and they have said, *only ring if it starts bearing down*.

Surely they're not going to leave her?

She fumbles for the bell-cord and pulls it.

The door opens.

*"I can't bear being alone."*

"You won't have to," says a friendly voice.

A slim young midwife is sitting beside Veronica, holding her hand. "She is holding my hand," thinks Veronica, feeling happy. It is not often a stranger holds your hand.

"Where do you come from?"

"From the Faroes," says the midwife.

She holds Veronica's hand in hers, warm and friendly. Now she is there, everything is fine. She is at Veronica's side . . . that's quite clear.

"How long can you stay?"

"Until twelve o'clock," says the midwife. "Then there's a change of shift, but I'll try to stay on a bit longer if I can."

Bredo comes, looks round and smiles. He has hurried and is out of breath. They have given him a pale blue paper overall tied at the back. He bends down and kisses Veronica on the mouth. His cheeks are cold and his mouth soft.

"How're things going?"

"Fine."

"Does it hurt?"

"Yes, but it's supposed to."

The morning sky is as clear as a glass of pink liquid, the sun rising transparently rosy, starting off the day. The earth has rolled quietly aside and where it has been dark before is now growing light.

Contractions are like nothing else on earth. They are strong and frequent now. Veronica feels a completely new kind of self-reliance and joy. The contractions are carrying her cheerfully away like waves on the ocean. Her womb is contracting regularly, working for the first time in its life, making the internal mouth of the womb open, steadily and calmly.

Veronica tries to breathe in the right way, as she had learnt to over the long months. The midwife helps her to remember the exercises. When the contractions come, Veronica takes a deep breath and then lets it very slowly out. In that way, her child gets the best supply of oxygen and at the same time she retains control over her body.

"It's funny . . . it's a Russian system, really, isn't it?"

"Yes," says the midwife. "They developed it in the 1930s in the Soviet Union and first brought it to Western Europe at the beginning of the fifties."

The brilliantly clear sky is framed by the bright blue curtains.

"What do you usually do?"

"I'm a secretary in a trade union," says Veronica. "I work in the office."

"And I work for the same union," says Bredo.

The midwife brings Veronica a bedpan, then feels her with her slippery gloved hand.

"You're seven centimeters open now, so only three left."

What a remarkable world of women, with one woman putting her hand up another woman's vagina.

"Now let's have a really good deep breath and push . . . one that will do something about it."

Bredo's face is close to Veronica's. He kisses her on the mouth. She is holding hard round his neck.

"Ssh!" he whispers, winking at her as he tries to loosen her grasp on him.

Will we ever sleep together again? she thinks.

He supports her across the small of her back, pressing his warm broad hand right in toward the base of her spine. The feeling of her bones sliding apart vanishes.


Veronica's body is working away, driving her. She is bathed in sweat, subjected to natural laws she has no chance of escaping. She can't suddenly cry out: "Stop, I want to get off! I've changed my mind." Or "Give me half an hour's rest." Impossible. She is completely in the power of her fate.

Abandoning her body to her surroundings . . . she must simply go on and rely on them helping her. There is absolutely no other way out.

As long as they speak kindly to her, as long as they come to meet her, she'll do anything! But she cannot stand hard words. If her helpers are hostile, then the battle is lost, and there will be incalculable consequences far into the future.

The midwife bends over her and wipes her forehead.

"I'm sorry, but it's past one o'clock now, and I *must* go. I had hoped that you would have given birth while I was on duty. But things will be fine for you now. I'll look in tomorrow to see how it's gone and what you've got."

To see what you've got? She is perfectly certain Veronica will have something worth seeing tomorrow!


At midday, a large heavy figure in a brown overcoat, stooping and bent like a drunk, comes pushing a little cot ahead of her along the prenatal corridor. With slow laborious steps, the figure heads for the glass window.

"Well, heavens above, it's Olivia!" The nurse almost drops the bedpan she has in her hand. "You are a clever one, aren't you, now?"

Patients come out of the wards and gather round Olivia.

"Let's see! May we look?"

Olivia says "ouch!" and steps aside, and an orderly says:

"I will . . . I will. . . ." and she lifts the little bundle up in the air for all to see.

It's a little redhead with sticking-out hair, a real living human being, with pink fingers and small nails and fine ears and eyebrows and everything as it should be.

"Oh, isn't she sweet?"

"May I hold her?"

"No, it's my turn."

Olivia is pale but collected.

"Can we see your scar?" says Marie.

"Yes, certainly." Olivia undoes her shirt and proudly reveals it.

"Isn't it neat?"

There's nothing to see except a vertical pink plaster on her flabby stomach. Is that really all? How well it has been done. They're really clever in here.

"What does your husband say?"

"He's fit to bust."

"Are you feeding the baby?"

"Yes, she's ever so good, ever so. She's dreadfully greedy, too." But nevertheless, Olivia is already giving her supplementary feeds, because they've advised her to do so down in the delivery ward, so that the baby doesn't become jaundiced.

"Watch out for supplementary feeds," says Signe, her finger raised. "The devil created them!"

"And Holger's coming to fetch us."

"What's it like down in Delivery?"

"They're awfully good, they really are. I can't speak highly enough of them."

Olivia is proud and smiles with her blue front teeth. She is like an encyclopedia from which they can find out everything.

"Did they remember to sterilize you?" Marie exclaims.

"They did." Olivia closes one eye. "I should think so, too."

"How on earth did you get down here?"

"Easy enough. Just took the lift down to the underground passage. Then I walked here. I got a porter to help me. Then I came up here . . . nothing to it."

During the pains—the cosmic loneliness. A loneliness of a wholly different nature from anything Veronica has ever felt before.

Is death like birth? Is natural death like natural birth? So severe? So solemn and merciless?

Bredo strokes her forehead.

She can hear herself jerking out words.

"My back hurts."

"Try to relax. Yes, that's right. That's fine."

The new midwife is standing beside her. She puts her light hand on Veronica's shoulder and gives her a wide smile. Her eyes are dark and lively.

"No, no! I'll never make it!"

"Yes, of course you will. Try to sit up, that's right."

"It's good that she doesn't agree with me," thinks Veronica. "Supposing she'd said: 'No, you won't make it.' Then I think I'd die."

"I'm going to be sick."

The paper bowl is filled with a strange mess, the contents of her stomach.

"Good," says the midwife. "Something'll happen soon now."

Oh, what will she do? The contractions come in swift waves, one after another. She is no longer herself in between them. She had thought she would be able to keep her self-control all the time . . . but she cannot. If only it would stop for a moment. If only she could have a little rest. But no, she has to go on, go on.

Supposing the child is stuck? Supposing it can't get out? Supposing it's not getting enough oxygen? Supposing the cord is round its neck . . . supposing something happens. . . .

The midwife listens to her uneasy body. The fetus is kicking—even in contraction, her belly bulges.

"The baby's fine."

"Are you from South Jylland?"

"Yes, from Sønderborg," she says. She has Veronica's life in her hands.

"I'm so thirsty."

"Rinse out your mouth, then spit it out."

She whimpers. It hurts so. It hurts so. Everything is heaving and pressing inside her, like a locomotive driving over her. Is being raped something like this? She clings to the midwife's arm. The midwife strokes her hair. "I love you," thinks Veronica. "You are my own earth-mother. You speak so quietly and calmly to the two student midwives bustling round the bed. My Hebamma, my Hevanna, my Earth Mother. Do not leave me.

"Without you, I cannot make it. Though children are being born in Vietnam as the bombs fall. Poor women had healthy off-spring in Warsaw's ghetto . . . with no help at all. My grand-mother had eight children in her own bed. If others can, then I suppose I must be able to. . . ."

She sees a black universe in front of her, the stars twinkling, a comet rushing through the cold room. She cries out in anguish.

"I want to push. . . ."

"One moment, hold your breath, hold it, that's right, fine . . . no, no, don't push. It's too soon."

She sees a globe in front of her, lit by the moon.

"Can you open your eyes."

She looks into the smiling brown eyes.

"Pant, now . . ."

Pant like a dog . . . she has learnt that. Pant and pant and pant, as the pains roll over her body. From top to bottom. From bottom to top . . . all her fibers contracting. Pant so as not to push before the mouth of the womb is quite ready, before the vagina and the baby are ready. Pant like a locomotive chugging uphill. Her tongue is dry, her throat strangled, her whole body pulling and pulling.

"Up on the bedpan now, so that I can have a look."

The midwife feels in her vagina and says, yes, and suddenly there is great activity in the room.

A little table is wheeled to the foot of her bed. People come in and stand in a semicircle, staring with round eyes, like owls on a branch.

"Now come over here if you want to see something."

Bredo gets up from his chair at the head of the bed and goes and stands by the midwife. He is pale and there is an uncertain smile on his lips.

"Hold your knees with both hands, now, bend your legs . . . that's it . . . now push when I tell you."

Blue and green float before Veronica's eyes. The contractions start rising like a cliff in front of her.

"No!" cries Veronica. "I can't!"

The rocky wall stands before her, quite vertically.

"I can see the hair," whispers Bredo.

The pain eases off, Veronica falls back on the bed, her eyes closed.

A new pain starts, rising and rising. . . .

Headlong, bloody, bursting . . . chunks of rock rolling down the cliff wall and hurtling into the sea.

"The head's showing now," cries the midwife. "Press down . . . as hard as you can . . . that's it. . . ."

Veronica hides her face in her hands, her bones cracking as they glide apart. The baby's body makes its way through the last soft part of the birth passage, a log gliding over a shore and on out into the sea—something large and firm and dark is thrust out of her body, out between her legs, a dark parcel, a bloody lump.

"Take it," cries the midwife. "Lift it up yourself."

"No, I daren't."

A tearing red and white feeling.

A strange slithering sound.

Then everything is quite still . . . an expanse of sea like a mirror.

"Guess what it is."


The baby's sex . . . like a cloven leaf. A little cushion. A girl. No, it's not true, it's not true.

The newborn infant kicks and squeals, like a landed fish. The strong little blue limbs twitching in the air, water scattering. Blue-white and purple, covered with fetal fat.

She is still tied to the mother ship by a hawser, to the spaceship

by her lifeline . . . the thick yellowish-white pulsating twisted cord.

Clip! And she is for ever an independent human being.

Veronica half-sits up in bed, tears streaming down her cheeks as she sees this dark little space-creature, this complete little Tutankhamen. *All pain has gone.* 3,600 grams, 52 centimeters. It couldn't have been finer.

They swing the heat lamp over the bed and place the naked child in her mother's arms. My little guest. My little new one. I dare not touch you, you are so perfect.

She kisses one of the long purplish feet and notices the slightly acid smell of the alien country the child has come from. How pretty she is. So incredible that it has happened. Is it really you?

There is a start inside Veronica, a jerk in her womb . . . and yet another contraction comes. The midwife puts her hand firmly on her stomach and presses hard and slowly in the rhythm of the contraction.

"Press down, now."

The placenta appears and is lifted away. It is large and awe-inspiring, a creature from the seabed, ruby-red, with blue and white veins and membranes, transparent and glistening.

"What's the time?"

"Five past three."

It has taken eleven hours since her waters broke that morning. Veronica squeezes the midwife's arm and kisses her hand.

"A thousand thousand thanks."


"Listen," says Marie. She knows perfectly well Tenna is tired, but makes her listen all the same.

"Yes," says Tenna, turning round.

*"Radio telescopes have registered the sound of an explosion resulting in the creation of the world. Very sensitive instruments have recorded the tremors that occurred when a fireball ten billion years ago started on its indefatigable growth.*

Marie raises her head.

"Well, what do you say?"

"Go on reading."

*Ten to fifteen billion years ago everything in space was gathered in an incomprehensibly compact super-star. For inexplicable reasons, it suddenly exploded, and pieces of matter were flung in every direction with tremendous force. From this arose the Milky Way and the galaxies that today we see moving away from us at dizzying speeds. The explosion persisted as the universe continued its violent growth.*

"You're to have stitches . . . you've a big internal tear."

"Oh, no, and I was just feeling so happy!"

They hand Veronica the mask.

"Breathe in deeply, then you'll have the finest crossstitching you can imagine."

All feeling has long since returned to her, and Veronica notices how every touch is like the sting of a red hot wire.

The pain strikes her like blue lightning, her whole body jerking. She feels like kicking out at the white figures. That needle in her flesh . . . her poor flesh. She breathes deeply into the mask and slips away, gliding into another existence between heaven and earth, hovering between bluish layers, sinking into dark holes, seesawing up and down on a gigantic cloth, seeing the white angel coming into sight at the end of a long tunnel . . . it is the midwife and her pupil between her legs.

"Lie quietly now! It's for your own good we're doing this!"

"But why the bloody hell don't you use an anesthetic?"

"Hey, hey, is that how you talk in your union? Because then the flesh swells up and we can't see where we're stitching, and it's not so neat. Take the mask, now. It's nothing. The stitches will go away by themselves."

"Hell's bloody bells!"

"What language . . . think of your baby!"

"Hell's bloody bells again, it hurts so. You've no idea what agony it is."

"Your husband will thank us for this."

Her violent inhalations again take her into no-man's land. She thinks she is in labor again. She has contractions. She is afraid.

127

Something's going wrong. The child is sideways. She cries out and notices someone shaking her.

"Wake up . . . you've got a little girl . . . her father's sitting over there by the window."

"It's a lie. It's a hellish lie!"

"It's a lie, is it?"

The midwife is standing beside her.

"You've had too much, my girl."

Veronica props herself up on her elbows and sees a dark figure silhouetted against the window . . . it's . . . it's Bredo, holding a bundle in his arms.

It's him! It's true. Oh, God, he's heard all that?

Veronica throws herself against the midwife and embraces her hips, almost tipping over onto the floor.

"You're a treasure."

"That I'm not!"

"Yes, you are."

Bredo carries the child over to the bed. When Veronica kisses her for the first time, it is like kissing light down or fine chamois leather, so soft she is, so softened by all that water that has surrounded her for nine months. What an eternity!

Oh, the little treasure! Look at her blinking against the strong light. Look at her little hands. She's so strong! How can she be so strong?

"What about a feed?" says the baby's father, putting her to her mother's breast. "Try now. Come on, have a bite, tiddler."

And she starts sucking. Smacking, too. Loudly, as well. Where has she learnt that? How clever she is. And wise. Oh, she looks so gentle, kind. So touching with that small closed face.

"Just think," said Bredo. "When I was standing there and saw her head coming out, it was quite round, like a stone ball. Her nose and ears were flat against her head. She looked as if she was made of stone, and I thought, will she survive? But I wasn't afraid, because everyone was taking it so calmly. When her neck was free, her nose started rising and her ears unfolding. Just like a little flower opening, and then out she came."

"What did you think about it otherwise?"

"It was much more natural than I had thought. No instruments and practically no blood. Only the midwife's hands all the time. *It was marvelous.*"

Two student midwives clear up the room, moving the trolley aside, taking away bedpans and turning out lights.

One of them pulls down Veronica's hospital shirt and washes her with a large yellow sponge. The cool water feels good. How thoughtful of them. There is a plaster on her hand where the needle had gone in.

Oh, it's all over now.

A doctor comes into the room and listens to her heart and lungs, takes her pulse, and goes away again.


So they are alone together with the baby for the first time, in the room that the winter day is already emptying of light. They lift the little bundle of life off the bed into the light from the bedside lamp.

Bredo's eyes are shining . . . how pretty she is, this little Sunday's child of theirs.

He takes his newborn child in his arms, and kisses her, stroking her head and forehead carefully, speaking quietly to her, as if to a small acquaintance.

To think that all these months, she has lain there being a girl, with the same fine little face. A girl above all girls. You are ours. Before we were two, and now we are three. Before we had nothing . . . now we have everything. A human being to send out into the world.

Bredo puts the baby down at Veronica's breast. The baby lifts her head. She's *that* strong. Her eyes are deep blue and calm, with large dark pupils. She hardly blinks, simply looking straight ahead with a firm convincing gaze.

She has small fat spots on her nose. Her mouth is a silky bow. Her small hands and feet are minute, dark, with mussel shells for nails. She still moves dreamily, slowly, as if filmed in slow motion.

She is still linked with that unknown country from where she has been fetched.

She is still, in this precious hour, halfway between fetal and human life.

An orderly comes in with a tray.

"Here we are, and the father too must be hungry, eh? Help yourselves, there's plenty more where that came from."

Never has anything tasted so good. Never has the tea been so hot. Never in all her life has Veronica been so happy.

From one world to another.

A sturdy little porter with short gray hair is standing by Veronica's bed with a high stretcher on wheels.

"Roll over, little mother."

Her limbs creak as she carefully rolls over on her side, away from the labor couch on to the stretcher. The baby has been dressed and is now wrapped in the check quilt and put alongside her mother, in the curve of her arm. They lie face to face, touching noses.

At the end of the stretcher are Veronica's shoulder bag, her sandals, her transistor radio and the orange dressing gown.

"Can I have a room of my own?"

The porter hums contentedly as he pushes the little family out on to the main stairs and over to the lifts.

"No, you certainly cannot, little mother. This isn't a hotel, you know. Single rooms go to those who need them. No, you're in Ward 1. Ten beds in there. It's the biggest of the lot, but it's also the nicest."

## MONDAY 6 JANUARY

The ultrasound apparatus has been on the go since early morning. You can feel it in the air of the room, which seems to hang like mist from so many people in such a small room.

Marie is lying on a narrow bunk; in front of her a large notice-board covered with newspaper clippings, reproductions, photo-stats, and letters.

She puts the palms of her hands on the paper undersheet to give her back some support. It is uncomfortable for her to lie like that, but there is no other way.

A young man with a black moustache rubs her stomach with groundnut oil. It is pleasing to see a young man again and feel his proximity.

He brings the metal arm of the apparatus closer to her stomach and then starts moving the arm back and forth and up and down in semicircular movements.

She has had ultrasonic treatment twice before, but this time the atmosphere in the room is quite different.

No one says anything, nor shows any sign of uneasiness, and yet she seems to sense the tension. The young man and the woman standing behind him with her hands in her overall pockets atten-tively follow the tracks on the screen.

They are looking for something. She feels a tickling sensation in the left-hand side of her abdomen, down near her groin. They are looking for the baby's head . . . yes, *that* must be it. They are trying to encircle it with smaller and smaller movements.

The young man lets go the apparatus and takes a photograph of the screen with a polaroid camera. He smiles encouragingly at Marie as he pulls the picture out of the camera.

But wasn't there a slight flicker in his eyes?

Then he takes a whole series of photographs.

The fair-haired woman looks at the photograph and at the screen, then sits down at the desk in front of the notice-board, her back to Marie.

They've found something, or so it seems.

"You can get down now," he says, switching off the apparatus.

"Are you looking for anything special? says Marie, looking questioningly at the fair woman.

"We're always doing that."

"What can you see?"

"We can see that the baby has lungs, liver, kidneys, and heart . . . we can see the size of the organs and their position."

"What else?"

"We can see the fetus has a *caput*."

Has a head? Why on earth should it not have a head?

There must be something in Marie's expression that makes the fair woman take a step back and look at the picture she has in her hand.

The young man rises noisily from his chair and the woman regains her equilibrium. Marie's heart thumps beneath her hospital shirt.

"But you have an awful lot of amniotic fluid," he says. "Your child's splashing about and thrashing around so it's almost impossible to photograph . . . you can see for yourself. Look here."

They put the series of scans in front of her on the table, a collection of semiabstract pictures of dotted lines, diffuse white surfaces, and trailing tracks that need special skills to interpret.

"How do you decide the baby's age?"

"We measure the size of the head."

"How large is mine?"

"Large."

"Should I go on asking for more details?" thinks Marie. "No, they're probably not allowed to give too much information, even less make diagnoses."

"Then what's wrong in my case?"

"To be honest, we can't find *anything* wrong."

The fair woman in the white coat stands in front of Marie. They are the same height and their eyes are exactly level with each other.

"But what does one do if *despite everything* something abnormal is registered?"

"If it's incompatible with life . . . then we'd induce the delivery."

They think, but they're not sure, that the child is encephalitic, water on the brain, flashes through Marie's mind.

The woman gathers up the photographs, puts a couple of them into Marie's file, then puts the whole lot into a large yellow envelope. Then she seals the envelope with a strip of tape and hands it to Marie.

Marie feels shapeless and foolish as she leaves the lift and goes into the silent prenatal department, her white stockings sagging round her ankles, as she has no garters to hold them up.

It is the middle of the day and most of the patients are asleep. The sister is sitting bent over the open daybook in the office. Marie hands her the yellow envelope.

"Well, how are things?"

Marie sits down by the little table, the pulse beating in her throat, tears pouring down her cheeks. Suddenly she can't control herself any longer.

"But what's the matter?" says the sister in surprise.

The tears run down into Marie's mouth.

"The worst of it is . . . that you don't *know*."

"Would you like a drink?"

The sister takes a key fastened to a chain at her belt and opens the medicine cupboard. She takes out a bottle and pours out a little glassful for her patient. Marie knows it well. It is a calming medicine that has nothing to do with alcohol. She has seen several of the other girls being given the same thing when they have felt depressed.

"Here . . . drink this down."

Marie nods and tips back the drink and blows her nose. A moment later, the tears cease pouring down, simply stop, and a strange *false* sense of ease spreads through her body.

She looks up at the sister, who is standing in front of her, leaning against the medicine cupboard with her arms folded, one leg crossed over the other, her head on one side.

"Well?"

"The worst of it is that one simply doesn't know what one has to adjust to. . . ."

When Marie slips back into Ward 0, she finds an orderly making up Tenna's empty bed.

"Where's Tenna got to?"

"She's having pains."

"Are you sure?"

"Yes, they've just taken her down to Delivery . . . only five minutes between contractions."

"Has a midwife been in to see her?"

"Yes, when you were down at Ultrasound. She's been examined. She was four or five centimeters open."

So they hadn't been able to stop Tenna's pains.

"Do you know if they've phoned her husband?"

"Yes, she talks of nothing else. They've phoned him, but he's got 'flu and a high temperature, so can't come. Poor girl. And it's five weeks too early, too."

Her body is young and strong and the pains are coming quickly, one after the other. No stimulant needed here, neither oxytocin nor drip.

But the patient is restless and anguished.

It is a hectic day in the delivery department, something going on in almost every room. This can be seen in attitudes to each individual patient. The door to Tenna's room often opens and a stranger sticks in her head and says:

"You haven't got a moment, by any chance, have you?"

The student midwife leaves the room.

Along the walls, standing or hanging, are various horrible machines, the compressed-air stand, oxygen-cylinders, suction apparatus, tubes hanging loose down behind the head of her bed.

Being left alone like this is the worst thing Tenna knows.

"I must pee," she mumbles.

"Raise yourself up carefully then, so I can get the bedpan in," says the student midwife.

"Oh, no, that hurts so."

"Now?"

"No, wait a moment."

"Now, then?"

The student midwife pushes the cold bedpan into place and the movement at once sets off a pain that tautens Tenna's stomach like a bowstring.

The sky is gray beyond the square window. Tenna is lonely. She has no energy to establish a relationship with the delivery staff . . . and they are too busy and too uninvolved to break down the barrier dividing them from the patient.

Tenna lies on one side with her eyes closed.

On the other stands the midwife reading her casesheet.

There's another knock on the door and the midwife leaves the room.

"I'll go mad if they keep popping in and out like that," thinks Tenna. "I'll never recover after all this."

No one tells Tenna to open her eyes. No one comes and sits beside her and talks to her. No one has time to hold her hand.

There are hot tears behind her closed eyes, and her mouth trembles slightly.

"I'm going to look and see how many centimeters you're open now," says the midwife, looking out through the window. "We'll have you up on a bedpan so that we can feel."

"Oh, no, please don't."

"I must be able to do my work, now, mustn't I? That's right, help me a little, will you . . . that's right."

She thrusts her cool gloved fingers into Tenna's warm tender vagina, where everything is at the same time so soft and so taut. With her other hand, she feels her stomach on the outside as it heaves and sinks with its small pounding load.

"All right," she says, getting down from the stool. "Now it's your turn."

The student midwife gets up and feels, her hands more hesitant, more uncertain than the other midwife's.

"It seems to me as if the orifice is open about eight centimeters . . . I can feel the square fontanelle—the head is engaged."

"That's right."

The student midwife places a paper sheet over Tenna's loins and gets down from the stool.

They whisper quietly together in one corner of the room, and the midwife jots down the result of her examination in the case-sheet.

In the bathroom, the shower curtain has finally fallen off its rail and is now lying carelessly folded on the window sill.

The hot water runs down over Marie's stomach, the smell of the shampoo tickling her nose. Her hair is soapy, and the scum collects down by the drainage grid.

A reddish-blonde girl is standing over by the basin, cleaning her teeth.

"What are you in for?"

"For observation," says the girl, spitting into the basin. "I've got a little boy at home, the sweetest kid you could imagine, but he has nothing in his head. The doctors say he's mentally defective, but they can't find any explanation. He looks perfectly normal and simply hasn't developed. He can neither eat by himself, nor walk nor talk."

"How old is he?"

"Five," says the girl, putting her toothbrush into its case. "And he's ever so sweet-looking." She smiles. "He's red-haired, just like me."

She starts brushing her hair with swift strong movements.

"The doctors advised us to try again. They say the chances of that happening again are minimal."

"Is it difficult having him at home?"

"Yes, it is. But we love him. You know what's the most important thing when you have a handicapped child?"

"No."

"That your *marriage* holds."

She looks at Marie with her calm dark-green eyes.

"You've no idea how many marriages break up because of a handicapped child. There are lots of men who say, 'that thing, that can't be my child!' They just don't want to accept it. As if it had been conceived by the Holy Ghost!"

"How has your husband taken it then?" says Marie, wrapping the towel round her head.

"Oh, he's a hundred percent involved. He's very fond of him. Though it hasn't been easy for him. We've had to change our lives completely . . . both as far as our social life is concerned, and to be able to look after him at home ourselves."

"What does your husband do?"

"He's an optician."

"And you?"

"I was a hospital orderly until we had the baby. But I've been at home ever since; I'm used to looking after other people."

She pulls at her hospital shirt.

"Do you think they're good here?'

"Oh, yes," said Marie. "But what are they doing with you?"

"Nothing except keeping me under observation. My estriol count isn't all that high. I had a baby born dead six years ago. They think perhaps there's a connection between these things."

She throws the wet towel into the laundry basket.


"You're not lying there crying, are you?" says the student midwife.

"It hurts so," whispers Tenna.

The student midwife puts her stethoscope against her patient's stomach. Tenna is lying on her side with her eyes closed, the spasms flashing across her closed face like swift clouds.

"Here . . . take the mask, then you won't notice it so much," says the student.

The black rubber threateningly approaches Tenna's mouth and nose from above.

"No, I don't want it," she says, pushing the mask away.

"Yes, try again."

"No, it makes me feel sick. I can't bear it. Take it away!" cries Tenna.

Her mouth and throat are dry.

The student midwife runs her soft cool hand carefully over her belly.

The midwife comes into the room, followed by a tall doctor.

"Well, how are things going?"

"They're not going at all," whispers Tenna.

Her contractions are more irregular. She can feel cold shivers between her shoulder blades and up the back of her neck, although her face feels quite hot. Hot and cold at the same time. Then the doctor puts his hard stethoscope against her belly in a very careless manner.

"Oh, no, take it away," cries Tenna.

He tries again.

"Take it away!"

Then suddenly she feels she must bear down, the reflex suddenly there before her with its ruthless demands.

"It's there now!" she cries.

"One moment," says the midwife. "See if you can pant and hold back a little. Yes, that's it!" She turns to the doctor and whispers: "We could have given an epidural, but it's too late now."

Tenna hears every single word.

A lamp is switched on with a snap and throws its sharp light between her legs. She is lying on her side, struggling like an animal that has been struck to the ground, the great muscle of her womb working independently of her will.

"Try taking a deep breath when the next pain comes."

Tenna screws up her eyes.

"Would you turn over on your back and get up on the bedpan? . . . That's it."

Now she's on the actual delivery bedpan, on the throne, the cold hard throne, endlessly distant from the white coats all round her.

The midwife feels again.

"Now you must bear down . . . it won't hurt any more from now on . . . fill your lungs full and then try to bear down two or three times during each pain."

She turns to her pupil and says:

"I think we'll give oxygen in the mask now."

Tenna presses her chin against her chest, holds on to the back of her knees with her hands, straddling with her legs, feeling the heavy, mercilessly demanding contraction come rolling over her.

The oxygen from the mask prickles her skin.

She bears down and screams. A thin stream of urine spurts out and the pain recedes.

"Put your feet down now and rest."

Her legs are trembling.

There are a lot of people in the delivery room now.

The midwife puts her stethoscope to her stomach and looks at the doctor.

Tenna sinks back into a trance, as if she were about to leave life on this earth.

Then a pain starts up again, and with it the primeval urge to bear down and eject the fetus . . . Tenna stretches every muscle in her young body and the child's head appears . . . she lets the air trickle out of her lungs and then fills them again . . . and bears down . . . feeling a fiery scorching all round her orifice.

"Wait a moment," says the midwife gently. "Bear down now, carefully now, now it's coming, yes . . ."


It is deathly silent in the delivery room.

Much too silent.

A tense vibrating silence.

Between her legs, Tenna can sense rather than see a tiny gray little body.

Then she hears the hissing sound as they suck the mucus out of the child's mouth.

"We'll have to take it out into the recovery room," says the doctor. "It must be sucked out a little more."

Sucked out more? The figures move, the door is opened and shut.

The midwife places her hand on Tenna's belly and says in a subdued voice:

"Try to bear down, quite calmly, just once more."

The great soft placenta glides down the vagina with the other membranes the child has lain in. The midwife carefully pulls the navel cord and the placenta falls heavily into the bedpan.

There are odd whisperings . . . *abruptio—insuffiens*. They stand beside the placenta for a long time.

"Do I need stitching?" says Tenna anxiously.

"No, not at all . . . not a single tear."

"Really?" says Tenna, relieved for the very first time.

At visiting time, an unusually tall man with glasses comes in carrying a very large child in a blue overcoat, a red-haired child with calm green eyes in his white face.

"That must be him," Rørby thinks, as she goes into Ward 0 with a pot of steaming hot tea.

"Well, how's the world revolution going, then?"

Marie puts her paper aside and Rørby pours out tea.

"You should have those flowers taken away," says Rørby, pointing a stubby forefinger at the bouquet standing on the floor by the television set. "Don't you know red and white flowers bring bad luck?"

"They're Tenna's," says Marie.

They hear the sound of children running along the corridor, laughing and boisterous. A chair falls over.

"Rørby, Rørby!" they cry. "Give us a poisonous green pop!"

It must be Signe's children. They are so small they still speak exclusively in the form of urgent requests.

The doctor is sitting on her bed.

"Is it dead?"

"No, it's alive. It seemed dead at birth, but we sucked the mucus out of its throat."

"What is it?"

"A boy."

"Is he terribly small?"

"He weighs 1,800 grams."

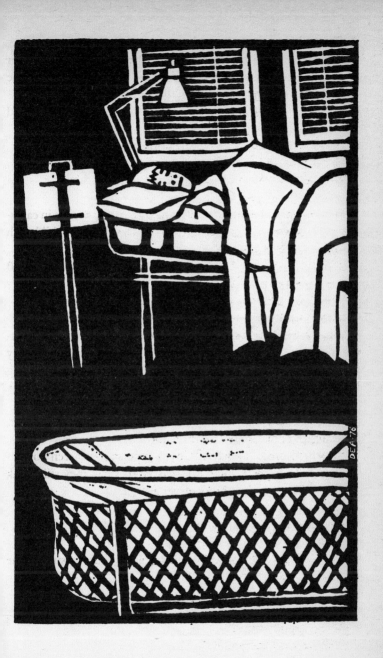

The doctor hesitates for a moment.

"But I'm afraid there's something wrong."

A gigantic bell begins to toll.

"There's something wrong with his feet."

He takes a deep breath.

"He *has* no feet."

For a fraction of a second, reality slips away from Tenna. Or she slips away from it. Her surroundings expand and she seems to see the doctor through a pane of glass. She sees him opening and shutting his mouth and she can also hear his words far away, but they do not impinge on her. She does not understand them.

She is icy cold. He's wrong. He's not talking about her—it must be someone else.

She hears him repeat everything all over again. The boy was apparently dead, but they have managed to bring him back to life. He weighs 1,800 grams, but would probably have weighed a few hundred grams more if he had had any feet.

A group of specialists are at that moment examining him in the pediatric department.

"What can I do?" says the doctor in despair. "It's not my fault."

No, naturally it's not his fault.

He walks up and down the room, trying to get her to understand what has happened.

"Will he have to live in a wheelchair all his life?" says Tenna.

"I don't really know much about that," he says. "But it is immensely important that the boy has his knee-joints."

Anders is standing in front of her, his face chalk-white. The doctor has left the room and they are alone.

"They said on the phone that I had to come, as there was something wrong with the baby. But they weren't allowed to say what."

"It's a boy."

"Yes?"

"He's awfully small. 1,800 grams."

"Yes?"

DEA·76

"But he's . . . he's got no feet. . . ."

Anders and Tenna look at each other for a moment, then the happy, good-natured Anders lies right across the bed and hides his face in the covers.

Time passes. They don't know what the time is.

They hold hands. They put their arms round each other's necks. They try to wipe away the tears from each other's eyes. They don't know what they're going to do, what they should think or believe. Only that a boundless grief has struck them.

Tenna straightens up. She has half an hour's headstart on him. She has had time to think a little more than he has. In some way she must try to give him courage and strength.

"All our silly lives," she says, looking into his feverish face. "Everything's been so small in comparison with this one single great thing."

She grasps his shoulders.

"We've been handed the challenge of our life."


Marie is standing by the big window at one end of the prenatal corridor, leaning against the wall and looking down on the empty building site where the snow has spread its white sheet over the sheds and equipment. She would like to talk to Signe. But Signe is asleep.

The inner city lies spread out in front of her, the inner city where she lives and works. Casting its blurred purplish light against the deep suspended sky. The inner city, with its rich floating stream of life, life that continues rotating all the time, the life that never stops.

Out on the water, great flocks of freezing birds are standing on the thin ice, ducks and gulls, their dead eyes half-closed and their circulation reduced.


They come and ask if they want to see him.

Anders nods.

They can't very well say they don't *want* to see him, can they?

A cot is wheeled soundlessly in to them under the light of the night-lamp, and they are alone again.

A tiny little fair-haired boy-child is lying in the cot, his eyes closed. They can hardly see that he's breathing.

They lift the quilt aside and look. They feel under the clothes.

He is two things, a little handicapped child, and their own flesh and blood.

How touching he is, their baby.

Anders lifts him up and walks back and forth with his son in the dark delivery room.

"But I love the little blighter."

"You're being given a single room," says the student midwife.

Tenna suddenly notices tears are pouring down the girl's cheeks. She neither sniffs nor wipes her face with her sleeve; just those tears ploughing two shining tracks down her face. Tenna turns cold.

No one may weep over her child!

Weeping she can manage *herself* . . . no one else need take the trouble.

"Are you good at knitting?"

"No, hopeless," says Marie, propping herself up on her elbow.

The redhead is standing by her bed with a little jacket in her hands.

"I was wondering whether you'd help me with this. What's that smell? Is it medicine?"

"Old Danish Bitter," says Marie, leaning over the edge of the bed and taking a bulbous bottle out of her locker. "Want some?"

The redhead nods happily and sits down on the end of the bed.

"Did you see my little boy? Oh, didn't you?" she says with disappointment. "My husband's bringing him in today."

That night a stretcher is brought up in the lift. The door opens and the stretcher is wheeled out into the deserted postnatal department. A tired young woman is lying under a blanket on the stretcher. She has no child with her, and because of that, she is given a single room.

That was Tenna's Twelfth Night.

The Day of the Three Kings, January the sixth, the thirteenth day after Christmas.

That day the sun starts moving again. After its return, it has rested for twelve days, and then on the thirteenth it starts rolling again, according to old folklore. The sun measures the sacred number of days, when nothing may turn, neither wheel, nor drill nor spinning wheel, while the portents for the twelve months of the new year are interpreted.

In the old days, school children walked in procession on that day—schoolboys, that is, for in those days no girls went to school.

They walked in procession, carrying a long pole with a paper star on top at the head. Three of the boys were dressed up as the three holy kings, Caspar, Melchior, and Balthazar. One of them had blacked his face so that he resembled a Moor.

Another was Judas with a large moneybag in his hand, and beside him was Joseph, a bent old man with an axe in his hand.

Last of all came the Virgin Mary with the infant Jesus in a bag on her back.

All of them in the procession sang a psalm, an antiphon, a star song, and wherever they went, people came out of their houses and stood in their doorways watching the children disappearing down toward the main street of the town.

## TUESDAY 7 JANUARY

In the examination room on Tuesday morning, immediately after his round, the doctor says:

"I hear . . . I hear you're rather troubled?"

So Sister has told him. Marie is greatly relieved.

"Have you time to talk . . . for a while?"

"Of course."

She thinks for a moment, searching for the words she has prepared. Then she starts.

"You see, I've heard that too much fluid might mean there is something wrong with the fetus."

"Where on *earth* did you get that idea?"

Pure comedy, thinks Marie.

"I've put two and two together," she says, her heart thumping. They look at each other in silence.

"I'd like to ask you to tell me the truth. I'd feel better about it if you told me what you know and what you think. I don't think the truth should be kept hidden. It serves no purpose, *ever*. I think you live a fuller life if you look reality in the eye. . . ."

They look at each other. Silence reigns in the examination room, and she notices he is now coming to meet her.

"It's not knowing that's the worst," she says. "Assuming there's something that isn't quite right with this baby . . . I'd get over it very much better and be able to work my way through it, as long as I've been sufficiently *prepared* for it beforehand."

"You're right in a way," he says. "But most patients feel better if they're not told too much. Some prefer to be told *nothing* at all."

"I won't talk about it, so it won't cause trouble on the wards," she says, feeling she is now talking past him. He is not really interested. "I quite realize that there's a certain responsibility in being a patient."

"Well, then, if you're really sure of what you're saying, then I can confirm your assumption that hydramnios may be associated with malformation. The two things are often found together. Before, we used to do x-rays, but we've gone on to Ultrasound now, as you know."

"I noticed up there in Ultrasound that they think my child is very large."

"I don't think it's *that* large. At a guess, I should say it's about 3,000 grams. But it's hard to say because of all that amniotic fluid."

He hands her her open file.

"I'd like to show you what I've written, so you believe what I am saying. Here, you can see . . . it says *nothing abnormal observed*,

149

and that's repeated here on the next page. So we can't *establish* anything. And your estriol count is fine . . . look at the diagram here. It's within the normal range. There's only one dip around the twenty-fourth of December. But actually it's quite common for estriol counts to be rather low over holidays. Perhaps you yourself weren't all that thorough with your urine sample!"

He smiles fleetingly. She clenches her fist in her pocket.

"But there must be something you can't see on the ultrasonic picture?"

"Yes, not everything throws back an echo."

"What doesn't give an echo?"

He hesitates for a moment.

"The gullet and the central nervous system."

The central nervous system and the gullet.

So it's round those two things attention is being focused.

"Do you think the baby might be defective?"

He looks at her with his dark brown eyes, then says:

"I don't *think* so."

He says he doesn't *think* so. She trusts him. He doesn't *think* so. But at the same time he cannot exclude the possibility.

Marie would like to ask him *why* he doesn't think so, but she feels that would be going too far. She might easily irritate him. There is an invisible boundary between them . . . a boundary she cannot step over without destroying their newly acquired trust.

She decides to ask one last question.

"How great do you think the statistical risk is . . . of there being something wrong in my case?"

"We—ell, round about fifteen to twenty percent."

They get up and shake hands.

"I hope I haven't said too much," he says.


"Did you have x-ray or radium treatment during the first three months of pregnancy?"

"No."

"Were you ill at all? Can you remember?"

"No."

"No severe influenza, either?"

"No," says Anders, looking at Tenna. "It's true. She hasn't been ill. We've lived perfectly normally."

"Have you taken any medication?"

"No, not that, either!"

The old doctor is sitting in the postnatal department with Tenna's hand in his. Through his hand she can feel a warmth that means she can keep on an even keel and not start crying. This warm good hand of his with its big veins and ribbed nails encloses hers in such a fatherly way.

"You're quite sure you haven't forgotten anything?"

"Quite sure."

"It must have happened very quickly," says Anders. "The hands and feet . . . aren't they formed in the course of a few days?"

"That was probably why it hurt so, then," says Tenna in a low voice. "It must have been those little stumps that were stabbing me in the side every time he moved."

The doctor looks from Tenna to Anders and then back at Tenna again.

"So we're faced with one of nature's whims. There's nothing in your medical history or casesheet that gives us even the slightest inkling of an explanation for what has happened. But it's happened and nothing can change that. It might be due to pollution, it might be due to so many things, it's just not possible to say. . . ."

He places his large hands round Tenna's one hand.

"I would advise you . . . *stop wondering about how it could have happened*. Try to stop thinking about it. Send people who ask about it packing . . . for most people will go on and on about the reason for the child's handicap."

Anders nods.

"But don't think you've already thought through it all and have got over the shock . . . because you *haven't*. There'll be reactions for many many months to come. And the next few weeks will be the hardest for you both. Relating to your surroundings will seem horribly complicated to you . . . much more complicated than relating to your child, because you'll probably cope with that perfectly well."

He nods to give emphasis to his words, then gets up.

"Come, let's go over and have a look at him. I'll tell the staff in Neonatal that you can come whenever you like, at any time of the day or night, and that you want to look after your child yourself."

Marie is like another person now. She is in a better mood. Why? She has had her worst fears confirmed so to speak. Yes, but she feels better now, for her fears have been given a name and a direction, and first and foremost because she feels she is now respected as a human being, a person they do not want to exclude from her own destiny. And most of all, *that* gives her a sense of security.

She gazes at the raindrops on the windowpane, opens the drawer in her locker and gets out pen and paper. For the first time for many days, she feels like writing to Zacharias and to her parents. Now she can tell them that they needn't worry, she is in good hands and trusts the hospital.

## WEDNESDAY 8 JANUARY

Suddenly Olivia's husband, Holger, appears in the doorway of Ward 0, his cap crushed in his hands.

"I only wanted to . . ." he says. "I only want to say thanks. Thanks for being so nice to Olivia."

Marie props herself up on her elbows.

"We're taking the baby home."

Before she can get a word out, he has gone as quickly as he had come.

The window is filled with a glowing morning sky, pale yellow and watery pink, occasional white clouds floating gently by.

"Every time I get slightly closer to the doctor, I am betraying my fellow patients."

Marie gazes out of the window, the same fixed idea whirling round and round in her head.

To a certain extent, the hospital is a reflection of society. The majority of patients will always *feel* and in reality *be*, deep down—at heart—hospitalized, with no experience of asking questions, and with no possibility of understanding their own cases as part of a larger social context. They do not understand what is being said, only realize that decisions have been made without themselves having the slightest influence over their own destinies.

Most of the patients do not know about or understand the methods of treatment that are going to make them well or halt their illness.

If the prognosis is bad, they do not want to be told the truth, because they do not know what to do with it. There is no one to help them use it for any purpose.

The truth about an individual is not enough to carry the individual along.

The truth about an individual is only meaningful as long as it can be placed in relation to the truth about us all. That is, as long as it can be used as a tool for a change in the prevailing circumstances.

During the course of Wednesday, for the first time Marie decides that she is going for a walk outside the building.

The red-haired girl is sitting in the deep armchair in the day room busy with her little pale blue and white knitting, the ball of wool dancing in her lap. She raises her head and smiles.

"Where are you off to in that getup?"

"I'm going down to Postnatal to look at a new baby."

Marie takes the lift down to the ground floor. She has put on her big coat, the grubby grayish sheepskin, which she can no longer do up round her middle. She has wound the long knitted scarf twice round her neck and thrown the ends over her shoulders, and she has the Peruvian hood pulled right down over her forehead. She has pushed her feet in their long white hospital socks into a pair of broad leather shoes. Slowly, she walks out of the main entrance and on along the great white building. The wind strikes her as she swings round the corner. She crosses the paving stones toward the large red older building that is so familiar to her, both from the time when she went there for prenatals in the maternity center, and then from the innumerable times she has looked down at it from the department window above.

She stops and pulls up her socks, straightens her hood, breathes in the cold January air with an *aaaah* and opens the main door of the red building.

Laboriously, she climbs the two flights of stairs until she finds herself outside the actual Postnatal Department.

She goes through the swing doors. The light comes in from one side.

She hurries along the corridor.

At the other end, by the opposite entrance, she hears a familiar voice from one of the wards. She puts her head cautiously round the door and looks.

Habiba is sitting heavily and awkwardly in bed on her broad tender backside. Her eyes are shiny and her cheeks red, the little black pigtail dancing joyfully on her shoulder.

She has in her arms the largest and chubbiest newborn infant in the world, with long black hair and a red bow on top of her head. The child has even redder and more balloon-shaped cheeks than her mother. Her eyes are dark, her hands broad and fat at the end of her strong little arms that stick out each side like on an old-fashioned doll.

On the coverlet in front of Habiba, in the dip between her outstretched legs, is a gigantic box of chocolates.

Beside Habiba is her older girl, Fatime, the dark-eyed daughter who has just pinched her baby sister's cheek for the first time.

Her sturdy little undersized husband is standing on her other side, his handsome dark head on one side. He is wearing a blue suit and a spotless white shirt, his hands clasped behind his back.

And there she is, the family's little Danish friend, sitting so trustfully at the end of the bed, bright and cheerful in her red costume and glittering ornaments, her candy-floss hairdo, smiling with her blue teeth. She waves to Marie, urging her to come on in.

"Have a chocolate!"

"Maria!" says Habiba, looking at Marie with her large kind eyes.

"Habiba . . . congratulations! She's really very fine, your baby."

"Yes, very fine," says Habiba, laughing her happy Turkish laugh.

"Is she starting school soon?" says Marie, for fun.

"Not understand . . . not understand," says Ibrahim.

"Nothing . . . I didn't mean anything," Marie hurries to say.

"Ow," says Habiba, lifting one of her buttocks.

"Habiba has *ow*, bad bad sit," says the Danish friend.

Fatime dives into the chocolates and takes one, then glances provocatively at her father before moving even closer to her mother, so that her mother almost falls out of bed with her new baby in her arms.

They all smile. They are all happy.

Marie has a feeling that now their ways will part.

The little family will go home to Næstved in a few days time and start cooking in oil and frying in fat on their Danish gas stove again. The neighbors will come and congratulate them, and the whole of the little Turkish community will visit them and celebrate the happy event. As usual the man will work harder at work than the others, and his employer will give him fifty kroner to buy something for the child.

Every month they will send a modest sum home to their account in Istanbul.

Habiba and Marie will probably never meet again, and have not even thought of exchanging addresses. Their relationship is about to dissolve . . . not forgotten . . . it can never be forgotten. It just doesn't exist any longer.


Veronica is making small talk with her baby. She scrapes her yoghurt cup clean and puts it on her table.

The baby is large and well-formed, lying on its back, its eyes open, and waving its arms about.

Now that she knows that she is the one to make this infant

flourish, she has begun to understand that it really is a privilege to be a woman. To be a woman is a privilege, and to have a child is a political statement. But it is not a statement that can be analyzed in isolation. It can only be analyzed together with other people.

She can't take her eyes off her tiny well-formed face, her dark-blue eyes, her fine curved nose, the bow of her mouth. Is she smiling? No, she can't be . . . it's much too soon, isn't it? She gives her forefinger to the baby and it grasps the tip and pulls at it without hesitation.

Her breasts are taut . . . a wet patch appears on her nightshirt. She unbuttons it and puts the baby to her breast. The tiny mouth finds the nipple and starts sucking eagerly and confidently. Her eyes close.

There is a jab inside Veronica's womb and she notices it with satisfaction. Every time the baby is at her breast, her womb contracts; in the course of a few weeks it will be its ordinary shape and size again.

Nature has built the most ingenious contracting mechanism possible inside her body.

"Oh, here you are!"

The South Jylland midwife with warm brown eyes is standing beside Veronica.

Veronica sits up higher in the bed. They shake hands and don't let go, but go on sitting that way.

"Are you glad to be going home?"

"Yes, of course, but at the same time I'd have liked to stay here much longer. This feeling of irresponsibility . . . it's so marvelous. Just being able to lie here enjoying your baby and being looked after in every way . . . it's just wonderful."

"Yes, I suppose it won't be long before you'll be tired once you're home."

"You know what . . . I can hardly bear the thought that this might be my last child. I can quite imagine having another baby in a fortnight's time!"

Veronica's cheeks grow red.

"I'm disappointed with myself that I didn't dare pick the baby up as you suggested. I was quite simply afraid to touch the living flesh. . . ."

"No," says the midwife. "No, I should have prepared you better. I've succeeded with some girls. They've actually pulled out the baby themselves . . . while I've stood there with folded arms and watched. But I'd had them for very thorough prenatal training, too."

"That one over there," whispers Veronica, nodding in the direction of an imposing woman three beds away. "She says that it can't be right, that I wasn't anesthetized. She says *everyone* gets an epidural."

"No, they don't. Firstly, there's not always time, and secondly it's not certain that there's any reason for one, either. You didn't have one, for instance . . . because I thought you should take part in the whole experience."

Every time Veronica thinks of her delivery, she feels a pleasant shudder . . . a profound and all-embracing sense of happiness. It was so concentrated, that experience of releasing life from her own life.

She thinks about her midwife's eyes, her hands, her voice, and what they have in common.

Veronica is not quite sure whether she isn't slightly in love with her midwife.

She doesn't give a thought to the fact that this midwife does an average of a hundred deliveries a year, and that she's worked for ten years. That's about a thousand deliveries, a thousand deliveries that have had their effect. Some deliveries have almost certainly been immediately forgotten, while others have left deeper traces. But for the midwife, this is her daily work, her handwork, her way of life.

For Veronica, on the other hand, it is something quite remarkable. She will only give birth to children once, or at the most very few times in her life. For her this delivery is something that will cast its light on the whole of the rest of her life.

They can hear the sister's calm voice coming from the kitchen.

"Now, Baska, this just won't do."

"Won't do, what?" says Baska in her Polish accent.

"No, it won't do, you carrying on long personal telephone calls in this way on the hospital telephone."

"No, no, not, no . . ." Baska's voice sounds guilty. "I only phoning my dear beloved brother in Katowice."

"Yes, but however beloved he is, you mustn't make personal telephone calls from the office . . . you must understand that."

"Understand, yes, yes," says Baska, trying to pretend that nothing has happened.

Toward evening, Marie seems to be having certain sensations in her body, rather like tensions in her back.

"No, it can't be pains," says Rasmussen. "It's probably just unease in your body, because you've been out for a walk today. You've a whole month to go, haven't you?"

But all the same, it feels as if something unknown has started moving inside her. A bell tolling. A signal winking. A voice whispering . . . *now*.

She tries to relax. She is feeling quite lighthearted in some way.

In the office the bony little gray-haired night nurse is doing a crossword, chewing on her pencil, staring at the black pane of glass and writing down the solution in the square field of the crossword with large capital letters.

Her night duty has a guilty secret.

A secret she indulges in every night shift.

Somehow she has found out what to do to turn her transistor radio on to the same wavelength the police use during their night patrols of the city.

Night after night, she follows Copenhagen's most secret life. She finds out about holdups in intimate massage clubs in Vesterbro. She knows when a man has fallen into the canal in Nyhavn and that the police have sent for frogmen. She turns up the volume when drug pushers are being hunted in the black quarter.

In Lars Bjørn Street, a window has been broken. A prostitute is lying bleeding on the pavement, her front teeth knocked out. A man has run off with her handbag.

The night sister knows all about that.

Life is lived in night-time Copenhagen. She is always there whenever anything happens. She makes herself a cup of tea, puts aside the crossword and listens to how the people at the bottom of the pyramid of society every night are kept in their place with an iron hand.

## THURSDAY 9 JANUARY

Very early on Thursday morning, on polling day itself, Marie gets up and takes a walk with her swaying stomach along the corridor.

The gray-haired night nurse nods at her from behind the pane of glass. She is used to patients taking little walks in the small hours. They sleep so badly, these poor women.

Marie goes into the w.c. and discovers she is bleeding slightly.

Something turns inside her. She leans over the basin and vomits.

Aching back, bleeding and vomiting . . . all signs that something is happening.

With her hands on the edge of the basin, she looks at herself in the mirror, her long brown hair framing the pale oval of her face. She sees a face that is almost imperceptibly beginning to change. It is no longer like her. It is like all the others just before they give birth.

She takes a shower and washes her hair, then she goes along to the office. The night nurse phones down to Delivery and asks what they should do.

"We'll send a midwife," they say.

A third year student midwife examines Marie in the little examination room. Yes, she's starting to dilate. She'd better come down to Delivery at once.

Marie slips into Ward 0, and quietly gathers up her belongings in the dark so as not to waken the others.

Signe is waiting out in the corridor, small and dark, her hair sticking out in all directions.

"Is it true?"

"Yes . . . I'm having pains."

Signe looks at her for a while, then takes her hand and gives it a squeeze. They have nothing to say to each other. At this moment, whatever is said can only be wrong.

Marie slings her bag onto her shoulder and follows the midwife.

At the far end by the exit, she turns round and sees Signe and the little gray-haired night nurse standing like two shadows in the light from the office.

In the warm dark pleasant delivery room, a stiff belt with a circular plate on it is strapped round her large stomach. The belt is connected to an apparatus, a fetal monitor that can pick up the smallest contractions in the womb and translate them into readable sign language. A dancing black needle draws zigzag lines onto a strip of white paper that coils down to the floor in a slow, ticking snake.

The curtains are drawn and only a small table lamp is alight. The delivery room is like a cave.

She dozes. She doesn't know how long she has been there when the door opens and the doctor comes in.

"Now, now, what's this? Are *you* here!"

He picks up the strip of paper and looks at the thin black track showing a slightly billowing landscape, a series of ragged mountaintops, one after another, then leveling out to a plain.

They are pains. She hardly notices them herself, except as a faint tension in her back. But they are working somewhere inside her body. They are contracting and relaxing round the lake where the blue fish is swirling round in the depths.

"We're going to take a sample of your amniotic fluid," he says. "You'll be taken to another room in a moment. I'll take a sample of it with a thin needle. It doesn't hurt, so you needn't be nervous."

The stretcher glides through a swing door, out onto the main stairway and in along a dark corridor, pushed by a white-haired old orderly in white jacket and black trousers.

"Tell me," says Marie, turning her head toward the old man.

"Yes?"

"If the baby dies . . . where does the mother go afterwards?"

"To Gynecology."

"Not Postnatal?"

"No."

He looks at her as if he had been thinking if there are any more important questions, I may as well answer them all at once.

The stretcher is pushed into a very small room with no windows, then placed under a lamp.

A pale gray cupboard with glass doors and a trolley are by her head.

The doctor walks round the room for a while, talking to the nurse.

"Now I'm going to do an amniocentesis," he says. "It's a test of the amniotic fluid. The fetus secretes small fat cells into the water. By analyzing them, we can see if the child is in a position to manage the respiratory function on its own. *Assuming* it can . . . then we'll try to deliver you today. If not . . . we try to stop the contractions."

"Is that the same thing as a chromosome analysis?"

Is there something more behind this business of the respiratory function? she thinks.

"Yes, it's taken in the same way. But that's not what's being investigated now. And you won't know the sex of the child, either."

The tips of his fingers glide over her stomach.

"We'll have an answer in a couple of hours . . . and then we'll decide what to do next."

The nurse hands him a syringe.

"Now I'm going to do it."

Marie looks up at the ceiling. She relaxes completely, lying like a dead body, while the thin needle penetrates through her skin and abdominal wall, into the womb through the membranes to the fetal water.

What color will it be? Amniotic fluid can be discolored in sickly cases, colors that together tell the gynecologist something.

"What does it look like?"

He shows her the syringe with the glittering fluid inside it.

"It's perfectly clear."

The white-haired orderly pushes her back to Delivery.

The belt of the fetal monitor is fastened round her belly again.

A student midwife draws back the curtains.

A pale winter sky appears, just like a film that has been going on all the time behind the cinema curtain.

Sounds from the streets round the hospital can faintly be heard.

"Do you mind being left alone?"

"Not at all."

"Try to sleep a little, if you can."

The monitor ticks faintly. She puts her lower arm across her eyes and slides slowly backward into a mirror-gray surface of shallow sleep.

She is back with her parents. It is a late summer evening and they are harvesting in the high warm darkness. The machines are constantly on the go, industrious as ants, up and down the slopes. Her father is standing like a shadow in the cornfield.

The hours go by. Now and again a doctor comes in and lifts up the monitor's long white tongue. Through half-closed eyes, she senses that the curves have leveled out. The pains have grown weaker and weaker.

"Looks fine," he says.

He would have said that under any circumstances.

The afternoon must have come. She is given tea and a roll with butter on it.

The child is moving inside her body, just as an astronaut on his lifeline floats weightlessly in space. A hump bulges out above one hip and moves quickly underneath her skin. She puts her hands lightly on her stomach, as she has done a thousand times before, feeling the small blows from the baby's limbs.

She thinks it's a boy; she doesn't know why, but she just thinks it's a boy.

For a very brief moment, she relaxes completely and imagines herself having a large healthy child, that everything is as it should be, that all this is nothing but a false alarm.

Then she tries to obliterate that picture, tidying it away just as you slot a slide back into its case.

A light hand brushes the hair away from her forehead. She looks straight up into her sister's face.

"Eva, is it you?"

"How are you?"

"Not so bad."

"I phoned by chance and was told that you'd been taken to Delivery. They promised I could come. What's happened?"

"It's started. My body's decided that for itself. They've taken a sample of the waters. Then they can see if the child can survive if it's born today. If its lungs are not developed enough, they'll try to stop the contractions."

"Great!"

Eva thrusts her hand into the pocket of her afghan coat and takes out a small flat parcel.

"I phoned Mother and Dad and they asked me to buy this for you."

Marie opened the box. Beneath a layer of pale yellow cotton-wool is a new watch, a beautiful simple wristwatch with Arabic numbers and a white strap.

"It's *just* what I wanted."

She puts the watch on her wrist and at that moment feels sick. She puts her hand to her mouth and looks helplessly round. Eva stretches out for a paper bowl standing on the table, and only just gets it to Marie in time as she vomits so violently, it spurts out.

Eva sits by her bed for a while, holding her hand.

"You must go now," says Marie. "I'm so glad you came. But this is no place for you. You go now."

"We've had the results from the test," says the gynecologist. He is standing beside her with her casesheet in his hand. "It says that the baby's lungs are sufficiently well developed, so we can deliver you today."

A deep sigh escapes her.

"You're relieved, I'm sure. You'll be taken to an operating theater now, and we'll puncture the membrane on the operating table. We'll try to let out the huge quantity of water as slowly as possible. There is a slight risk involved. There might be a prolapse of the umbilical cord or the placenta may start to detach. *If* that happens, we can do a Caesarian within a few minutes."

"You mean . . . it's not certain you'll do a Caesarian?"

"No. A normal birth is always preferable, if possible."

Marie looks at her watch.

"We're just getting up some blood . . . and we can intervene in about an hour."

The doctor goes away and a midwife comes in.

"Good morning," she says, shaking Marie's hand. "I'm going to assist in your delivery."

She clatters about with a washing bowl.

"I'm going to shave you."

The razor blade is cold, the water tepid.

"Can I have an enema?" whispers Marie.

"I don't think that's necessary . . . but if you want one, all right. . . ."

"Have you a denture?"

Marie points at a molar.

"That won't matter."

She looks up into the great operating lamp with its dazzle-shade of circular rings. It looks like a collection of cells, a fertilized egg just about to divide.

The operating theater is full of people standing in a silent circle round the operating table. Most of them are student midwives come to watch.

A burly, broad-shouldered figure in an ultra-marine overall, blue cap and blue mouth-mask comes through the door. He says something. She recognizes his dark eyes.

"I'm glad you're here."

The consultant gynecologist nods.

The walls are of white square tiles with gray seams between them. On the floor, the gray tiles have black seams. The corners of the room are rounded and fade away. She isn't sure whether the room is oval or rectangular.

A white-clad anesthetist is sitting to the left of the operating table, holding her wrist lightly, looking absently round the room.

On her right is the slender midwife wearing white uniform with short sleeves and a narrow transparent plastic belt of the kind worn in the fifties.

For Marie this is an extremely unusual day, for all the others an ordinary working day. That is comforting. They are not doing this for personal reasons. They're doing it because it is their job.

Her hips are lifted high up, her legs parted into a pair of leg-holders, her pelvis leaning so that her left side is lower than her right.

All those eyes resting on her poor child's entrance into life.

In this dreadful position, she tries to block out her own self. All this has nothing to do with her. She is simply a tool of some primeval ritual occasion.

Between her legs she can just see the high priest's back and the tapes of his mouth-mask tied at the back of his neck.

His back tenses. He lifts his hand and gets a hold on the fetal membrane with his pointed instrument. The membrane bursts. She feels the pressure from his strong hands. They hold hard so that only a little of the water can pass.

The drops fall slowly down into a dish or bowl.

"Did I say something?" she thinks. "Or is it that I wish *someone* would say something?"

A thousand small needles seem to be pricking her face and hands and white stars appear in front of her eyes.

"Try to breathe more calmly," says the anesthetist quietly. "You're taking in too much air because you're nervous."

Nervous? Is she nervous? It doesn't feel like that to her. On the contrary, she feels a kind of security and clarity from being so irretrievably faced with her own destiny. The process has started. In an hour or two, it will have ended. And no one can change anything.

Drops fall into the vessel. The tension in her body eases. Her stomach shrinks. The time-glass runs out.

Now and again one of them on the fringe of her field of vision touches her arm.

A sense of nausea sits astride her chest like a witch.

"I feel sick."

"It's the pains starting," whispers the midwife. "Just keep quite calm."

"That's that," says the doctor, letting go of her. He turns round and pushes back his cap. His forehead is damp. "Measure how much there is at once."

Marie looks at her watch. Half an hour has gone by.

"It went well," he says. "None of the complications that might have arisen have done so. There's nothing to prevent the rest of your delivery from being perfectly normal."

Marie is placed on a stretcher and pushed out of the operating theater.

When they come into Delivery, a terrible, whimpering and un-bearably anguished scream comes out of one of the rooms.

Marie puts her hands over her ears.

"I don't want to hear it."

"Who's that?" her midwife asks a passerby, who looks like the senior midwife.

"It's the patient in Ward 10. The A-twin has just been delivered. Look at this . . . how she scratched my arms."

A copy of the evening paper is lying on a chair.

Right across the first front page it says: *Half a million people choose to abstain from voting*.

It is the third time she has been pushed into the same delivery room. The curtains have been drawn again, as evening has come. The room is small and cozily warm, with an interior like brown velvet.

The midwife and a student bustle round, like small animals scratching among fallen leaves. The student has a bad cold. This troubles Marie, but she says nothing.

The senior midwife comes into the room.

"Shall we telephone your husband?"

"He's in Greenland."

"Isn't there anyone else you'd like to have with you?"

"I have a sister, but I don't think this is anything for her."

"Are you sure?"

"Yes . . . no . . . yes, I am. If there's anything wrong with the baby . . . then . . . I've had enough time to be prepared for that. But it's much worse for her. She isn't involved in the way I am. Don't you think?"

The senior midwife says: "Hm."

"Don't you think so?"

"It's an ethical question . . . I can hardly answer that."

The senior midwife and the midwife look at each other.

Then it's decided. No one will be with her.

"I see you need a bedpan," says the midwife, pushing one under Marie.

Marie closes her eyes and tries to make the effort.

"I can't."

"Try now . . . otherwise I'll have to use a catheter, and I prefer not to have to do that."

"I'm sorry, but I can't."

The midwife pushes a tube into her urethra. It's not too bad. In fact the whole business is not nearly so bad as expected.

The midwife lays her hands firmly round her flabby belly and feels.

"The baby isn't large," she says. "I don't think it weighs more than 2,500 grams."

"2,500 grams?" Marie sees a wheel whirling in front of her. Sparks fly. That's much smaller than expected.

"It's lovely and quiet here," she whispers. "Thank you."

"I'll see to it that it goes on being quiet," says the midwife.

"Won't anyone be coming to watch?"

"No, there'll be just us . . . and a doctor. I think the baby will be born in the course of the next half hour. Breaking the membrane has opened you up a lot."

Marie closes her eyes and puts her hands on each side of her head.

Because she herself has a mother, she can bring out the motherliness in others, in this case the midwife. This midwife will not leave her in the lurch.

The room is a golden amber color. She gabbles Rasmussen's little prayer:

> *Mother Mary, lend me the keys thine*
> *to open the door to these loins of mine*

The contraction comes creeping up over her slack belly. Her body tenses, the womb working, a pain at the same time soft and hard. *An invigorating pain.*

"Take the mask . . . there's no reason to be brave!"

She shows Marie how the mask is used. "Like this. Breathe deeply and calmly. Hold it in your right hand. Listen now . . . it's supposed to sound like when a window-catch keeps rattling."

The student midwife smiles. She's nice. As long as she doesn't come too close with that cold.

Hazy from the gas, Marie sees one vision after another. The vision is quite still, for a long time, all the details crystal clear . . . before dissolving away.

She sees a young Vietnamese standing immobile in a forest of high reeds. Endlessly, slowly, he bends the reeds aside. She shivers. He sees miles of burnt and blackened countryside.

As far as the eye can see, devastated land and defoliated trees.

"Ssh," whispers the midwife, as the door opens.

"Who is this little girl lying here?"

"What?" Marie starts up, dropping the mask over the side of the bed. "Has the baby come?"

A tall fair doctor in a white vest, unbuttoned white jacket, and circular steel-rimmed glasses is standing at the head of her bed, the fair hairs on his chest sticking out above the vest. He turns to the midwife.

"What's the matter with her . . . has she had too much?"

The midwife does not answer.

"What little girl were you talking about?" says Marie in terror.

"I was talking about *you*," he says. "You were so big before with all that fluid, and now it's gone, you're so small . . . that was all I meant, Marie."

Heavens, was *that* what he meant. He is the doctor who had admitted her into hospital that day in December when she had been for a prenatal checkup. He's friendly. He calls her Marie. *At last a doctor who uses her Christian name.*

Now he's probably thinking about how careful you have to be when you talk to a woman in childbirth, thinks Marie. I could misunderstand what he *really* means.

The delivery room's amber-colored lighting and the student with a cold. Between her bent knees she can see the dark slender midwife.

Again, from far, far away, another pain comes traveling down the landscape of her body. Marie breathes as deeply as she can into the black mask, drawing the gas right down into the bottom of her lungs and hearing the chatter of the regulator fading like a car starting and driving away.

She is sitting with Zacharias at the bottom of the ocean. They have their arms round each other. They are at anchor. The water is bottle-green and clear. Water plants sway back and forth, rocking with long slow movements. Endlessly far away up there is a ship, its dark keel just visible below the surface of the water.

The green water.

The many layers.

Zacharias and she are standing on a large open swaying ice floe, meters thick, covered with glittering crystals of snow. The sky is a steely blue. In the distance, they can see great floating white icebergs with purple shadows.

"It'll all be over in a moment," whispers the midwife.

The ice floe dips and creaks.

"I felt something sliding down," cries Marie.

"One moment, wait a while," says the midwife. "Let me just see."

She gets up on the stool and feels how far the womb has opened, and as if she were giving orders to attack, she says:

"Bear down when I tell you; now!"

They wait in silence for the contraction.

A moment later, it is over. A child is born. But it is not a real child. There is something wrong. It is taken away. It can live only for a few days. A priest comes in a long black coat, white collar, brown trousers underneath the coat. He has a bowl with him. He wants to baptize the child. It only takes a few minutes. So that it isn't damned as a heathen, it will be forgiven its sins and allowed eternal life. She cries out no. She doesn't want her child baptized. He turns his back and leaves. The child dies. The death certificate has to be signed. They ask if it is to be buried. She doesn't want her child buried. Nothing is to be done with it. Will it just be thrown away?

A great sense of sorrow over the meaningless and humiliating process her body has gone through . . . and despair over having brought a small incomplete life into the world make all lights go out for her.

"Come on, now . . . bear down quite calmly . . . downwards . . . that's right . . ."

Marie sees a window in front of her, an old-fashioned window divided into six panes and painted blueish-green with pink and white decorations. It is open. Outside it is summer, and there is a garden in light and shade out there.

She hears a high note in the mask. It is herself whimpering.

The pain has reached its limit. Then she senses a strange tearing, rasping, shuddering feeling.

The doctor and the midwife are standing symmetrically leaning toward each other, working with something between her legs.

Marie closes her eyes and lets the mask fall.

Everything is over now.


The door opens and a whole lot of people come into the room, just like at the stadium when the gates are opened. They lift up the child and put it down in a glass box, turn round and the doors swing back behind them.

It is quite still. It is empty. In the aquarium, the water is green and the bubbles rise slowly to the surface and burst.

Marie is flat on her back, shivering with cold.

"What did it look like?"

"Perfectly normal."

She opens her eyes wide.

"No."

"Yes, she's well formed, very thin and very long and very beautiful," says the tall doctor with a wide smile.

"And her throat?"

"We put a tube down her throat at once . . . there's a passage all the way down."

The ball of fire dances in the air, suns bursting out of it.

If the child is beautiful . . . then it can't be deficient . . . then it can't be damaged.

"It's not right . . . you're not telling me the truth."

"Yes, I am."

"No, I'm dreaming. I've been dreaming all the time. And it's still a dream."

"I'll pinch your arm," he says with a smile. "Then you'll know you're awake."

He pulls a chair up to the head of the bed, sits down, and crosses one great long doctor's leg with a white clog at the end of it over the other. Then he starts rocking back and forth on the chair. He is happy, and she could have kissed him on the mouth. And pulled him down to her in the bed. And lain close to him. And been embraced by him. If only she could!

She hides her face in her hands, the tears pouring out between her fingers.

"Oh, God, how wonderful, how pleased I am, how wonderful, how grateful I am, oh, how marvelous!"

"Perhaps she should have a drink?" says the doctor quietly.

"Why on *earth* should she?" says the slim midwife, from the opposite corner of the room.

It's good that midwives are women.

The student with a cold is sitting on Marie's other side, holding firmly with both hands round Marie's stomach to give support to the emptied womb during the contractions. Her eyes are red-rimmed and she smiles broadly in a friendly way. Her cold doesn't matter any longer.

"Do I need stitches?" says Marie.

"No tears anywhere."

At that moment, little Rørby appears in the doorway with her hands on her hips and her head on one side. She has come from Prenatal and in through the secretive delivery department.

She bends over Marie and hugs her.

"Congratulations, Hansen, my pet!"

"Thank you, Rørby, thank you. I love you!"

Then she is gone. Marie's face is streaky.

"You'll find yourself blubbing quite a bit in the next few days," says the doctor. "You must be prepared for that."

The midwife shows her a little photograph in a plastic folder in her wallet. It's of four smiling children in a row, first a girl with fair plaits, then three small fair-haired boys.

"They're mine," she says. "The youngest is only two. I just wanted to show you, to say I understand you so well."

She puts back her wallet.

"This is the best day of my life," says Marie. "I've never been so happy about anything before. . . ."

"Yes, it's an experience," says the midwife.

A pediatrician with square rimless glasses comes into the room.

"We're just examining her in the pediatric department," he says. "We'll give her a contrast of barium and take x-rays to see if there is passage all the way down. She weighs 2,580, just enough for her to be with you down in Postnatal. I think I can almost promise you you'll have her back before midnight."

People all over the place, the door opening and shutting. The delivery is over, the excitement ended. There is no reason to lower your voice. They tidy and clean up, bowls and bedpans and all the rest put away.

Perhaps they'll keep her under observation. But she doesn't mind. She is so relieved, as if she had no body at all. She lies repeating:

"I'm so happy, I'm so happy!"

*"Oh, I'm so happy, I'm so happy!"*

Who said that? It is the senior midwife, again standing at the foot of her bed, with a determined expression in her eyes. So clearly that's enough!

Marie is given a cup of tea.

Then suddenly a completely different midwife is standing by her, a tall slim young one with very short hair. She looks familiar.

"She's terribly pretty, your baby."

"Have you seen her?"

"Yes, I've just been holding her hand in Neonatal."

"Why do you think they thought she was so big?"

"All that fluid . . . it distorted the whole picture. Seven liters! I measured it myself."

She looks radiant, the midwife. Is that right? Is it really true that they are all happy when a delivery has gone well?

What a job they have!

## FRIDAY 10 JANUARY

Gray everywhere. Where am I?

A nurse is leaning over Marie's bed.

"They've just brought your baby in."

My baby! I'd almost forgotten you! We were pushed along the underground passages to Postnatal last night, you and me.

Marie leans over and looks into the cot with a delighted shiver at the sight of the dark little head with shining hair just protruding onto the checked mattress. The child is lying on her side, a rolled blanket behind her for support. At the foot of the cot is a stone hot-water bottle wrapped in a nappy.

She is asleep, the tiny profile gravely outlined against the sheet, her hands in front of her mouth, fingers as thin as threads.

There she is, the tiny creature. Oh, I recognize you from last night.

The mothers are in two long symmetrical rows, in white hospital clothes, their babies in their arms under the light of the lamps. Their bosoms are bared, the babies at their breasts.

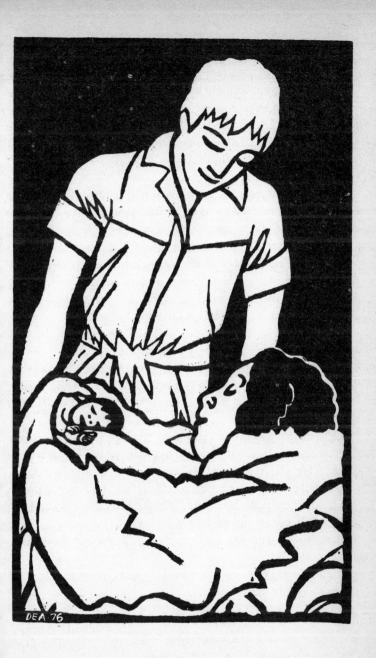

Small sucking noises, groans, and subdued talk can be heard. What an utterly woman's world!

The ward is large, rectangular and painted pale gray, thin morning light sifting in from three sides through immensely tall old-fashioned windows with long cadmium-yellow curtains. The fourth wall is taken up by a long narrow cupboard and the door leading out into the corridor. Alongside the door is a white wash basin, half-concealed by a screen.

Ward 1 is the largest ward in Postnatal, ten beds in all. Marie has asked to be allowed to go there that night, into this particular ward, where you find yourself in a community.

The beds are wide and comfortable. On the wall above each bed are two blackboards with the patient's surname written alongside the time of the baby's birth, its birth-weight and length, as well as the mother's temperature, pulse, and stitches, if any. Farthest down is the Greek sign for a boy or a girl.

They get up the very first day here, mothers going to the w.c., and showers as early as a couple of hours after delivery.

And here you look after your baby yourself. The baby is in the ward all day and not taken out until nighttime. In the smaller wards, they are allowed to keep their babies all round the clock if they want to.

Here there is individual breast-feeding, which means the babies of 3,000 grams birth-weight and over can be fed whenever the mothers feel like it. Babies with lower birth-weights, like Marie's, have to be fed at definite times, six times every twenty-four hours.

The mothers walk back and forth between the beds and the long baby-table in the middle of the ward. They change their infants, wash them, talk to them, weigh them, and enjoy each other's company.

They also enjoy the very special delight of being in this ward after a successful delivery.

But although they reckon with some patients getting up the very first day, Marie feels black and blue all over, as if a steamroller had driven over her and crushed all her joints.

She simply cannot get out of bed. She just lies twisting her head from side to side, hoping someone will in the end come over and say something to her.

It isn't easy to discover when a round is taking place in Postnatal, for even if the staff try to keep some kind of order, there are always mothers getting out of bed to fetch something they've forgotten, or changing their babies.

A blonde woman doctor, apparently not much older than Marie, moves soundlessly from patient to patient, asking as few questions as possible.

Marie props herself up on one elbow, and from her bed can see her baby being undressed, put on the scales and weighed.

"2,470 grams, as against 2,580 at birth last night," calls the nurse.

The figures are noted down on a chart lying on the locker together with various photostats, stenciled papers, and advertisements for disinfectants, paper napkins, and contraceptives. The figures are wholly abstract. They mean nothing to Marie.

The doctor puts her little finger into the baby's mouth and feels her gums, then puts both hands round the narrow head and presses carefully to feel the fontanelles. The baby whimpers as her professional hands glide down toward the collarbones and then out along her arms. The minute fingers are counted, the nails and lines of the hands studied. Then she feels the pulse in her groin and looks at her labia. She goes on down the legs, counting the toes, looking at the nails and letting her thumb stroke the silky soles of the child's feet. She grasps both of the baby's knees, pressing out the curled legs sideways—which looks horrible—to hear if the hip-joints creak.

Finally, with one hand she lifts up the weeping child by her feet, turns her over and lets her forefinger run down her spine.

She strikes a light blow on the under sheet each side of the child, who starts waving her arms and legs about.

"Yes," says the doctor, without looking up. "She's O.K."

Just as if, thinks Marie. If the doctor were really honest . . . my baby isn't the most perfect she has ever seen.

All along the long baby-table in the middle of the room lie these small red and kicking creatures.

"Does it matter if I stay in bed?" says Marie.

"Oh, no," says the nurse, a young girl with her long hair gathered at the nape of her neck. "You just stay there. I'll show you how to look after her. Look, now. The first stool is dark and sticky and is called meconium. But in a few days it'll turn pale yellow and sweet-scented if it's a breast-fed child. Wash her like this. With this sponge. Dab carefully with a towel afterwards. Dry her between her legs from top to bottom, never from bottom to top. Powder her carefully round the neck and under her arms and behind her ears and in all the places where damp builds up. But remember . . . never powder and ointment at the same time, because that can get sticky. You put the nappy on like this . . . preferably not too loosely. Otherwise it's uncomfortable. Then on with her vest. And the sleeping bag is tied with tapes at the back. There we are. Isn't she lovely?"

She puts the white child into Marie's arms. Marie feels like a Madonna in gold and red on an old picture.

"But you must watch out she doesn't get cold. Babies with low birth-weight find it difficult to keep warm. You must fill the hot-water bottle now and again, wrap a nappy round it, and put it into her cot with her."

Marie nods and tries to remember it all. She snuffles at the baby, who smells so good, clean and aromatic.

"Try and feed her now," says the nurse. "But no longer than ten minutes each side. Otherwise she'll get exhausted. She has to learn to suck as well as stimulate you. It'll take a couple of days before the milk comes. Until then, she'll get something called colostrum. It's yellowish and very easily digested. It's good for the baby because it contains important antibodies. . . ."

"I very much want to breast-feed her," says Marie, looking questioningly at the nurse. "Do you think I'll be able to?"

"Yes, of course you will. We'll help you get going. Look now . . . hold her to you so that her cheek touches your breast; that's right. Then she'll instinctively turn her head towards the nipple and open her mouth."

The nurse stands there watching them.

"If you get tender, you can rub in a little lanolin ointment. And sit so that you're really comfortable. It's important that your back is supported."

Marie shivers with delight when she feels the baby's silky lips against her breast for the first time, an unknown longing fulfilled, an ancient loss, the name of which she does not know.

Yes, what an utterly woman's world. During the last twenty-four hours Marie has sunk down through soft layers, one after another, through light and shade, down to this clean snow-white bed in Postnatal.

Together with the waters and the baby, the tension has vanished, slipped into the earth like rainwater, only her feeble body and equally feeble little soul lying like an old sack on the bed.

The baby sleeps, quite self-evidently, at her bare breast.

The baby is her own flesh and blood. She has been formed and has grown inside her, been thrust out of her body through the gateway from one world to another. Alive. Well-formed.

A rainbow curves its great arch above the Postnatal department.

A tall, fair, good-looking woman comes over to Marie.

"Welcome and congratulations," she says in a deep soft voice, holding out her hand. "How are you?"

How friendly they all are. And this is the Senior Sister.

For some reason Marie finds tears in her eyes and can't get a word out. She wants to say something, but the words stick in her throat.

The Senior Sister bends over and looks at the sleeping child.

"How sweet she is," she says. "I've read your casesheet and realize you haven't had an easy time at all."

She is giving her patient time to collect herself.

At last Marie manages to get a word out.

"I'm so tired, so tired, I don't know why . . . I just feel so. . . ."

She doesn't know whether to say . . . *peculiar* or *empty inside*, because she doesn't know how she can define the feeling she has.

"I understand very well how you feel," says Sister. "I was dead-tired myself when I had children. It's quite natural. I'll tell the sisters here that they must help you with the baby until your strength comes back a bit. If there's anything you don't understand, just ask."

She turns to the next bed.

A tiny shrunken creature is lying there, all crooked. She has had nothing when the others were given breakfast. All you can hear from her is a sigh or a sob at regular intervals. There is a drip above her bed, a bottle turned upside-down and fastened to a frame, a tube carrying clear liquid to a thin arm lying hidden under the bedclothes.

"Well, Mikkelsen, how are you today, my dear?"

A little drowned cat turns her careworn face up to the tall white woman . . . and a thick porridgy sound comes out of her throat.

The sister puts her hands in her pockets and leans over the bed.

"We'll be taking the drip away soon. Oh, are they yours?"

She points to two photographs in the twin-frame on her locker.

"Yes," says little Mikkelsen, wiping her nose with her sleeve. "Yes, they're mine all right!"

"You've a lot to be grateful for, then, haven't you?"

In this way, the sister goes from bed to bed, talking quietly to each patient. She makes time to listen to them all. Some of the patients light up with pleasure, others start crying at once. She is used to both. Nothing frightens her any more.

"Why are you lying in that strange way?" Marie whispers to her neighbor.

"I've been sterilized," sniffs the little body, looking over the edge of the bedclothes with large dark eyes.

"Haven't you had a baby, then?"

"Oh, yes, they're looking after him in the office."

Suddenly the consultant gynecologist, a trifle breathless, is standing by Marie's bed.

"I thought I'd come and see what you had," he says with a smile, leaning over and looking at the sleeping child.

Marie blushes. She wants to shake his hand and thank him.

But she can't find the right words.

*Everything* previous to all this, the many weeks in the prenatal department, the conversations, the examinations . . . and now yesterday . . . the puncturing of the membrane on the operating table . . . it's too vulnerable . . . it is something between him and her that cannot be expressed in words.

He nods. He has no need for thanks. He looks at her for a moment and then is gone.

Gone to one of his many activities, up on his round in Prenatal, in for a gynecological examination, out to do a Caesarian.

Marie is utterly confused and *exhausted* when he's gone.

There is a strange and utterly special odor in the ward, a sweetish smell of infant stools and urine, of the discharge between the mothers' legs, of the milk that leaks from breasts and stiffens on hospital shirts. Of sweat mixed with the scent of dazzling hothouse flowers and the smell of chlorine and vaseline.

Women and babies smell alike at first after confinement. Milky. Acid. Sweet-sour. Slightly sickening. A very special smell, a smell the body gives off only at this time in life.

The Postnatal corridor is very long and dark and high-ceilinged. To the left between the window niches are cupboards and refrigerators, trolleys, and chairs stacked on top of one another. To the right are the doors into the various wards and to the office and day room.

Caesarian patients or patients who have had difficult deliveries are in the smaller wards; also women who have had twins, triplets, and even quadruplets.

There is a great deal of life and movement everywhere in this department.

Nurses walk swiftly back and forth with trays in their hands. A doctor and a tall midwife are standing talking confidentially together, leaning against a window sill.

Wearing all kinds of possible and impossible dressing gowns, mothers walk with straddling legs and dragging feet, their hair untidy, their backs bowed, constantly moving between beds, bathroom, and day room.

A baby yells. A window-catch is hooked on. Laughter can be heard from one of the rooms. A nurse comes out, followed by an orderly. They are literally doubled up with laughter, slapping their thighs. They put their hands to their mouths and, groaning and giggling, they straighten up with tears in their eyes.

They do nothing to hide their amusement.

No one had that much fun in Prenatal.


"Hullo, there!"

It's someone Marie knows, quite a young girl, not very big. Now, who is it? Of course, it's Connie from up in Prenatal. Seventeen-year old Connie from Hundestad, who was in Ward 5 with Karen-Margrethe.

"Hullo, yourself. So you're in here, eh?"

"Yes, I'm in that bed over there . . . by Mrs. Holm. I had a little girl this morning," says Connie proudly. "And what did you have?"

"The same—there she is."

"Oh, isn't she sweet," says Connie, bending over the cot with her hands on her knees. "Congratulations!"

"How did it go for you?"

"So so. I had quite a cut. It hurts like hell. I simply can't sit down, only lie down or stand up. The stitches . . . they really pull! I was too narrow, the midwife said. It's often like that with young girls, even if we're the best at having children."

Connie smiles proudly as she stands there, shifting her weight from one foot to the other.

"How did things go for the others up there, the ones I knew?" she says.

"Well, Olivia, you know, the big one in my ward . . . she had a fine girl weighing 3,500 grams. The consultant herself did her Caesarian."

"And the Turkish woman . . . what happened to her?"

"She had a girl too . . . a giant of four and a half kilos. A fine child. She already looks like a schoolgirl."

The picture of Habiba and her huge little doll in her arms comes alive to Marie.

"She must have gone home to Næstved yesterday, I think."

"And then, you know, Yvonne . . . what happened to her?"

"She was delivered at the same time as me yesterday. She had two girls. Terribly small and born much too early. They're in incubators in that department for newborn babies. I wonder if Yvonne's in here in this department, by the way . . . in one of the little wards? I expect she is."

Connie's face has changed, her features softer in some way. She looks healthy, her cheeks red and hair curly. You could hardly believe she had given birth to a child a few hours before.

"And that one . . . the one you talked to such a lot . . . the one with the three little girls?"

"Signe? She's still up there."

I wonder if Connie has heard anything about Karen-Margrethe? I'll say nothing if she doesn't ask, thinks Marie.

But Connie must have read her thoughts, because she immediately exclaims:

"I've had a letter from Karen-Margrethe. She says would I like a job in their paper shop in the autumn. Isn't that nice of her? I was terribly pleased."

"Do you know what happened to her?"

Connie nodded. But they don't talk about it. They shudder . . . and think of their own sleeping children.

"Listen! Is she breathing?" Marie bends hastily over the edge of the bed and puts her arm down to the baby to feel her breath against her hand.

For a brief moment she sees her baby dead before her, unmoving, outstretched, with closed eyes and half-open mouth. Marie puts her hand on her heart.

They are given clear soup with forcemeat balls and dumplings in it, pale green and yellow pieces of leek, celery and carrots floating about.

Then they have veal cutlets with steamed peas and large yellow potatoes.

Connie waves gaily to Marie from her bed. She is lying on her side and is having great difficulty getting the food into her mouth.

From twelve to half-past one is rest time. Sister says they should try to sleep, as they have a greater need for rest than they think. "And remember, when you all get home, things won't be so easy!"

The room is white all over. The babies are satiated and silent, making contented little grunts and tiny snores.

Marie shuffles her pillow and quilt under her body, pushing bits and corners beneath the small of her back and between her legs, under her cheeks and across the back of her neck, until she is lying comfortably in her warm nest.

Sleep prickles her skin, irresponsible and swaying; it's like sleeping in a cradle.

It's like when you roam round the Sjælland countryside at the end of April or the beginning of May . . . at the time of year when the buds are bursting out, when the fields take on their first blurred pale green, when the damson tree's white flowers begin to appear in the woods . . . and you feel everything is too great to hold it within yourself. . . . Marie feels the same way in this postnatal department. Everything is too great for her to be able to hold and understand it.

She would like to have time to stay and see the same picture over and over again.

The little baby is lying on the quilt between her legs, the child's forehead clear and vaulted, her hair dark and silky soft. The color of her skin is pale brown with a touch of yellow in it, two pale roses on her cheeks. Her fine eyebrows are a trifle slanting, the corners of her mouth drawn down.

She yawns and pulls up her legs beneath her a little, still without opening her eyes and with a slightly troubled expression on her face.

For every hour that goes past, the child moves farther away from the fetal condition, the distance between the baby and the womb growing longer and longer and between the baby and humankind shorter and shorter.

The door opens and the first visitors start crowding in. The mothers hurry off to their beds to settle themselves in them in a decorative manner.

Visiting hours are twice a day. They are not so afraid visitors will bring in infections with them here and conditions are very free. Families and friends come with presents and flowers and sit on the sacred beds, lifting up the infant and passing it round from arms to arms.

Even older brothers and sisters can come too with special permission.

There are no thick panes of glass here, separating the family from its new member.

An embarrassed young boy is sitting on a chair beside Connie, dangling his feet, the palms of his hands pressed together between his knees, his shoulders slightly hunched up round his ears. He looks up at the ceiling and then down into the cot, then out of the window. He doesn't really know what to say. Connie lies there grimacing over her stitches as she tries to find something she can tell him.

In the bed on her right is the imposing Mrs. Holm, looking at her nails.

If Mrs. Holm is large, her husband is even larger.

He comes tiptoeing in in brown socks and black lace-up shoes, carefully and self-effacingly making his way along the baby table, his hat in one hand and a parcel in patterned paper in the other.

The first thing Mrs. Holm says is:

"What did you buy me?"

He holds one great hand by her ear and whispers something, while with the other hand he presses the present into her lap.

*"Oh . . . you great i-d-i-o-t!"*

Mrs. Holm cringes.

"But Marchen. You said . . . I thought. . . ?"

"Thought!"

He is not allowed to see his child at all. Perhaps it doesn't matter much, because Mrs. Holm has started telling him what to do about dinner.

"It's in the freezer, don't forget. And when it's thawed. . . ."

"Was that your husband?" says Mrs. Holm genially.

"Who?" says Connie.

"That young person of about fourteen or fifteen sitting by your bed."

"Oh, *him* . . . that's my little brother."

Connie flushes and looks searchingly round, as if seeking support. Then she decides to pick up her baby and say: "Grandad'll find a nice nickname for you, he will."

"What a way to hold the child! . . . You'll have to watch out you don't drop it."

Mrs. Marchen Holm has a lot of good advice to give a young and inexperienced mother.

The January day is not long, shrinking and fading away as it is drawn out of the window. It retreats out of the room, leaving darkness in its wake, drawing it out of the corners and the walls.

Plates of open sandwiches are brought in, sandwiches with liver paté, brawn, eggs and tomatoes, fish and cold beef.

Connie enjoys the food. She has to make sure she eats as much as possible before she goes home to her mother's awful stews again. But Mrs. Holm suffers.

"Oh, I can hardly get it down. Could I possibly have some mineral water to wash it down with?"

Little Mikkelsen is gradually cheering up.

The orderly takes the drip away. She sits down on the edge of the bed and looks at the two color photographs standing on the locker top.

"Are they really yours?"

"They certainly are! Rudi is seven and Randi four. Like hell they're mine. The pets."

Little Mikkelsen puts her head on one side and looks important.

The orderly twists and turns the photographs.

"Who's looking after them now while you're here?"

"Their daddy's doing that."

"Can he stay at home then?"

"Oh yes! He's just got a disability pension. He's smashing at looking after the kids."

"And what are you going to call this one?"

191

"Rolf or Robin . . . Robin I expect."

"Rudi, Randi, and Robin . . . Nice."

Marie can't contain herself.

"You could call him Roland. There's something called the Song of Roland."

"Or Rudolf," says the orderly.

"No, that's his dad's name."

"But what about Rune or Rory or Rex?" Marie persists. "You could call him Raphael, too, or Richard or Roger."

"No, better Rasmus then, for God's sake," cries Connie, from over in her bed.

"What about Roy . . . Roy Mikkelsen?" says Marie. "Doesn't that sound good?"

"Where do you get all those names from?" says Mrs. Holm.

"Oh, nowhere special," says Marie, gesturing with her hand.

They don't know that *What shall we call it* has been her favorite game in Prenatal.

Mrs. Holm is lying with her arm under her head among soft piled-up pillows, holding her paper in her outstretched hand . . . good gracious, if she isn't a little long-sighted!

"Listen to this," she says, starting to read aloud. "Doesn't this sound interesting?"

"*Yesterday you voted for a new Prime Minister. Today you have the chance to make him keep the promises made during the election campaign. The election is settled, but Denmark's future Prime Minister has not yet been chosen. Regardless of who will lead Denmark through future troubles, you now have a chance to influence him* . . . doesn't that sound good . . . *Write an open letter to Denmark's future Prime Minister. You can give him your honest opinion, good advice or ask him questions. We shall ensure your letters get there, and with over a million readers behind us, we know the Prime Minister will listen and reply* . . . that sounds fascinating, doesn't it?"

"Who *did* win the election?" says Marie, looking round the ward. "Does anyone know?"

"Wasn't it the Social-Democrats?" a voice says.

"Oh, *no*, not them again, please!" exclaims Mrs. Holm. "It'll be nothing but chaos."

"I've got today's paper," says Connie, holding it up so that everyone can see it. "Listen now, all of you . . . *Hartling must go . . . the result of the election is a draw. The bourgeois parties have seventy-eight seats, the workers parties seventy-three and Glistrup has twenty-four.*"

"What happened to Erhart?" says Mrs. Holm.

"*Erhart is the election's great loser. He lost ten seats and is now down to four,*" Connie went on.

"Ha!" laughs Mikkelsen. "Serves him right—the stupid fool."

"I really can't agree with you there," says Mrs. Holm.

"It says here, that *Hartling was so successful he defeated himself—he won twenty seats but can't use them for anything.*"

"What happened to the Communists?" says Marie.

"They got seven seats and went ahead with one."

"Well, I'm going to write to my candidate for the premiership all the same," says Mrs. Holm, turning over with her paper in her hand.

"Stand up straight!" a voice calls out, as Marie walks past the open door of the office.

"What a sight you are!" says the evening nurse, coming over to Marie. "That nightshirt must be at least five sizes too large. Where on earth did you get it? You look like . . . you look like someone from a geriatric ward."

She knows how to express herself, Marie thinks, stretching out her arms in the far too long sleeves.

"There now, just you stand still and let me do this."

With brisk movements, the nurse rolls up the sleeves several times, so that Marie's hands are visible.

Then she takes a step backward, screws up her eyes, and puts her head on one side.

Marie goes on down the corridor to the table with a white cloth on it and helps herself liberally to coffee and cheese sandwiches.

The nurse shakes her head in despair.

The mothers walk back and forth to the table and help themselves, putting thick slices of white bread with a liberal layer of butter on them onto paper plates. Tea and coffee are served in plastic mugs.

Some of them go back to their own wards, others go and sit on the red sofa to talk and watch television.

The day room is narrow with a high ceiling and spotlights. There is a pay phone on the wall inside the door, enclosed in a plexihood.

Above the low red sofa is a pair of framed lithographs and some color prints by well-known artists, mass-produced graphics and typical hospital art. They say nothing to anyone. They just hang there, having cost a certain sum of money.

The women have spread themselves round the assorted chairs, smoking, talking, or watching the television grinding on. The screen looks gray . . . it's a long time since anyone bothered to adjust the picture.

A bony little woman in a high starched cap comes along pulling a tinkling trolley full of medicine jars. She stops in the middle of the room and asks in a friendly but at the same time quite sharp voice whether anyone wants anything for the night, sleeping pills or laxatives or what?

"How are you, Mrs. Holm? Have your bowels opened today?"

"I've got such terrible hemorrhoids!"

"Is there anyone else who wants anything?"

"I've got hellish after-pains," says little Mikkelsen. "Didn't get a wink of sleep last night. And I'd like something for my stomach. What you gave me yesterday was useless."

"Didn't it help?"

"Not a jot."

"Try two glasses of liquid paraffin then . . . and here's some Magnecyl with codeine . . . take two each time."

"I'm afraid I can't sleep," says Marie. "Can I have something strong that's sure to work?"

"A Doriden . . . will that do?"

"Thanks. And a glass of syrup of figs."

It sounds so Old Testament.

The babies are wheeled out for the night. Marie puts her hand on the night nurse's arm and says:

"Please watch her carefully, won't you? She's so small and so new."

"Don't you worry, you try to get some sleep. You need it. It's more important than you think. I promise you we'll watch over her carefully. She'll come in with us in the office, where we sit. In that way we can keep an eye on her all the time."

My little one. You're going to spend the night in the office now.

All the lights are out. Marie's thoughts whirl round and round. Her body feels tender, her ribs broken.

She has swallowed the sleeping pill and taken the opportunity to wash it down with alcohol.

She must remember to write to Zacharias. She must tell him that he's become father to a girl . . . four weeks too soon. That will be something of a surprise.

Marie puts her new watch on her right wrist, so that she won't forget to send him a telegram the next day.

For the first time for many months, she can lie on her stomach, a flat stomach, loose, empty as an old sack, like a laundry bag. Oh, to be allowed to sleep for a hundred years. Oh, to feel sleep coming creeping over you, strong, irresistible. To be able to sink back completely and abandon yourself to the night.

One single light flickers in the ceiling.

A skidding taxi stops at the edge of the pavement.

Far into the night, a terrible scream penetrates through the pipes behind the head of her bed, the scream tearing the silence apart. A voice cries no-no-no! Marie thrusts her fingers into her ears, closing her eyes tight and pressing her body down against the mattress. A moment later, she doesn't know whether it was herself screaming, something she had dreamt, or even whether there are any pipes behind her bed at all.

She notices that she is bleeding.

She pulls the cord. A blue light goes on. The night nurse comes and changes the drawsheet.

## SATURDAY 11 JANUARY

The skinny little newspaper woman comes along with her heavy newspaper trolley. She soon catches sight of Marie, whom she recognizes from Prenatal.

"Goodness!" she says, clapping her hands together. "Have you gone and had a little one too, now. May I look? Oh, how sweet! Congratulations!"

And she starts selling papers from her trolley.

Mrs. Holm reveals a talent for organization and succeeds in arranging things so that no two patients in the ward buy the same things. Everyone buys something different . . . different dailies, different magazines and different sweets. In that way there's something to pass the time with.

Marie is standing by the baby table with her naked baby. What was it she had to do now? She looks round. What do the others do?

There are four babies on the table. She can't help comparing hers with the others, first looking at one of them, then back to her own. There's a clear difference. Her child is much smaller and weaker, like a plucked chicken. A tiny little concentration-camp child with long thin legs and joints that creak.

Perhaps it has been like a kind of concentration camp for her, before she was born.

But at the same time, she is very beautiful, *definitely* the most beautiful of them all.

No one should think a mother doesn't know what her own child looks like!

"Born too soon, was she?" says Connie.

"Yes, a month."

With clumsy hands, Marie tries to get the baby's vest on. Her arms are so thin and hands so incredibly small, she is afraid of breaking something as she squeezes the limbs into the clothes.

"What does one do?"

"Like this," says Connie, changing places with Marie. "One corner of the nappy down between her legs and the other round her back, then fasten it like this. D'you see now?"

Quickly and professionally, seventeen-year-old Connie dresses the matchstick child.

"How is it you're so good at it?"

"I've looked after my sister's children."

Marie has also changed the nappies of children in the kindergarten but that was quite different. Some were disposable nappies, and anyhow the children were larger and quite different to hold.

Think of those three- and four-year-olds . . . the parents really have had them a long time!

The room is full of morning light, the beds snowy white and everything orderly and tidy.

In the cupboard there's as much clean linen as you want.

A lovely long weekend lies ahead for the mothers, a weekend when they only have to look after themselves, enjoy their babies, be visited by their families, take a shower, read magazines, talk and sleep.

No great demands are made on them.

They are respected for what they are.

It is like coming into paradise.


Cut flowers stand on the locker tops, mostly tulips, with long stiff stalks thrust into the hospital's shiny aluminum vases.

Brilliant yellow tulips, dark red tulips, pink tulips with translucent glass-green leaves, with no real scent, for they have not grown in real earth out in the country, but have been forced and wrapped in cellophane like ready-cooked chickens.

Red flowers are good for women with new babies, for red is a life-giving color. In the old days, baptismal clothes of newborn infants were always red.

Yellow is good, too, as it offers protection against all evil.

But white brings bad luck. Red and white flowers may not under any circumstances be mixed. If a bouquet of that kind were delivered to the maternity department, the staff would separate them at once.

Now and again the main door would open and a uniformed messenger would come in with an immense floral arrangement wrapped in rustling tissue paper, an extravagant visiting card fastened to it with a pin.

There would be no ordinary flowers like roses, tulips, aconites, or hyacinths inside the tissue paper. No, there would be an artistically arranged bouquet tied up with a colored silk ribbon, the flowers so unusual that no one in the department would know their names.

The messenger disappears into a single room where there is sure to be . . . at least that is what Mrs. Holm says . . . a royal or aristocratic person, while Mikkelsen, on the other hand, has heard that a famous model is in there, or is it an actress? Anyhow, one of those people you see in weekly magazines.

The person with the most flowers in Ward 1 is undoubtedly Mrs. Holm. She has twelve long-stemmed, almost black red roses tied with a pink silk ribbon on her locker, and then she has a little bouquet of rosebuds in a vase as well.

Above her head on the window sill is a whole row of handsome bouquets, azaleas, freesias with cotton-grass and sprays of coral.

Marie is slightly embarrassed that she has no flowers, not because she misses them, no, not at all, but she can't bear the thought that the others might think her miserable because none of her kin had thought to send her some!

"Oh, you little pig you, you've gone and messed yourself up again."

Mrs. Holm speaks to her baby in carefully studied tones.

It's her third child. She already has two girls.

She is the only one in the ward to have had her breasts tied up. The nurse has helped her by putting a firm bandage right round her chest.

She doesn't want drooping breasts.

While the others are feeding their babies, she sits there with a bottle. It's all so much easier, because you know exactly what the baby is getting.

On Mrs. Holm's left, Connie is groaning over her stitches. On her right, in the bed by the window, a big woman lies with her great coarse feet with curved toenails and scratched red soles sticking out of the end of the bed. She is married to a blacksmith and has had a fourth son. Mrs. Holm has suggested they should exchange children, but the blacksmith's wife replied: "Thanks, I think I'll keep what I've got."

The blacksmith's wife is sitting propped against the pillows, gazing at her sleeping child in the strong light from the window. His face is quite slack, the mouth large and full, the nose thick and slightly flat, a vigorous child.

She tries to wake him up. She sticks her thumbs into his hands, pulls him slowly up, then lets him fall back on to the soft bed.

"Hey, you . . . wake up now . . . time for food!"

He carefully opens one deep blue eye, then hurriedly shuts it again.

Then he yawns and wrinkles his nose, gazing straight ahead with a calm firm gaze. Wide awake.

The blacksmith's wife unbuttons her hospital shirt, revealing blue veins crisscrossing her full brown-spotted breast. Confidently, his mouth seeks the dark nipple while the little hand strokes her bare skin.

He sucks contentedly. At first the nipple was cold and tasting unpleasantly of lanolin, but now it's dark and more alive. He sucks and the milk runs straight into his tiny stomach.

After feeding intensely at each breast for the stipulated ten minutes, he burps and falls back with a sigh, his free arm falling out sideways.

He's asleep again, the little drunkard.

In the bed by the other window, opposite the blacksmith's wife, lies a thin hairdresser with her pale baby in her arms. She is one of the many unmarried mothers. In this ward alone there are three—Connie, Marie, and herself. In the other wards there are probably many more. The hospital cannot refuse them, and traditionally never has.

Marie is in the bed on the hairdresser's right. Her Eskimo child has been changed and handed to her by the nurse.

The baby softly and delicately takes hold of the nipple with her lips. Then she dozes off. Nothing much has been achieved. Marie feels uncertain.

"How's it going?" says Sister. "Are you getting her to take it?"

She glances at the weight graph on Marie's locker, where it says: *Saturday*, *3rd day*, *2,310 grams*. The baby is losing weight rapidly.

"You must try to get her to feed, Hansen. Her kidneys must be got going. All babies lose weight during the first few days, but little ones like yours shouldn't be allowed to go down too far."

"But what shall I do?" says Marie unhappily. "I try and try, and I do just as you tell me to, but she gets tired so quickly and stops. And I haven't the slightest idea how much she's getting."

"Try milking it out and put it into a bottle. She might find it easier that way. The bottle is easier to drink out of, as the milk runs more quickly. Then she won't get so exhausted. Then we can check her weight now and again."

The nurse turns to the next bed.

"Well, Mikkelsen?"

Mikkelsen lifts her untidy head from the lumpy pillow. Sister helps give her support for her back and to wipe her nipples.

"Give me the little pet, then," says Mikkelsen with a determined expression on her face.

The little pet complains about everyone and everything, but with a firm grip on the back of his neck, the nurse manages to get him started.

"Ow, the little devil," his mother groans.

There is a Pakistani girl on her right, sitting there in a brilliant black silk coat with gold and silver threads woven into it, her 3,500 gram baby in her arms. The baby has been helped out with a suction cup, a handsome dark child with a large brown patch on its skull.

The Pakistani woman has lost heart completely. The baby won't take the bottle of valuable expressed drops of breast-milk. The nurse looks at her with a troubled expression.

The last woman in the row, farthest away in the darkest corner of the ward by the linen cupboard, is called Sidenius. Her fine golden hair lies spread out like a fan on the pillow. She has had a weak boy who cries in a high thin voice. Sidenius just lies there, anemic and without initiative. The delivery has been long and unhappy, and now she just stares up at the ceiling, distant from everything and everyone.

There is one more in the ward.

A very small little black-haired boy, a light brown mulatto, for some reason is all alone. He is looked after by the staff all the time.

Where is his mother? She can't be dead, can she? Even today, women do occasionally die in childbirth, even in special departments like this.

The women walk past his bed and glance down at the little boy. When they see his fine, well-formed face, their throats tighten. He looks so abandoned, lying there, so loveless.

Then someone plucks up courage and asks the sister why he is there.

"He's going to be adopted," she replies. "His mother is only fourteen."

Connie's good humor has suddenly vanished. During the morning's round, the doctor has heard something like an indistinct creaking in one of the baby's hip-joints. The child is to be examined again in an orthopedic department.

Perhaps the baby's hips are dislocated.

In one of the other wards, Connie has seen a child like that. They set the little legs out at right angles, bent at the knees. The splint has to stay for three months. Then the hips recover and the child won't limp . . . like Mikkelsen does as she waddles round the room.

It's just that it looks so awful with the splint on.

Connie is eating her tomato soup, the spoon stopping halfway between plate and mouth, great tears rolling down her cheeks.

"Don't worry," says the nurse. "Your baby will be examined in a special department. Three out of four sent there come back guaranteed nothing wrong. We just don't like taking risks here."

Half an hour later, a taxi comes to fetch them. The nurse puts the baby in a baby carrier, Connie puts on her fur jacket and goes as well. They are going to a specialist in Blekdamm Road.

A physiotherapist in a loose white shirt and dark blue trousers is standing in the middle of the ward, talking about how important it is for the women to do their exercises, and that they should gradually start training up their muscles again.

"Remember," she says, "Your pelvic muscles have been under great strain during your labor."

Two fingers are missing from one hand and Marie can't help wondering if she had been born like that.

Marie is lying on her back on top of the bed, one hand on her diaphragm, her knees slightly bent.

"Don't let your legs fall to one side suddenly. You might pull your stitches, or at worst break them. That's it, now stretch your legs, cross your feet, and squeeze."

The physiotherapist looks round.

"Squeeze now, calmly and slowly, one-two-three-four-five, then relax and breathe out. That's it. Think of your womb as a lift you're sending up to the first-second-third-fourth-fifth floor."

Mrs. Holm groans loudly. She can't really localize that lift. The blacksmith's wife bursts out laughing. She's pressed the wrong button.

"You can do this exercise at any time and anywhere, when you're having a midday rest or when you're waiting at the bus stop. Even when you're holding the washing up."

"My husband'll have to do that," says the blacksmith's wife, her face scarlet with laughter.

While they are resting at midday, the hairdresser has a visit from the social worker, who has a red band in her hair. The social worker pulls up a chair and they whisper together for a long time. Mrs. Holm pricks up her ears to catch what it's all about. Something to do with benefit, social security, and application forms.

The hairdresser is given a paper that she signs with numbed movements.

Then the social worker turns to Marie and says:

"What about the paternity? Has that been established?"

Connie returns happily with her infant in the baby carrier. It was a false alarm. Nothing is wrong and the child need not wear a splint.

Mrs. Holm is standing in front of the basin, putting her hair in curlers. She twists and turns her head, looking at herself from all sides and touching the rolled curls lightly with the tips of her fingers.

As she puts a thin hairnet over her head, she exclaims:

"It really is awful . . . they do *nothing* but use us as *guinea pigs*."

Marie suddenly raises herself up on one elbow.

"Signe! How nice to see you."

The black kimono leans over the white figure, and for a brief moment Marie feels Signe's great firm belly against her own slack one.

"Where's your baby?" Signe says, looking round.

"There . . . at the end of the bed."

She leans over and looks at the sleeping child.

"I can't tell you how pleased I was when I heard how it'd gone. How sweet she is!"

Every time anyone says something positive about her baby, Marie feels a mixture of pride and joy she has never experienced before.

"It's just that she's losing weight so quickly."

"It's great you're in such good hands."

Marie leans back and looks at Signe. Signe's hair has grown a little longer, but it's still just as untidy. Her face is pale. Signe looks isolated and suddenly Marie feels for her. Her friend is still at that painful point in the past . . . when you still haven't given birth.

Marie touches her arm.

"How are things up there in the old ward?"

"I'm being discharged tomorrow. The baby's been large enough for a long time," she says, patting her stomach. "Linda's been admitted again."

"Linda?"

"Yes. You'll go and see her before you go home, won't you?"

"Of course."

"Where are you going when you're discharged?"

"To my parents in Jylland . . . on holiday with the baby."

Marie sees herself on the ferry up on deck with a basket in her hand. The baby is sound asleep inside it. The wind blows and the waves have white tops on them.

"How do you get on with your mother?"

"Well," says Marie. "Really well. And with my dad, too."

Signe nods nervously, her hands running up and down her kimono, perhaps wanting a cigarette. Then she says:

"There's something I can't help thinking about. I often think relations between girls and their mothers are rather bad. Don't you? If you look round here, for instance, don't you think that lots of the girls we've met have a *hell of a time* with their parents. But they all reckon things are going to be all right with their own children. I suppose one must hope. . . ."

"I don't know how certain they are, . . ." says Marie.

"But in some ways, I've a shrewd suspicion that you can't shed things so easily. That bad things are inherited. . . !"

She plays with the belt of her kimono.

"I often think," says Marie, "it's almost difficult to admit that you get on well with your parents, as if people will think you're not an independent person if you do."

"Yes, it's quite hard nowadays to come to some agreement with the old. It's devalued. It counts for nothing. And the result is a whole lot of unhappiness. What will become of the girls lying here, and their husbands . . ."

Signe nods from one bed to another.

". . . if they have no one more experienced to help them, and who really *likes* their bandy little kids? This business of *liking* . . . you have to *learn* it. As you learn from your parents and pass it on to your own children. It's not something you know just like that."

She smiles.

"They say that they're crazy about children up in Greenland."

"Yes," says Marie happily. "So they say."

"What are you thinking of doing now? . . . Are you going to go on working at the kindergarten?"

"I want to go on studying, really. I know I'm twenty-eight, but . . . well, I'd like to do social studies, or go to the Institute of Education. Preferably the alternative one in Jylland, if it's possible to have your child with you there."

"Your man's training to teach, too, isn't he?"

"Yes. We may well consider going to work in Greenland, both of us."

Marie clasps her hands behind her head.

"Signe . . . I understand now much better what you said to me once up there in Prenatal. You said the world becomes smaller, but at the same time more concentrated when you have a child. I can already see my world becoming limited . . . *it's as if I only had room for this child and nothing else.* But what worries me is that I understood nothing before. I've never shown any special solidarity toward other girls. I've always been much more interested in men. Not until now have I begun to understand other women."

"You know," said Signe. "Tenna . . . she. . . ."

The afternoon is beginning to draw out, winter darkness penetrating into the ward, rolling in like a wave, pushing the light ahead of it.

The blacksmith's wife is taking a little walk with her son. She carries him round the baby table, over to the basin and door, then along the row of beds and over to the big window, holding his hand in hers and giving it a kiss.

"Why are you in here?" says Marie.

"Well, we had those three boys, and we really did want another one. But then I had two miscarriages quite close to each other. I was terribly down. So I was referred to this hospital and they helped me have Junior here."

She looks affectionately down at the sturdy infant body.

"It's almost as if the hospital had given him to me as a present."

"How do you live . . . with so many of you?"

"In three and a half rooms and kitchen."

"Is there room . . . six people?"

"Oh, yes, it's fine. You see, my in-laws live quite close. The two elder boys are always round with them. They have their dinner and do their homework there, and they sleep at their place, too. So it works out very well, really. We've never had any baby-sitting problems with our lot. And we won't with him, either."

She walks over to the table on her sturdy legs and large calves. Her buttocks are round and high, her brown hair falling over her shoulders.

She looks down at her son with radiant eyes as he wriggles about on the plastic undersheet.

The main door opens and closes. There are visitors all over the place.

Visiting mothers with new babies has always been a popular entertainment. It is hard work when it all happens at home, but here there's no need to go to all the trouble of tidying up the house and providing food and drink for your guests. The framework of hospital and its regulations protect the mother.

It is strange seeing the women's families, incredibly intimate in some way. What is also strange, husbands and wives so often resemble each other. Small undersized women have a tendency to marry small undersized men. Like to like, much more than Marie had imagined.

But what is most noticeable when you see the family is that suddenly you also see their surroundings.

207

The equality of class that reigns in the ward when the patients are alone suddenly vanishes when husbands appear.

By their clothes, their faces, their teeth and hands . . . their flowers and presents, their way of speaking, the men always reveal the couple's social standing.

Working-class, middle-class and upper-class . . . the woman and her child are a puzzle until the moment her husband comes up to her bed, and then it is solved quite clearly.

Mr. Holm has been given permission by the staff to bring their two older girls with him into the ward for a brief visit to their mother. They are six and eight. They stand there at the end of her bed with their hair neatly brushed and recently cut, wearing pale blue buttoned-up coats. They have inquisitively approached their new little sister, but each time their mother has put them firmly in their place.

*"Careful! Don't touch her! Don't cough like that near the cot! Don't wipe your nose on your sleeve!"*

Now they are standing as quiet as mice beside each other, hardly daring to breathe.

The skinny little hairdresser alongside Marie is being visited by her mother. They whisper away and suddenly the mother raises her voice and says:

"But, don't you think you *ought* to get married?"

"Oh, *Mum*!" says the hairdresser, glancing anxiously round.

There is a colorful group standing round the Pakistani's bed, the men with dark curls over their foreheads, one wearing a canary-yellow shirt, another a red one, and the third a blue one. An older woman in black is holding the baby carefully in her arms, rocking it from side to side.

Sidenius's husband is sitting with his back to the ward and the Pakistani family.

He picks up his child, holds it for a while and then puts it back again. He looks at his wife, who just stares up at the ceiling. They say nothing to each other.

Eva leans over Marie's bed, holding her little niece wrapped up in the check quilt.

She blows at the closed eyes and sees little spasms crossing the face. She whistles a tune and the child clearly reacts to the sound. She gives the baby her forefinger and feels a weak grip round the very tip.

She may be tired, the tiny mite, but all her senses are certainly intact.

"Isn't she turning slightly yellow?" says Marie. "That worries me rather."

"She'll soon pick up in the next day or two. Don't worry."

Eva strokes the baby's head. What does she know about it?

"Our women's group is getting off the ground now," says Eva, raising her voice. "We're six now. An unemployed porcelain painter from the Royal Porcelain factory, two girls from Christiania, a nurse, and someone who's studying for her higher examination. It's really exciting. We meet every Thursday evening at one of our homes. Wouldn't you like to join when you're discharged?"

Marie is not listening.

"Will you send a telegram to Zacharias, when you go? I've written it out here. He's in a hotel in Holsteinborg. The address is there, too."


What a relief! Visiting time is over.

The little motherless mulatto is lying on his back, snuffling. There is no full breast for him. His small hands wave about in the air, his mouth drawn down pitifully, but his eyes cannot cry tears yet. If only one could pick him up and put him to one's breast.

Mrs. Holm stands with straddled legs at his bedside.

"Sleeping around like that . . . she shouldn't be allowed to bring children into the world."

Then she slowly goes back to her own bed:

"Oh, I've got such terrible hemorrhoids."

"I think I'll get someone to take a look at you, Mrs. Holm," says the nurse.

Mrs. Holm nods desolately.

"Could you change my baby for me?" she says. She's gone and messed herself again, and I simply haven't got the *energy* any more."

The mothers are there in the lamp-light, two rows of lying or sitting women, in white hospital shirts. One raises her head and nods to the evening sister. Another is sitting with a breast-pump. A third has switched off her lamp and gone to sleep. A fourth is feeding her baby. A fifth and sixth are looking at their kicking infants lying on the quilts in front of them. A seventh is reading a magazine. The eighth is sitting on the ninth's bed, talking confidentially.

The ward is like a lantern at night, golden, hovering.

Mrs. Marchen Holm is telling little Mikkelsen something frightfully important, straight over the head of Connie, as if she didn't exist, but that doesn't worry Connie in the slightest. She hasn't yet realized you can exhort other people to do or not to do this that or the other.

She is alive. She is vegetating. She is experiencing an utterly inarticulate sense of well-being as she lies there with her baby girl in her arms, taking in the very scent of her. She is not worrying about why it's so pleasant. It just is.

When she's discharged, she will go home to her parents and younger brothers and sisters. Dad and Mum will no doubt cope with all the problems in their usual rough and ready manner.

"Yes," Mrs. Holm is saying. "There I was at home, running the house and all that, cleaning up the girls' room. But that's not enough in the long run, is it? And then I decided that if we went and had an afterthought then at least I'd have *that* to devote myself to. We had decided on a boy. And when it turned out to be a girl, I actually said to the midwife: *'I want to give it back! It's a changeling!'*"

From midnight to six o'clock in the morning, the babies are all placed in a long row out in the corridor, the smallest and the most recent taken into the office and a napkin placed across the top of the cots so that the light won't shine in their eyes.

The night nurse is talking on the telephone, a cup of steaming hot coffee in front of her. A slim young orderly is changing the nappies of the little Pakistani baby.

Quiet breathing out there in the corridor. Marie walks slowly from cot to cot, looking at each one. There is a long-skulled baby with red cheeks and fair eyebrows, and a huge baby, lying on its stomach with tiny clenched fists each side of its fluffy head. Then comes her little acquaintance, the lonely mulatto, with his fine curved mouth and pale brown face.

You can't hear them breathing . . . they are quite soundless . . . but you perceive it. They are resting in their secretive sleep. They are being swung, rocked, carried away in nappies in their infant dreams.

This whole long row of infants has been born in the course of the last five or six days. All of them have the solemn dignified faces of the newborn.

Here they lie . . . infants . . . utterly abandoned to the adult world they've been brought into.

In thirty years time, they will be the ones keeping the wheels of society turning.

The mothers have left small handwritten notes on the blue and white check covers. *His bottom is sore* is written on one of them. Another says *Please wake my mummy at two o'clock because she wants to feed me herself.* A tiny creature with sticking-out hair has a note fastened with a safety pin to the cot-side, which says *No supplementary feeding, please, my breast-milk is in the refrigerator.*

Marie thinks she hears a sound she recognizes. It must be her own baby whimpering. She recognizes the baby's voice right through everything else. It is the same for all mothers. The feelers are out.

"I must imprint all this on to my mind properly," Marie thinks. "I can always go back to Paris, but this . . . it'll never come back again."

What now, then? Someone is shaking her shoulder. It's quite dark and everyone is asleep. What on earth. . . ?

She sits up in bed, her head heavy, stickiness between her legs.

"You left a note to say you wanted to be woken," a black shadow in front of her whispers. "You wanted to feed her yourself. Have you changed your mind?"

It's strange hearing a stranger whispering.

Marie looks at her watch. It's two o'clock. That's right. She wanted to feed her herself.

She swings her feet down, fumbles for her sandals on the cold floor, then for the dressing gown on the back of her chair. Then she follows the orderly, creeping past the sleeping women.

There is great activity out in the corridor, which is quite unexpected. Although faint sounds have penetrated through to her, cries from distant shores every night, she had not thought so much went on.

Most of the babies are awake and hungry, moving in their cots and waving their arms, smacking their lips and grunting. A few are yelling. Mikkelsen's little pet Robin is making the most noise.

The night nurse darts from baby to baby, changing nappies, changing sheets, giving bottles and glucose-water, and making sure they all bring up wind.

"Come on," says the young orderly. "You can sit in the day room, where you'll be left in peace."

The orderly finds the right cot and pushes it ahead of her to the dark room that smells slightly of tobacco. They don't switch on the lamp . . . the light from the door is enough.

Marie sinks down on the sofa, undoes her shirt, and settles the little bundle right down in her arms.

"Come on, now, little one."

But the baby does not want to open her mouth. She twists her head away, as if pleading not to be disturbed like this in the middle of the night.

The orderly is standing like a ghost in front of them, black against the lighted doorway.

Marie is anxious.

"Can you help me?" she whispers.

The ghost sits down on the sofa and puts her cold inexperienced hand round Marie's warm breast, at the same time trying to support the baby's neck. But the baby does not want to wake up, not even when they click fingers against the soles of her feet. She doesn't want the breast. She doesn't want anything at all!

"If only I could get hold of the proper night nurse," Marie

thinks. "She knows what to do. But she's got such a lot on her hands with all the others. I really can't bother her."

"You little mite, you."

The baby reacts with weak dismissive gestures. Marie doesn't know what to do, and the orderly has lost interest.

"It's probably no use," says Marie shaking her head. "And I suppose you've got other things to do."

They get up together. Marie puts her baby into the cot and pushes it back to her place.

The night nurse will probably give her something instead? A little glucose-water? Or a supplementary feed? The child must have something, mustn't she?

Marie creeps through the dark ward back to her bed.


## SUNDAY 12 JANUARY

The sky is dark gray, and while the beds are made and the floor scrubbed, the patients all lie with thermometers in their mouths.

Marie has a bad day. It starts by dropping her thermometer on the floor, so the nurse has to sweep the dancing quicksilver into the dustpan. Then she happens to put the new thermometer in her tea so that it shows way above normal.

Even at that hour of the morning, it is clear Mikkelsen has cheered up considerably. She starts gadding about the ward, from the washbasin to the linen cupboard, past the baby table and over to the window, her gait like a seaman's. Her old hip injury makes her waddle from side to side. She holds her son straight out with her bare arms so that his head wobbles from side to side, then gives him a kiss slap on the mouth . . . sweetie, mother's little sweetie-pie.

The weekend staff approve. They admire the Mikkelsen way of life.

Little Mikkelsen borrows the department's expensive set of curlers. It is like an enormous jewel case with a shiny red lining. In front of the wash basin, she carefully rolls one strand after another round the thick metal rollers.

She tries out possible names for her son. Rolf Mikkelsen. Robin Mikkelsen. Does that sound better? They could call him René, too, of course.

The babies are weighed and changed. Marie's little girl is now down to 2,260 grams. Sister gives her a long look and says now we really *must* see that she gets something inside her, whether she wants to or not. She is clearly slowly turning yellow.

Marie can see it herself, approaching jaundice. The little girl looks Indian, golden, slim and long.

The nurse draws a chair up to Marie's bed, pours the breast-milk into a bottle and settles down with the baby. Marie lies on her side with her hand in her hair, watching them both. It's been a long time since the baby opened her eyes. She is constantly sleepy, withdrawn, and without appetite.

Marie doesn't know what to think or do.

A quarter of an hour later, when the child has taken no more than about twenty grams of milk, the nurse says: "I must speak to my colleagues about this."

Twenty grams? That's the same weight as an airmail letter, isn't it?

She can't be dying, can she? Marie turns cold all over. This child of hers who has come through all those troubles . . . she can't be lying there quite quietly giving up the ghost in this hospital ward, can she?

On her way down the ward, Sister stops by the Pakistani's bed. As usual the baby has thrown itself back, crying, refusing to take food from the bottle.

The nurse stretches out her hand.

"Can I just have a look at the bottle?"

The Pakistani hands it to her.

"Goodness gracious me, did you ever see such a thing! There's no hole in it!"

Little Mikkelsen is standing in front of the mirror, letting out her curls one by one and putting the curlers back into the lined case. She is so small, she can hardly see the top of her own hair in the mirror.

She waddles over to her locker, gets out her hair spray and sprays her new hairdo with a hissing sound. Then she sits up on her bed and sets about painting her toenails. Spreading out her toes, she says:

"Oh, all right, all right, sweetie-pie! Not so much noise!"

Sweetie-pie is making the most noise in the whole ward, and Mikkelsen is proud of it. There's certainly spunk in the boy.

Leaning comfortably back against her pillow, she takes a lip-stick out of the drawer and with swift practiced movements sets about painting her mouth a bright shiny red.

She rubs her lips together, pressing them against a paper nap-kin, at the same time rocking the cot in an attempt to get sweetie-pie to quiet down.

Then she leans back happily, expectant and well-prepared, ob-serving life in the ward.

Sunday is a festive day for the patients. The doors constantly open and shut and people pour in and out bringing flowers and presents, the air full of jokes and witticisms.

A thin man with a horse-face comes into Ward 1, in a brown cardigan with a white zigzag pattern on it, and brown trousers and large brown shoes.

He embraces little Mikkelsen and she gets off the bed. They put their arms round each other and move off, she holding her thin arms round his square hip, and he putting his knobbly hand round her shoulder. Together, they waddle along the corridor from one side to the other, now and again out of step, like a boat loading at the quayside.

He bends his long head down and looks deep into her eyes. After a while, that painted mouth melts into his thin mouth in a corner of the comfortable day room.

Chat, calls, and laughter go back and forth in waves across Ward 1. The visitors stand in closed circles round each bed, gossiping.

Yet no one has so many visitors as Mrs. Holm.

Fourteen-year-old relations look at the child, turn on their heels, and look vaguely out of the window. Women-friends with fat necks and fat hands, in tailored brown coats and white ankle-socks, pluck at the silent infant and let out little yelps or squeaks, tripping round the ward floor.

Mothers and mothers-in-law in their black Persian fur coats from the northern suburbs of Copenhagen put their heads on one side and look affectionately at Marchen as they let out tender sighs and say . . . "Isn't she lovely!"

Mr. Holm stands to one side, pressing his long embarrassed figure against the radiator as he adjusts his tie.

Marchen receives a shower of presents, pink and blue tissue paper piling up under her bed. A large plastic elephant with a collar is blown up and placed on the window sill alongside the many bunches of flowers.

Little Robin Mikkelsen has been abandoned by his parents and crossly tosses about in his cot. Marie bends down and gives him the comforter. The small wrinkled hands are waving angrily about in the air. The comforter is the first substitute in his life . . . but there will be many more after that.

The blacksmith's wife brightens and puts aside her knitting.

Her husband has come through the door. He is of medium height and strong, wearing a blue raincoat and carrying an umbrella over his arm. His head is broad and his hair short. She gets off the bed and holds out her hands. He hangs up his umbrella on the radiator and pinches his wife's bottom. She smacks his fingers. Then he throws his arms round her and plants a damp kiss on her warm motherly mouth.

Little Connie has no visitors. She has raised her magazine right up to her face and is studying an advertisement on the back of it with interest, at the same time keeping watch out of the corner of her eye on Marchen Holm and her various visitors.

*For a mere 7.50 a week you can teach yourself English.*

"That'd be something for me."

*More and more employers are demanding a knowledge of English. If you want to know more about your work and/or your hobby, the best books on the subject are nearly always in English. There is only one language that can be understood in nearly all countries: ENGLISH. With no money or obligation, send for your prospectus on English by the Natural Method.*

"I might have a go at that," she thinks. "I must do something for the child's sake."

Sister is standing at the end of Marie's bed.

"We've decided . . . that we'd better move your baby to the ward for new babies."

A lump comes into Marie's throat.

"She's beginning to get sluggish. We must check that jaundice. We would be able to cope with her here, too, but we haven't enough staff."

Marie's eyes begin to swim. She looks down at the immobile little baby at the bottom of the cot. She hasn't moved since she was put there.

Marie feels the whole ward staring at her. All Mrs. Holm's visitors fall silent and turn round to look.

"Now . . . at this very moment?" whispers Marie.

The nurse walks with bowed back, pushing the cot ahead of her, Marie keeping up as best she can alongside her in her crumpled white dressing gown, white socks, and plastic sandals. They get into a lift. It's icy cold. They get out into the long white underground passage that runs right under the length of the hospital. They turn left, walk straight on for a while, then turn right, passing a stretcher going in the other direction. Then they come to another lift and are sucked up two floors. It is the same part of the hospital where Marie had been in Prenatal and Delivery. She knows it inside-out.

They walk up the main stairs and through a wide doorway on which it says NEONATAL DEPARTMENT, *No unauthorized ad-*

*mittance*. Then they suddenly find themselves in a pleasant little corridor with a low ceiling, on one side a kitchen where a large woman is washing bottles, on the other two narrow doors, each with a glass pane set into it. One clearly leads to where the babies sleep, the other to the incubators.

Marie and the nurse are standing in front of an unknown person.

"We've got a little one here who is three days old and is dehydrated and has a high hemoglobin count."

"Oh, yes, well, we can soon see to that."

The child vanishes into the ward and a moment goes by before Marie is given a receipt, a piece of paper on which is stenciled:

*To Mrs*—then the word *Nansen* has been written in with a ballpoint—*Your child has been admitted to Department NN and has been given number NN29*—the number added by hand. *Your child will be shown to you every day between 11 and 12 o'clock a.m. The child can also be seen by relations once during the first half hour of visiting hours. Enquiries will be answered on the telephone daily between 8 a.m. and 8 p.m.*

To Mrs. Nansen, it says. Her name is Hansen. Well, it doesn't matter. The nurse signals that they must hurry back, as they have no further business there. Marie pulls up her socks and silently they make their way back like two shadows through the long white tunnels to Postnatal.

All the time, Marie tries to persuade herself that it is for the best. The responsibility has been too great.

But she cannot wholly escape the thought that she is carrying her child's death certificate in her pocket.

Marie drifts aimlessly about the department in her white dressing gown and sandals, with drooping shoulders. Her ribs still hurt like hell, almost more than before.

The refrigerator door opens and shuts. The monotonous hum of the breast-pumps sounds like a bass note amongst the sounds of clinking, tinkling glass.

Propping herself against the wall, a Caesarian patient hunches her way along to the day room.

The doors into most of the wards are open. Suddenly the whole department whirls round in front of Marie's eyes, like a ship keeling over, at once losing its shimmer, its enchantment.

All she sees are sad mothers sitting there sadly with their sad infants. She feels superfluous. Smoke rings rise like signals from the w.c. compartments. She goes and takes a shower, for what else can she do?

Under the hot water, her breasts open . . . a faint white mist runs down her body. She dries herself on a white towel and puts on a clean nightie. It is all pointless.

The evening sister who thought she looked like a geriatric patient helps her with the breast-pump and shows her how to equip the small bottles with name, number, and date and put them into the refrigerator.

The evening nurse goes over to Mrs. Holm's bed.

"Please turn over."

Mrs. Holm is just reading a recipe for baking dough. *Baking dough consists of flour, oil, water, yeast, whipped whites of egg and salt and white pepper. For one packet of lobster-tails, you need a dough made of 100 grams flour.* Mrs. Holm puts aside *Food and Guests*, turns over and reveals her large pink typically Holm-like backside.

"You haven't any hemorrhoids at all!"

"What, none at *all*!"

With a furious jerk, Mrs. Holm sits up in bed again and looks askance at the nurse briskly vanishing from the ward.

*Spain is at present going through a wave of strikes despite the authorities' firm measures.* Marie lets her eyes glide over the surface of the paper, reading the headlines and the first two lines of each article, letting the letters and words sift through to her brain. But she doesn't really understand what she is reading.

*Member of Parliament, Lars Emil Johansen, was the clear victor for the election in Greenland. He is the only one of the four candidates in Greenland who after the count has certainly. . . .*

What will Zacharias say about having a child? What will it mean to him?

Perhaps it would be best to move in with him . . . fairly soon? Find some commune where they could live. She is no longer so certain that she can cope with all this on her own.

*Weekend Market. Two female Abyssinian kids for sale. Fine pedigree. Answer to tel: no: . . .*

Who knows whether her child will ever grow into a person?

*US Air Force lead bombing raid on South Vietnam. Saigon (Reuter). On Friday, the Liberation Forces of South Vietnam destroyed over five million liters of fuel at an oil depôt near the town of Pleiku.*

*At about one o'clock on Friday, a robbery took place in a take-away sandwich bar in Nørrebro Street, and two women assistants were threatened with knives. . . .*

She is standing by the dark window out in the corridor, resting her arms on the window sill and staring down at the faint contours of the low buildings. She can hear the television grinding away in the day room.

"Hansen . . . perhaps you could go over to Neonatal with a little milk for your baby?"

Marie starts and turns to the evening sister.

"May I?"

"Of course you may! Can you find your way on your own?"

Marie nods and goes over to the refrigerator to take out the tiny plastic bottle with name, number and date on it, and puts it in her pocket . . . down with the receipt for her child. Then she hauls up her socks and gets into the cold lift.

The long white shaft stretches on, getting smaller and smaller and ending in a black dot at the end. It is so empty in this mole tunnel. Marie feels someone's eyes boring into the back of her neck and turns round quickly, her hand clutching the milk bottle. But there is no one there, only fear drilling into her back with its cold eyes.

Now and again, the tunnels branch off in other directions, a number on the wall, a code you have to know so as not to get lost.

An orderly walks past her with an empty stretcher, the bed-clothes hanging crumpled down one side. He is whistling, the sound fading away like a gramophone when the volume is turned down.

Her hands and feet are cold. She tightens her dressing-gown belt to keep in the last of her body-warmth.

Now she's in the evening-quiet Neonatal department, the infants sleeping in their cots and incubators in the dim light. Behind the glass pane, she can see a couple of white contourless figures gliding by.

She is clutching a bottle containing fifty grams of breast-milk, a yellowish white bottle that she is beseechingly holding out in front of her.

The evening nurse's face is oval and pale. She has white teeth, pale yellow hair, and pale blue eyes. She is very small-waisted and slightly shorter than Marie.

"Would you like to see your baby?"

"Oh, yes, please, yes, please."

"What's the number?"

"Twenty-nine."

The sister disappears into the low pleasant ward and comes out into the cold electric light of the corridor with a little white bundle.

Marie holds her baby in her arms. She weighs nothing. It is like holding a trembling baby bird.

She is quite still.

All Marie can see is this tiny dark creature. Will you ever become a person? Will you ever leave here alive?

The child opens her eyes and looks at her.

She kisses the lonely mouth and with the tips of her fingers touches the baby's face and hair quite lightly, as if reading braille.

She goes back through the long white mole tunnels, thinking about Tenna. Tenna, who had walked here with her strong dark yellow milk for her little boy in his incubator. A short little boy with legs ending just below the knees. He has been moved to another hospital now, quite near to where Anders and Tenna live.

Tenna had walked many a time through these underground shafts, every day and every night, to see her handicapped child.

"If *she* could, what have I got to cry about?" Marie thinks, the tears pouring down her cheeks.

The shimmering black and white negative of the hospital night; so desolate here . . . despite all those sleeping people.

Marie lies with her hands behind her head, gazing up at the ceiling.

Then she pulls the covers over her head and starts crying quite soundlessly so as not to waken the others. She cries and cries and cries, emptying herself of all the tears she has in her eyes onto the soft material of the bedclothes.

First her baby swam in all that crazy water and now, three days after her birth, she's becoming completely dehydrated.

What have I not brought upon the poor little creature!

Now in the night, it's as if the buildings all fall and the walls split apart and collapse. Now the dams open—letting loose the gnawing tension and anguish of the whole of the last month.

Here in secret, down under the covers . . . on the night between Sunday and Monday . . . here the whole defense system disintegrates.

## MONDAY 13 JANUARY

On Monday morning, Sister walks slowly from bed to bed, speaking to each of the patients as usual. She is wearing her red knee-length socks today.

"But what's this?" The blacksmith's wife, robust great woman that she is, is crying, tears cascading down her cheeks.

"May I have a look?" says Sister.

The blacksmith's wife gets out of bed, unbuttons her shirt, and hauls out two gigantic brown-spotted breasts, swollen and hot, milk dripping down both sides of her powerful body.

The blacksmith's wife wipes her nose with the back of her hand as the sister feels under her arms.

"My goodness, it is running, isn't it? Enough for the whole department."

"It hurts so, it hurts so . . . I get such afterpains every time I feed him, I almost explode."

"I'll go and get you something," says Sister. "Don't worry about it. We'll do something for you."

A little while later, Sister is standing in front of Marie.

"How are things, my dear?"

Her voice is soft and deep.

But Marie cannot get a word out. She just blinks rapidly.

Sister is calm, smiling down at her.

"Would you rather be in a smaller ward?"

"No, thank you," whispers Marie, her face distorted. "I'd prefer to stay here."

"Don't worry about your baby being over there in Neonatal. They're feeding her through a tube for a few days, then they'll give her a bottle and then you can take her home. We probably would have been able to manage, but such a tiny little mite needs a whole person to herself to look after her. Over there, she'll get all the professional attention she needs."

"I'm so scared of going to see her," Marie wails. "I'm so afraid of what she'll look like with tubes and things. . . ."

"Well, then, perhaps your sister could go and see her? She comes here every day, doesn't she?"

The tall fair sister smiles. She clearly thinks the child *ought* to be visited. But she doesn't deny Marie's assumption . . . that the baby is lying there with tubes and things, looking *awful*. Perhaps she hasn't understood how anguished her patient is.

"First and foremost, you must try to decide for yourself what suits you best. For instance, you could go into town in the daytime and then sleep here at night . . . if that's what you would like."

Yes, that *would* be marvelous. But wouldn't that be taking advantage of the system? Marie looks up at the tall sister.

"If you prefer it, we could discharge you now, then we can admit you again when your baby has got to two and a half kilos. Then we can help you get a good routine going."

Marie clasps her forehead. Imagine! This is supposed to be a large institution and yet . . . it has so much understanding and kindness toward individual patients. She can hardly take it in.

"Think about it for a while," says Sister, turning on her heel to go to the next bed. "Don't forget today is your fifth day. The fourth and fifth are often difficult . . . easy to feel down. It'll pass. Anyhow, you're not going for examination today . . . not until tomorrow."

How can a person take things so calmly? So unsentimentally? Going from bed to bed and being confronted with all these problems?

If only one could be like her, then at least one would be of some use to one's fellow human beings.

The sister has hardly left when Marie begins to have regrets. How could she be so cowardly, not daring to go and look at her own child!

Of course she wants to see her baby. She would dare anything anywhere.

Just before half past eleven, Marie sets off with the little plastic bottle containing seventy-five grams of breast milk.

It says on her receipt that the babies in Neonatal are shown every day between half-past eleven and midday, so now she mustn't waste a single minute.

She is clutching the receipt in her pocket, almost like a cloak-room ticket you have to keep if you want your coat back.

The wind is whistling faintly in the white tunnel, the sound echoing hollowly, the lights fixed in the ceiling throwing their cold blue light down on to the figure silently fleeing like a shadow along the gray concrete floor.

Mothers whose children have been taken away from them go along these passages underneath the National Hospital . . . because the baby for some reason requires intensive care.

The women walk back and forth between Postnatal and Neonatal. They walk down here, as it is actually warmer than above ground in the tearing January wind.

Here they walk, hunched and tired in their own dressing gowns, their figures clumsy, their stomachs still far too bulky, feeling miserable and uncertain. They have not passed the test. Their children are not as they should be, and neither are they in themselves. They have suffered defeat and feel worthless.

The anxiety that something might happen to the baby makes them feel cold.

Marie gets into a lift, is sucked upward, spat out, then is once again in Neonatal.

The greenhouse and conservatory of the newborn.

The door into the kitchen is open and she can see the large woman wiping her hands on a dishcloth and putting bottles into a gray cupboard hanging on the wall.

Marie creeps over to the door and peeps through the narrow glass pane into that secretive incubator-country.

She sees young doctors in white trousers and white short-sleeved vests walking round as if in uncharted country. Only the tropical helmets are missing, for it all looks like a journey of exploration in distant southern climes. They are moving back and forth in the warmth and humidity, keeping behind the twelfth door of the saga a kind of preliminary stage of life under observation.

She can see seven or eight transparent Plexiglas containers coupled to the electric circuit and various pieces of complex apparatus.

Above the incubators are small heavy metal boxes with handles and push-buttons and dark green screens that blink and dance out pale green tracks in an intricate system of drawn graphs.

She can hear the sound of bubbling water as if from underground springs or rivers.

She is back in a warm swampy *primeval world*, where human kind once came into existence.

Pistons pump up and down, clocks tick faintly, small rabbit-cries rise from the treasure chests, a hollow humming sound always in the background.

Forest everywhere . . . a wicker-work of green branches and leaves.

In the chests small figures lie in the multifarious light . . . ancient Aztec gold created by the most skilled artist-craftsmen.

But no, it is an ordinary weekday in the department for new-born babies. No alchemy, no mystique connected with it. That forest . . . is the cables, cords, tubes and drips casting their shadows up on to the walls and ceiling.

The children in the incubators are those who have been ejected too early from the mother organism, either because it was not in a state to retain them any longer, or because the climate in there had suddenly become too harsh.

Others have at the very last moment been released from the body's stranglehold via a Caesarian.

Some of them are even below 1,000 grams in weight . . . the weight that is otherwise the borderline between miscarriage and newborn.

There they lie . . . Winter's Children . . . in their mechanical wombs of glass and steel, condemned to survive.

Red and green or transparent tubes carry nourishment through their nostrils down into their stomachs or through their skin into the bloodstream.

They are children born too early, and children with a fault somewhere, children with visible or invisible inborn defects, children for whom some complication has arisen during or after their actual birth.

One of them has meningitis and a far too pale pink skin. Another has faulty heart valves and is apt to turn the color of bilberries. One has a broken arm from a complicated Caesarian birth. And there . . . a drug addict on a cure.

Some of them are having blood transfusions. Some lie in respirators. Others are receiving oxygen or lie immobile in sharp light, their eyes bandaged. Some tremble. Some have drawn breath in the womb.

A new patient is carried in, an absolutely new baby brought into the world a moment ago, its life hanging on a thread. The first day is the most critical in a human being's life. More people die during the very first day than during any other day in their existence.

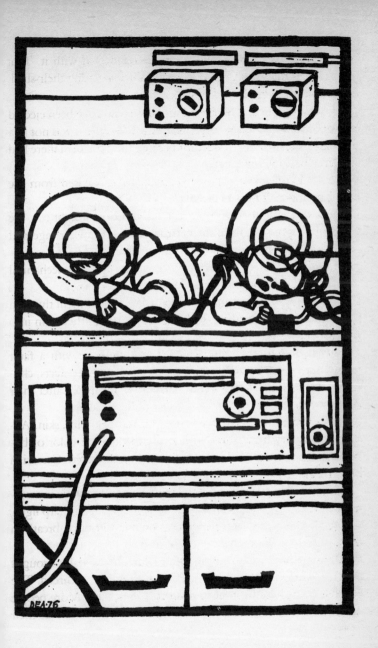

"Little Lukas's father is on the phone."

"Oh, God, what shall I say to him?"

"Tell him the truth."

The young doctors are sitting on high stools, observing their patients through glass walls. They talk, gesticulate, and laugh.

They listen to the news on the radio, which can be heard faintly in the background.

A nurse is carefully carrying a little surgical patient. His head is swollen. He resembles a monster, a monster of the kind you read about in ghost stories. They have wound a white bandage round his neck; his tongue sticks out, stiff and thick between blood-red lips, bubbles coming from the corners of his mouth.

She carries him round between the incubators, kissing his pale little hand, and looking down into his gentle eyes. They are clear and look straight back at her. He is not newborn. He has been there a couple of weeks and has already had several operations.

She whispers something to him and he turns his heavy little head toward the sound. He tries to smile, but the smile is nothing but a twitching round his eyes. She sees it at once and smiles back.

He has been baptized long ago. He has his own independent first name. Most of these children have . . . large, solid adult names betraying the dreams and hopes of their parents.

No trouble is spared to ensure their survival, to get them to cope with life as well as possible. No treatment is too demanding or too expensive.

This country is a closed country. No unauthorized person is let in.

But if, like Marie, you happen to see it . . . if only through a glass pane in a door, then you cannot help thinking about how dearly bought life is, how beautiful it is. And how cruel it is.

But her own child is not in an incubator. She is in one of the side rooms, in the ward where the relatively larger and stronger children are.

A nurse hands patient number 29 through the door. Marie takes the bundle, leans against the wall, and looks down into the

231

narrow infant face. Her head has slid down onto her shoulder. Her breathing is scarcely visible.

"When she's got up to 2,300 grams, you can look after her yourself and feed her," says the nurse. "Then you can try breast-feeding her again."

Marie nods. She is holding the butterfly-light hand in hers.

"I was so worried that she was lying with a tube in her nose all the time."

"Oh, no. The tube is pushed down in a second, just before feed-time. That's nothing to worry about. Her bilirubin count is also going down. You can see that for yourself . . . she's not nearly so yellow now."

So the door hasn't slammed behind you, Marie thinks. You'll be coming back to me again, you tiny mite.

The dark young doctor comes out into the corridor and joins Marie as she stands there in her crumpled nightie, with her tired face and sagging socks. And there he is . . . tall, clean, well-educated, and cheerful.

"Couldn't you tell me what you know?"

"Yes," he says. "She is what we call a dysmature child . . . long and thin. We used to call children under five pounds premature. But that definition didn't take into consideration gestation age, intrauterine malnutrition or hereditary factors . . . or for instance large premature children born to diabetic mothers. Your child has partly been born too early and has partly starved in the uterus. She may have at one time weighed more than she does now."

Marie has to swallow and her eyes brim.

"Naturally there's a connection between this and your hydramnios. Were you ill during your pregnancy? Did you have a bad attack of 'flu? High temperature? No? We'd be glad if you could write a report for us on the course of your pregnancy. Would you do that? Good. But don't worry now . . . we can't find anything specially wrong with your baby. All the tests we have taken have turned out quite normal."

"Can I rely on that?"

"You can rely on that."

"You're not hiding anything?"

"We're not hiding anything."


It is quiet and peaceful in Postnatal.

"I'm glad you've come back," says the blacksmith's wife. "Could you hold him for a moment while I go out?"

Marie is pleased to do that, and the little fattie is transferred to her bed. He is twice as big as her own child at the moment.

She is aware that the blacksmith's wife has begun to hand her child over to her so that she shall not miss her own child too much. But sitting there with the little boy does not make her miss her own baby any less. On the contrary, almost. Her own body just feels soft and weak, the milk coming into her own breasts and dripping slightly.

Marie can't bear other people feeling sorry for her, but at the same time, she wouldn't have dreamt of saying no to holding the little boy, even if her own child had been lying alongside. So why should she say no *now*? That would seem very strange.

Marie is slightly in love with this little blacksmith boy. He is so incredibly touching and solid, she feels a kind of gratitude toward him.

The tiny creature is firm and warm. *He* has no body-temperature problems. He makes small snuffling noises through his soft full mouth, and he is short and sturdy, just like his father. How happy his father must be! Marie experiences the wonderful living feeling of sitting with a large full-term newborn baby, making his presence known, making demands, and showing his very special form of devotion.

Then he tries putting his fingers in his mouth. No, that's too difficult, even if he's managed it several times during his weightless existence in his mother's womb. His mouth turns down and a small expression of despair comes into his round face.

She can't really say he is beautiful. He is slightly too coarse for that. Her own baby is in every way much prettier. But he's just so wonderful.

"If you have him adopted," she says, when the blacksmith's wife appears again, "put me down on the list, won't you?"

"I don't think my husband would agree to that," says the mother proudly.

She leans down and smooths out the sheet in the cot, her backside sticking up in the air.

"Look what I've got for you!"

Sister comes in with four bottles of red wine in her arms.

"What on earth. . . ?"

"Senior Sister thought you needed something to cheer you up . . . there were so many of you sniveling in here this morning. So now you're to have this." The nurse uncorks the bottles.

The women raise their glasses to each other from their beds. It'll be good to eat and drink and then have an after-dinner snooze.

All along the Postnatal corridor, the monotonous sound of the breast-pumps can be heard.

Marie is sitting on the edge of her bed, her nightie unbuttoned and one hand round her breast, the other holding the transparent glass pump. The milk squirts out in thin fan-shaped ivory-colored spurts toward the inside of the glass, then gathers and runs down into the container in broad uneven ribbons.

Now and again she switches off the machine and pours the milk into the small disposable bottle on her locker.

"Isn't it irritating, that business?" says the blacksmith's wife, her great bumpkin at her breast.

"Yes, it is in a way . . . But I'm only too glad to do it."

"I knew someone once," says Mikkelsen, "Who milked herself and sold the milk. She made a *fortune*."

The evening nurse is standing in the middle of the room, inspecting her troops.

"That's right. Everything's going fine."

"You're fine yourself," says the blacksmith's wife.

Connie slips over to Marie, giggling, her hand in front of her mouth.

"You know what? The wastepaper basket caught fire in the day

234

room just now. It flared up. It was him . . . you know . . . Terrible Olfert! He'd thrown his cigarette butt on top of some paper towels. You should have seen his face!"

A very tall and slim midwife with short hair glides soundlessly into the ward on her soft clogs. She waves to Marie and goes over to the blacksmith's wife, who is deep in a copy of *Home*.

The blacksmith's wife brightens, grasps the midwife's hand, and stretches out for the cot.

"No, don't pick him up," says the midwife. "I can see him from here."

"Oh, I'm so pleased you've come," whispers the blacksmith's wife. "There are one or two things I want to ask you."

She feels a very special dependency on this young woman, who on Thursday night had helped her child into the world. It is not *just* dependency, but almost a love relationship.

The midwife knows this perfectly well and she had come to wind up the relationship. She tries to meet half way the need she knows the patient has to talk about her confinement, to air the whole affair, so to speak.

"What is it you want to know?"

"Do you remember towards the end of the bearing down pains, when. . . ."

It is in every way important for a woman to be able to talk about her confinement. It is *the* experience of her life. Should she then keep it all to herself?

For centuries, this collective experience has been stowed away, confined to closed female circles as childbirth superstition, filled with confused notions, taboos and old wives' tales. Now, when women are beginning to be more aware of their own situation, the whole picture is starting to change.

A woman has the same need to talk about her confinement and the same natural right to do so, as people need to talk about their holidays abroad.

In the same way as when you have been to Paris, you wish to see your slides and films and recount your observations—in the same way, a woman likes to talk about her confinement, which seems to her a far more authentic experience than the sight of the Eiffel Tower.

The very act of relating your experiences serves several purposes. The words give shape to the shapeless. Impressions become more defined and lucid, and therefore easier to deal with in the future. Talking about it gives identity and self-confidence, and also creates a certain distance to events that have influenced you too strongly.

It could well be said that a midwife has a comprehensive and exceptional job. She doesn't only prepare a pregnant woman for her delivery and support her during the actual drama. She also has, to some extent, to help the woman cope with the experience afterwards . . . and help make it settle in a reasonably acceptable way into her consciousness.

The midwife of the blacksmith's wife knows this, so between these two women a feeling of solidarity arises that extends far beyond temporal matters.

But not everyone can or wants to . . . or generally even gets a chance to express herself.

Even if there are so many common features in the mothers' situation, at this moment, immediately after the confinement, their situation is very varied.

For one of them, the delivery has involved an experience that will give her strength and self-confidence for many years to come. To another, it has been a defeat or a humiliation she cannot overcome just like that.

Birth is for good or evil a revelation. No lies, no hypocrisy, no dissimulation can stand up against the enormous natural force that birth is . . . not even in our highly civilized society.

Birth is a mirror that shows a woman quite clearly her own physical and mental state . . . the strength in her environment . . . or the weakness. Not to mention the treachery in her environment.

There are women for whom giving birth is a shock . . . in the same way that rape is. An assault that brings things to the surface, the existence of which she was quite unaware.

A forgotten pain appears. A tormented sense of loneliness breaks out.

Take Sidenius, for instance.

There she is in the darkest corner of the room, staring with wide-open eyes up at the ceiling. Distant. Anguished. Quite slowly, something is overcoming her. She is gliding away from the world around her . . . and the world does not seem to be noticing.

Or are the staff aware of it, after all? They are the ones who look after her child while she lies there so apathetically.

Her husband comes every evening to see her. He sits uncertainly and in silence at the bedside. He does not know what to do or what is expected of him in this situation. He just sits there with the baby in his arms, looking at it. He looks at his wife staring at the ceiling. Then he leaves at the end of visiting time.

Marie wonders whether she should go over there and try to talk to Sidenius for a while. But she is quite aware of a warning light winking. Dare she?

No, she daren't.

She does just as all the others.

They simply pretend the problem doesn't exist.


"Lend me your *Extra*, Connie, will you? It's so good to send you to sleep."

"There's an awful story in it."

"Those people should be shot, they really should," says Mrs. Holm, quite unasked.

The ward is being made ready for the night. The babies have been wheeled out into the corridor, only little Mikkelsen is still struggling bravely with her little screamer.

Marie twists the bedside lamp in toward her and unfolds the paper.

What on earth is all this about?

That one's dead . . . and that one, and that one. Three foreign children from the same doctor's family, a family she has read about in the weekly mags dozens of times . . . three of the children are dead! A fourth child has been admitted to hospital in a very weak state. A fifth child has been returned to Vietnam. By their adoptive father—a medical consultant.

Dead? *Three* children! That can hardly be a coincidence, can it?

Inside the newspaper are pictures of the whole family, happy and smiling, at a time when everything was peace and happiness, the parents in the middle, surrounded by their large colored flock of children . . . which for some reason they have now maltreated.

Marie looks round the dark room. Except her own, all the lamps have been switched out.

Vietnamese, Korean, Thai children. The Danish children are out in the corridor. In the ward for newborn infants is her own . . . an Eskimo child.

She turns out the lamp.

Children are only children for so few years. For adults, childhood is a measurable period of time. For children it is an eternity.

It is extremely risky to be a child.

It would be better to be . . . a tree.


Marie lies on her back with both hands on her slack stomach, looking up at the dark gray ceiling, where the shadows dance and blend with each other like water.

She closes her eyes. An unpleasant, inexplicable picture appears on the inside of her eyelids, a terrible close-up torn out of context. It resembles a tuft of hair in a red crack in the skin. It moves slightly, a living lump. A deformed detail.

She presses her hands so hard against her eyes that stars appear. She keeps her hands there to get rid of the picture. But it returns over and over again. With the same demarcation.

Then she sits up in bed with her eyes wide open, staying like that for a long time, staring out into the dark.


## TUESDAY 14 JANUARY

Drops of water hang in the air and the windows are misty.

Marie is in a queue for the two showers in the bathroom. She is listening to the hot water spattering against the floor. Taps are turned on and the water rumbles through the pipes, which start whistling.

The two women in front of her are lean and beautiful like natives of an Indian tribe or bony like female cats just emerging from their hidden place of confinement.

Empty sacks ready for refilling.

White bandages lie alongside the stacks of clean linen.

There is a smell of soap and shampoo and skin cream. The girl who first comes out through the door is as shiny and red as a boiled lobster.

It is her sixth day, and a day late, she is to go for the routine gynecological examination. She is wearing the cleanest and starchiest hospital clothes, her body clean and hair newly washed as she stands outside the examination room waiting for her turn.

The blacksmith's wife comes out.

"What happens in there?" says Marie.

"He just puts a finger up you and says squeeze. If you've had stitches, he takes them out. Then he talks about contraceptives for a while. Nothing special at all. Takes three minutes."

Inside is the consultant she knows so well. It is nice to see him again.

"Well, how are things, then?" he says, swinging his chair round toward her.

"Fine, thanks."

He turns his back on her as she lies down on the gynecological chair.

"Can you slide down a bit," whispers the nurse.

He leans over her. She closes her eyes. He pushes his fingers inside her cold and rough vagina, and feels.

"Is my womb still very large?"

"No, it's contracted very well," he says, his gaze directed somewhere into eternity above her head. "It's amazing how skilfully nature has arranged things. When you think how extended it was."

She draws a deep breath and tries to relax.

"Squeeze together now . . . that's right."

"Will I ever be myself again, do you think? Internally?"

"Yes, of course you will. Thank you . . . you can get down now."

He sits down at his desk with his back to her while she pulls on her pants.

"Have you thought about what to do so that you don't get pregnant again?"

"Would a coil be a good thing?"

He smiles as he notes something down in the casesheet. She isn't quite sure why he is smiling.

"Phone me here some time in March . . . and I'll insert one."

She notices the conversation is coming to an end, but she wants to extend it, so she says:

"Isn't it peculiar? First my baby swam round in all that water, and then three days after her birth, she was dehydrated."

"That's life," he says hastily, still leaning over her casesheet.

"If I want to have more children . . . do you think I risk the same thing again?"

"That would be very unusual . . . no, I don't think you need fear that at all."

He gets up and they shake hands.

"I'm very grateful for everything you've done for me."

"It's my work."

She feels a sudden despair, and does not know where it has come from, or what she should do with it.

She sidles out of the door.


Today the trip through the underground passage seems to Marie to be slightly shorter. The first icy impression is beginning to disappear, or is it that the situation is beginning to stabilize?

She straightens up and looks ahead, her body apparently slightly sprightlier.

Inside Neonatal, she is told that she must wait a moment. She thrusts her hands into her dressing-gown pockets, leans against the wall and looks round.

Everything is gray and white and low-ceilinged and really quite

pleasant. She can hear the tinkle of glass from the kitchen, a cupboard door slams shut, subdued music pours out of the radio, and there is a smell of coffee.

A young man in an Icelandic sweater and white painter's trousers comes in. He stops, hesitates, looks questioningly round and then goes over to the door with a pane of glass in it.

He fishes a crumpled piece of paper out of his pocket and puts it flat on the glass in front of his face. A moment later, an incubator is wheeled in front of him on the other side of the glass.

Inside the incubator is a tiny naked child.

He puts his hands on the pane of glass and bends his knees slightly, then taps out a little Morse signal with a large crooked finger. He tries to smile, but the smile fades. His white breath is like mist on the glass.

"She's so like . . ." he whispers. "My little treasure."

He glances upward at the nurse's half-moon shaped face with his forehead against the glass. Appealing.

She takes the incubator back and pushes in the plug.

He stands there. He looks Marie straight in the eye for a brief moment, then turns on his large dirty clogs and leaves.

Marie is asked to come into the baby ward. She is given a white coat to wear and regards it a mark of honor.

So many days have passed since the birth, they can now easily let her in. The risk of her bringing in a puerperal infection is now almost minimal.

Marie looks round. The babies don't look at all bad and suddenly she notices that they are going to survive; most of them, anyhow.

She goes over to the high pale-gray little cot where her own baby is. When she sees her, so small and thin, sleeping on her side, she is filled with a deep onion-shaped sense of happiness. There you are, my little friend, with your lovely glossy hair. My mussel shell. My valuable treasure. My own living flesh and blood.

"You can pick her up if you want to."

The nurse is standing in front of her.

"Things are going fine. We feed her through the tube and with a bottle, alternately. But I don't think she's very good at sucking. Perhaps we should look into her sucking reflex."

Marie pricks up her ears. Sucking reflex?

"What about the jaundice?"

"Almost gone. Shall we try weighing her?"

Marie undresses the child. It is like unfolding a paperclip.

"2,280 grams? That's the same as yesterday!" exclaims Marie in fright.

"She'll probably weigh a bit more tomorrow. It usually goes in fits and starts. From tomorrow onward, you can start caring for her yourself. Then you'll gradually get used to it."

"Does your own baby get the milk you bring over?"

"Of course," she replies, in astonishment at such a naive question. "Of course your child gets the milk you bring with you! I can certainly guarantee that! Breast-milk . . . that's an expensive item. Do you see that little milk can? We get one like that every morning from Fuglebakken Hospital. It costs a fortune. If your child doesn't need all the milk you bring, we give what's over to the other children, of course. Expensive drops they are, I'll have you know. You must do what you can to get breast-feeding going when you get her home. You've no idea how important it is, Hansen."

When Marie bends down to pull up her socks before leaving, she almost puts her head into a blue dressing-gown. She looks up. It's Yvonne . . . Terrible Olfert's Yvonne from up in Prenatal.

"Hullo, are you here?"

"Yes, I've been in to look at the twins."

"Congratulations."

"Thanks."

"How are they?"

"Well, I think . . . they're terribly small. One's in an incubator, and the other's just been moved over to a cot in here this morning."

"Shall we go back to Postnatal together?"

"Yes, let's. I hate walking through those awful basement tunnels. I'm scared of being attacked."

They go down to the basement of the building in the lift, and a moment later they are in the long white underground shaft.

"How are you feeling?" says Marie, straightening up.

"I'm flaked out."

Yvonne has tears in her eyes. She walks very slowly with straddling legs and stiff knees. Marie holds out her arm, but Yvonne does not take it.

She looks straight ahead and says:

"The first twin was born quite normally. But it took ages and was awfully hard work. But then . . . meanwhile the other one had twisted and turned so much that it couldn't come out. They didn't dare do anything else but a Caesarian. So now I've stitches in my stomach as well as down there. You can imagine what fun that is."

Her face is hard and angular.

"And that man of mine at home is so impatient and keeps asking when *am* I coming home. He doesn't understand at all that everything takes time."

Yvonne wipes her eyes with her blue sleeve.

Two orderlies in white jackets and black trousers pass them in great style and disappear with long brisk strides.

"The older boy has fallen off his bike and broken his arm. And the younger one is so wild at day nursery . . . they say they won't keep him there much longer."

There is a faint rustling of the wind in the shaft, and something far away rattles. They both shudder as they go on, Yvonne's feet white and knobbly in her slippers, her hair untidy, her back hunched.

For her, childbirth has not been one of life's great highlights. On the contrary, it has been a series of humiliations and disappointments, perhaps in the end one of the most oppressive events in the whole of her oppressed life.

She had not asked to become pregnant. She has not even looked forward to her confinement. The twins . . . they are just something forced on her and her husband, against their will.

Marie and Yvonne swing into a side tunnel where the ground rises slightly toward a heavy dark temple door.

Marie presses the button.

Yvonne seems to brighten slightly.

"You get attached to the only nice people you meet here. I was thinking about her, you know, that big woman . . . you know the one I mean."

She looks at Marie slightly irritably.

"The big one who washes up the bottles in Neonatal. She's the *only* one *I* can understand. All the others . . . they don't say a thing. Or else they stuff me full of Latin."

The lift sinks to the bottom with a sigh.

They open the heavy door and get in.

Inside the big ward in Postnatal, most of the women are getting ready to leave. They have been there for five, six, or seven days. Now they are to be discharged.

"What about you?" says the blacksmith's wife.

"I'm going home tomorrow," says Marie.

The blacksmith's wife is standing with her great ninepinlike legs sturdily thrust into a pair of high-heeled shoes with straps and cork soles. In honor of the day, she has put on a new tight blouse that makes her bosom look extra rich and swollen.

She has put a pile of folded paper towels in each of the cups of her great bra, so that the blouse won't be soaked through before they get home.

Sister has asked whether she wouldn't like to stay another day until the tension in her breasts has gone. But the blacksmith's wife thinks she has been here long enough now. She wants to go home to her boys. All of them have been reckoning with that.

She puts civilian clothes on to her fat little boy, the whole outfit brand new, purple and white, and she's knitted them all herself.

"Doesn't he get the others' cast-offs?" says Marie.

"Oh, no, he's to have things of his own!"

He has a hood put on his head, a real hood with ear-flaps, ribbons and bobbles, and mittens without thumbs on his hands.

The blacksmith opens the door with a crash and steps into the room, just as if he owned the whole world, which in some ways he does. He goes over to the window, hangs his umbrella on the radiator, puts the baby-carrier on the table, and gives his wife a smack on one of her big buttocks.

Then he lifts the family's latest production up high, lets him go on a little flying trip and gives him a smacking great kiss on the mouth, then carefully puts him in the carrier beneath the purple and white check cover.

He flings out his arms, nodding in all directions.

"Well, thanks a lot, girls, for everything . . . see you again when we have our next!"

"Now, just you stop that!" says his wife, twisting her forefinger into her temple, as she throws up her eyes and sticks out her tongue.

She goes from bed to bed, shaking hands with everyone.

The nurse gets a big hug.

"Thanks a lot, sweetheart. You've been lovely, you have."

"Leave the little dumpling to stay here with me," says the nurse. "I could do with a little lad like that."

There are no limits to the number of takers for that boy.

The blacksmith grasps hold of the carrier, but the nurse shakes her head and takes it from him. She will be the one to carry the baby down the stairs and out to the car. The hospital's responsibility does not cease until beyond the main entrance.

Mr. Holm comes pussy-footing along the baby table, the baby-carrier in his left hand and his hat in his right.

He strews the contents of the carrier on to the bed. He has brought everything; quilt, underclothes, outdoor clothes, cap, gloves, extra nappies and plastic pants . . . everything is pale blue in case it should be a boy.

He has brought his Kodak Instamatic and dutifully snaps one picture after another of mother and daughter.

Suddenly Mrs. Holm exclaims in great horror!

"You've forgotten the baby's blanket!"

"What do you mean, Marchen, dear?"

"You've forgotten the blanket . . . *the baby's blanket*."

"?"

"You'll have to go home and fetch it."

"Is that really necessary?"

"*At once!*"

Her face is quite distorted. She is standing there in her dark tailored coat, already starting to unbutton it.

He puts his soft hat on to his high Holm head and sneaks on tiptoe back along the baby table and out toward the exit.

The nurse comes in.

"Why has your husband gone?"

"He had to drive home to fetch the baby's blanket."

"Where do you live?"

"In Birkeröd."

"But, *listen* now. You can easily borrow one from us."

The nurse hurries out and comes back a moment later with the crestfallen husband, who is shaking all over.

Mrs. Holm offendedly clicks her suitcase shut.

Little Connie watches the others being discharged one by one, last of all the thin hairdresser. She and her baby are fetched by the grandmother. They go round politely saying goodbye with their cold hands.

"And my mother," says Connie. "She *promised* she'd come!"

She has tears in her eyes.

"Isn't it rotten of her."

"You can borrow what you need, and then you can send it back afterwards," says the nurse.

"But how shall I get all the way back home to Hundested?" whispers Connie, looking down at her baby.

During the course of the day, the big ward is filled again, new mothers being wheeled in on stretchers with their newborn infants in their arms.

Marie sits there like an old hand on her bed. She knows it all inside out. She welcomes them and can answer questions and in general put the newcomers to rights.

"Where's your baby?" someone asks.

"Oh, it's nothing," says Marie, glancing away. "She's over in Neonatal to gain a bit of weight. Nothing to worry about."

The others shudder imperceptibly.

Late that afternoon, Connie's mother and older sister appear.

"You can keep my *Extra* if you like, because I'm going home now," says Connie to Marie.

Connie's mother and sister are small and look very alike.

They have brought a baby basket with them and a whole lot of knitted baby clothes in a plastic bag.

Now they are walking round telling Connie what to do, pulling out drawers, and opening the doors of her locker to see if she's forgotten anything. Then they change the baby on the baby table and tell Connie she must remember to say goodbye properly.

Darkness has already begun to fall, and they have to catch a train.

Connie goes round in her leather jacket, shaking hands.

"Here's my address?" she says to Marie. "Don't forget now you know someone living in Hundested."

Then the nurse lifts the baby basket with the child in it and walks ahead of the three small women out of the ward, out into the corridor, down the main stairs, and out through the main entrance.

The women come together in Postnatal wearing the same white clothes and for the same reason. For five days, they live together in the same ward. They eat the same food and do roughly the same things. They are looked after by the same people and get the same treatment. On the fifth or sixth day, they leave the ward, this dreamland where everyone is equal, or at least more or less equal. They return to their respective classes, to their compartments, their place in life. Their fellowship is dissolved and never returns. They no longer hear from each other and, at best, they read about each other in some statistics.

In their different levels of society, they actually live separately, without knowledge of each other's activities and doings.

They have not the slightest idea what life is like for the other women, what they think, believe, or feel. They don't even know if they have experienced the birth of their children in the same way.

Time begins to drag for Marie. She really has no business here any longer.

She lies leafing through Connie's *Extra*.

There is a huge headline on the front page: *Children tied up in washhouse at night*.

On the middle spread is an aerial photograph of a house and she reads the caption. *This huge mansion belonging to a doctor in Klarup is like a fortress or a prison, a giant house surrounded by a high fence and inside a garden surrounded by walls.*

Marie's thoughts flit hither and thither.

She must try to free herself of the hospital, however difficult that may be. The hospital has protected her, and the staff have helped her.

Now she feels split in two, the one half wanting to leave, to go home, back to life and a varied humdrum existence.

The other half wants to stay in this enclosed well-ordered world with its sharply defined contours. She would be able to go from department to department here, being dressed and undressed, food being served to her and her child cared for, constantly an object of care and attention, without having to take up a definite stand about anything.

She turns over to page twenty-eight.

*With a heart-shaped hairdo, the masseuse is dressed in sexy corsets and suspenders, genuine stiletto heels and long boots, long-legged and with a delicious bust. French underclothes, suspender belts, stockings for men, and rubber clothes available. Specialities: French foam-bath, Greek, Spanish, Italian, French, etc., German to a lesser degree.*

How on earth will things go for the infants she has got to know here? The hairdresser's child? The little mulatto? Connie's baby? Yvonne's twins? Gertrude's, Olivia's, and Mrs. Holm's children?

Whatever happens, they will all have very varied upbringings.

Some have been discharged fat and well and will become physically and psychologically broken during the course of the next six months . . . a finishing touch that will affect the rest of their lives.

Others leaving the hospital weak and underweight will grow strong and self-confident in an environment that has enough time and energy to look after them.

*The future foretold. Hitler's destiny. World War Two.*

The mothers and fathers will do all they can, whether they are Mikkelsens or Erichsens, Holms or Hansens.

*Bad nerves and other psychological complaints treated. Smoking cures. Free catalogue.*

But there is a vast different between *what* can be coped with from family to family.

Some of the parents will start the wild sexual feud as early as a few weeks after the baby's birth . . . what none of Marie's generation can quite escape.

One of the children will perhaps die in an accident . . . another be simply murdered. A third within the near future will have a bank-book of its own and appear in photographs in *All for Ladies* magazine.

*Gentlemen! Looking for a nice escort to visit you at your hotel? Would you like a little exclusive pleasure privately or at your hotel? Open every day.*

It is not actually so difficult to predict the newborn child's fate as one would imagine. All you have to do is to look at their mothers and fathers, and then their social background and the rest comes by itself.

*Bondage Chili or dark Amber, both of us for 150.*

What will become of all those children in Neonatal? Many of them, as early as in the womb, have been objects of the greatest attention. The mothers have been admitted to Prenatal to rest . . . perhaps for as long as several months. Then the child comes into the world under the supervision of various professors, consultants and midwives. Then a couple of weeks in an incubator in Neonatal, where under the control of leading specialists, they laboriously manage to bring their weight up by fifteen grams per day.

Then they say goodbye to the child at the hospital entrance.

The child is sent home to two parents who may not have the slightest idea how to look after an infant, who have never learnt anything about such things, who have more than enough to do getting through the day themselves.

After two weeks, the mother can no longer breast-feed, so goes over to artificial feeding, and from that day on the child will continue with artificialities right through its life.

*Loans granted only on own signature. Premium bonds bought and sold. Your money placed at twelve percent. Executed in twenty seconds.*

The child, from whom the sacred glow of radiance of birth has long since vanished, will within a few months be attacked by influenza, inflammation of the ear, bronchitis. It will become feverish, whiny, irritable . . . and six months later, it is no fun any longer.

Meanwhile the mothers and fathers hurry back and forth between home and work, depending on the amount of cheap labor society requires.

Inadequate day-care. Repeated visits to hospital. Understaffed day-nurseries. Overcrowded primary schools. Special classes. Bad out-of-school arrangements. Small apartments. Insufficient leisure occupation. No point in life.

Defenseless victims of advertisements, entertainment, and political demagogy.

The parents' sense of standing outside, of being shut out from an overall view and insight into their own existence, that sense of impotence, of let it go . . . that they hand on to their children. It is their heritage.

Those expensive incubator children . . . what are they heading for?

The flowers left behind by the patients are on the tables and window sills.

In Mrs. Holm's place is a cold garden of drooping flowers, twelve dark-red roses with long stalks tied with a pink silk ribbon and a little bouquet of withered rosebuds in a vase of their own, freesias, cotton-grass, and coral branches all bowing their pale heads.

They are there because flowers should not be taken home from a hospital, as that means bad luck.

They stand there belonging to no one and to everyone, until the staff throws them out.

Marie takes the blacksmith's winter aconite over to her own locker. That couldn't really bring bad luck, could it?

Tomorrow she is to go home. The new crop of women will stay, then they will be discharged, then another bunch comes. And all the time, the big ward will keep its continuity, because there will always be girls from the previous lot filling in the gaps until the next round.

And the ward will fill and empty as regularly as a lake.

The brittle little nurse in a starched cap comes in with her tinkling trolley of pills and medicine jars, asking if anyone wants anything for the night.

"A Doriden."

"A glass of syrup of figs."

"And how are you, Mrs. Vesterhavn? Have your bowels opened?"

## WEDNESDAY 15 JANUARY

Early in the morning, Marie is lying in bed, her arms behind her head, taking a kind of quiet farewell of the hospital.

Sometime at the end of next week, as far as she can see, she will be given her baby back. The baby will have to be fed every three hours, all round the clock, until she weighs 3,000 grams. That could take weeks. Marie has a hard time ahead of her.

She thinks how wonderful it would be if she could accept Sister's offer to be admitted again when the baby is discharged from Neonatal.

That would be an incredible help.

But could she come back to the ward without being a real patient with blood between her legs and drooping shoulders . . . and stay there taking up a bed?

She can't really make use of the nurse's generous offer for anything at all . . . because Marie doesn't know what she wants herself . . . or what is best for her and the child.

She has never had a child before, and neither has she been in hospital before. She does not know what demands can reasonably be made by a patient . . . or what is possible to accept.

But couldn't one accept everything? The sister knows perfectly well what she is doing. She isn't just saying things she doesn't mean, is she?

But perhaps it would be better to try to manage on her own . . . as millions of women have to.

"I'm going home before lunch," says Marie.

"Oh, yes? You must do as you wish," says the sister. "You're quite welcome to phone here if there's anything you want to ask."

"What's the best way of getting a nurse from the Child Care Center to come home?"

"Phone them today, now, immediately, from the office."

"And I'll have to get hold of a breast-pump."

"You can hire one from Falck's."

Marie's old clothes have been put in the ward after having been hanging in the hospital wardrobe for thirty-one days.

They look gray and wretched, with an old smell about them that utterly dismays her.

Worst of all is her old sheepskin coat, which has once been white. She folds it up as best she can, puts it on the seat of a chair, and pushes the chair under the bed.

Her trousers are miles too baggy. She has worn them when her stomach had been enormous. She puts them on and stands there holding on to the waistband at the sides. With her large leather shoes sticking out from below, she looks like a cross between Donald Duck and the Three Little Pigs.

Now she understands better why the other women talked so much about what clothes they were going to wear when they were discharged. These are under any circumstances all wrong!

This time she doesn't go down along the underground passage to get to Neonatal, but walks above ground along the internal hospital roads, on stone slabs, curbstones, and asphalt, even trying to balance along a long iron pipe lying beside the road.

The air is sharp and damp.

"You see, wipe her mouth with a small bit of cotton-wool dipped in a little solution of borax and glycerine. She likes that . . . she licks it up. Then put a couple of drops of groundnut-oil into her bathwater and feel it with your forearm to see if it's the right temperature."

Marie is writing down everything Sister says in her notebook to make sure she will remember it all.

"Don't really wash her . . . with soap, I mean . . . only her bottom. Just splash a little of the lukewarm water over her. Like this. Mind she doesn't get water in her ears. Then take her out, wrap her in a towel and carefully pat her dry."

The baby weighs 2,320 grams today, and Marie is allowed to care for her herself. The child opens her calm deep-blue eyes and stares.

"Brush her hair like this . . . carefully . . . you see? Do you want to try feeding her? Then we'll check-weigh her first with her clothes on."

Marie puts away her notebook, unbuttons her impractical old jersey and puts her baby to her breast, embarrassed at having to force the smell of old clothes onto her.

The nurse leaves the room.

Marie strokes the baby's hair, sunk in thought, gazing out of the window at gray roofs and the uneven contours of the city against the leaden January sky.

Suddenly she sees the child is lying immobile in her arms, with her eyes closed. She feels the tiny forehead . . . it is quite cold. The blood in her veins turns to ice. She can't be dying, can she? Is she dead?

Then the baby yawns and all Marie's muscles relax.

The sister comes back.

"Well, shall we weigh her again now?"

They put the baby on the scales.

"Heavens, haven't you got any more into her?"

The child weighs five grams more than when she started to feed.

"But what shall I do?"

"Never mind," says the sister consolingly. "Don't be so scared of her. She's much stronger than you think."

Marie straightens up.

"You've been there with her now for a whole quarter of an hour. She's probably totally exhausted. I'll see that she gets something inside her for her next meal . . . with the tube, if nothing else."

How on earth will I cope with her at home? thinks Marie.

She stands outside Neonatal, thinking for a moment, gathering her wits, then walking resolutely upstairs until she finds herself outside her old department.

Prenatal looks gray and silent there in front of her. She walks past the day room, where there's a patient she doesn't know. She creeps on, past the sluice, the office and the kitchen, right down to the end of the corridor and into her old Ward 0.

Strange women are in three of the beds, sitting there in a strange way. In the fourth is Linda . . . in her old place by the window.

"Hullo, Linda! Signe told me you were back. How're things?"

She has begun to ask questions in the same tone of voice as the staff.

"All right, thanks . . . congrats, by the way. Is the baby all right?"

"Yes, fine. She'll probably be discharged in a week's time. Are you having pains, or what's up with you?"

"Water started trickling out, and there's a whole month to go, so . . . well, they say I should try to hold back a little longer."

It is the same pale Linda, with the same long thin legs sticking out at the end of the covers. She has tears in her eyes.

"Allan and I are separating," she whispers.

"Are you sure?"

"Yes, it's been hellish back home. Total chaos when I got back. Not a bill paid, but he'd bought a stereo setup for cash . . . 6,000! Everything was in a muddle, and there was a bloody awful atmosphere, too. Then he drinks . . . he simply *can't* take being unemployed. And then there's been other women, too. So I just got blasted angry about the whole thing."

Linda's mouth trembles.

"Don't you agree it'd be better if we separated *before* the baby's born?"

Marie looks at her and doesn't know what to say.

"But how can we arrange everything? I just can't imagine. He doesn't know where to go, and he says he just refuses to go back to his parents. His dad's unemployed, too. I'll have to keep the apartment . . . now I'm going back with the kid. Don't you think?"

"Can't you talk to the social worker about it?"

Linda smiles.

"You must hear my horoscope for this week. *It appears that you cannot see the wood for the trees. Stop flying so high up in the clouds. You cannot strike root if you have no contact with the ground. Wednesday morning will be a good time to solve a number of practical problems, especially those connected with written or educational matters.*"

She puts her magazine on the locker top and clasps her hands round her drawn-up legs.

They sit in silence for a moment.

"How're things otherwise here?"

"Oh, not so bad, but it's not such fun as it was when we sat watching television together in the evenings. We've stopped doing that. And we don't drink anything, either. It's sort of got quieter here . . . if I can put it like that."

Marie looks at Linda's pale bony face beneath the thin hair; Linda, who is only twenty-one; Linda, who in a month's time or so will give birth to the child she has so hoped will change and improve her life.

"I do hope it'll be a girl," she says. "I thought I'd call her Judith. Don't you think that's nice. Listen what it says in *Naming Your Child*." Linda leafs through the little book. *Judith, Hebrew, Jewess. The Book of Judith in the Old Testament is about the widow Judith, who killed Holofernes when he threatened her birthplace. English Judy; Danish Jutta, Jytte.* Have you decided what to call yours?"

"No, I don't seem to have any ideas."

A little while later, Marie is in the office.

"Oh, but how nice!" says the sister, pushing back her chair. "Sit yourself down. How is she, your baby?"

"Quite well, as far as I can make out. I've changed her myself today and tried to feed her."

"Is she pretty?"

"She's the prettiest thing I've ever seen, and I promise you that's not a lie."

"What do they say about her otherwise?"

"That she's all right. I'm being discharged today . . . in a little while. I'll take a taxi straight to Falck's and hire a breast-pump. Then I'll keep on trying to express at home and then come and visit her with the milk once or twice a day."

The sister closes the daybook she has been working on.

"I've come to say thank you and goodbye," says Marie. "I've had marvelous treatment in this department."

"That's good."

"By the way," says Marie, suddenly remembering something. "That red-haired girl who was always knitting and was so cheerful, the one with the backward boy. I liked her so much. How have things gone for her? Is she still here?"

The sister looks out of the window.

"She's not been discharged, has she?"

"No."

"How is she, then?"

"Do you really want to know?"

"Yes, of course."

"Her baby was born dead this morning."

"*No!*"

"Yes, I'm sorry to have to tell you, but that's what happened."

Marie stares in rage at the sister.

"But it can't be possible? Here in hospital . . . when she was under constant supervision?"

The sister shrugs her shoulders and gives her old patient a long calm look.

"These things happen . . . very occasionally. It's called inexplicable intrauterine fetal death."

The redhead . . . she had walked straight into the lion's mouth with her eyes open.

I must get away from here, Marie thinks.

*And I can't do it quick enough.*

A moment later, she is in Postnatal, nervous and breathless.

She pulls the chair from under her bed and shakes out her flattened coat, gathers up her belongings and starts stuffing them into the coat's large cloth pockets. The green pamphlet *ABC of Political Economy*, Neruda's *Memoirs* and the morning's papers are put into one pocket, her toilet bag and sandals into the other.

All the small stenciled papers, prospectuses, and advertising pamphlets of good advice about this and that she puts in a pile together with the letters she has had from Zacharias and her parents. Then she wraps her dressing gown round the lot and puts the bundle into her shoulder bag.

She puts on the wretched sheepskin, winds the knitted scarf twice round her neck, pulls the Peruvian hood down over her ears, lifts up her bag . . . stands in the middle of the room and says "'bye" . . . and vanishes hurriedly through the door.

The tall fair sister in her short-sleeved coat and red knee-stockings is in the office, talking to two nurses. Marie leans against the door-frame and waits.

"Oh, it's you!"

"Thanks for everything," says Marie.

She flings her arms round the tall blonde woman and embraces her awkwardly . . . she is beside herself and can't get a word out. The sister flushes, and supporting herself on the edge of the desk, pats Marie lightly on the shoulder.

"Get home safely, now, won't you?"

Marie turns and rushes out into the corridor toward the exit, almost crashing into the shiny aluminum trolley of food for lunch . . . roast pork, red cabbage, boiled potatoes, with strawberry jelly and pickled gherkins. The smell is marvelous.

Oh, hell, I should have stayed for another half an hour!

But there is absolutely no way back now.


She goes out into Tagen Road and on past the old military hospital to the triangular park at the North Avenue crossroads.

There is a statue of Steno and a small black magnolia tree in the grass. In a few months' time the magnolia will be in bloom, its remarkable pinkish flowers on its bare branches.

She stands on the edge of the pavement, waiting for the light to turn green.

The clouds are low and the traffic roars past along the trunk road, which runs on, wide and noisy, across the bridges in toward the inner city.